MYSTERIOUS
TEMPLAR

MYSTERIOUS TEMPLAR

BY

ADRIANA GIROLAMI

BOOK ONE OF THE

TEMPLAR TRILOGY

Cover by Adriana Girolami

THE AUTHOR

 Adriana Girolami was born in Rome, Italy. Books were always available in her home and at an early age she was encouraged to read by her parents. Adriana's creative, artistic nature was apparent even as a child and she delighted in drawing pictures on the pristine sands of Italy's coast line during beach outings. She immigrated with her family to the United States following her father's untimely death and later attended The Art Students League in New York City. Soon she embarked on a satisfying career as a portrait artist and illustrator, but still longed for the freedom of the written word. The author remembered all those wonderful and exciting books that stimulated her imagination as a child. She favored distinguished, historical authors such as Sir Walter Scott and Adriana's personal favorite, Alexander Dumas. She wrote her debut novels, the "Knights Templar Trilogy" containing *Mysterious Templar, The Crimson Amulet* and *The Templar's Redemption*. Being a professional artist, she made the illustrations for the cover of the books. In her spare time she enjoys physical activities. Jogging faithfully, she plays racquet ball and has a black belt in Kenpo Karate. She loves to travel and has visited many different countries throughout the world. She currently lives in Florida.

ISBN-13: - 978-0-9962483-8-9   Print
ISBN-10: - 0996248382
ISBN-13: - 978-0-9962483-9-6   E
ISBN-10: - 0996248390

Timber Creek Press
Imprint of Timber Creek Productions, LLC
312 N. Commerce St.
Gainesville, Texas

ACKNOWLEDGMENT

The author gratefully acknowledges Mr. Ken Farmer. His dynamic, creative personality and vision is instrumental in the publishing of the "Knights Templar Trilogy".

DEDICATION

In loving memory of my wonderful mother, Lena, who always encouraged me to follow my dreams. She introduced me by example to the beauty of the written word.

Contact Us:
Published by: Timber Creek Press
timbercreekpresss@yahoo.com
www.timbercreekpress.net
Twitter: @pagact
Facebook Book Page:
www.facebook.com/TimberCreekPress
214-533-4964

This novel is a work of fiction. Names, characters, places and incidents are either the products of the author's imaginations or are used fictitiously. Any resemblance to actual persons, living or dead, business establishments, events or locales is entirely coincidental.

ENDORSEMENTS

Anthony Flacco, New York Times best seller. - A Brilliant debut novel.

Aditi Saha, reviewer Kolkata, India: The most beautiful Historical Romance. The storytelling of the author is really one-of-a-kind and with those shocking twists and turns, the story becomes more compelling as well as interesting. This book is a total page-turner from its very first page.

Nancy J, Cohen, author "Bad Hair Mystery Series":
A Romantic Historical Adventure

Duncan H. Haines, author "Ben Candidi Mysteries":
Evocative...Resonates with the spirit of Ivanhoe and Rebecca

Brian Benson, author "Brent Dulac detective series"
Who say's romance is dead?

HISTORICAL FICTION WESTERN

THE NATIONS by Ken Farmer and Buck Stienke
Audio version: www.tinyurl.com/NationsAudio
HAUNTED FALLS by Ken Farmer and Buck Stienke
Audio version: www.tinyurl.com/HauntedFallsAudio
HELL HOLE by Ken Farmer
Audio version: www.tinyurl.com/HellHoleAudio
ACROSS the RED by Ken Farmer & Buck Stienke
Audio version:www.tinyurl.com/AcrossRedAudio
DEVIL'S CANYON by Buck Stienke

SY/FY

LEGEND of AURORA by Ken Farmer & Buck Stienke
AURORA: INVASION by Ken Farmer & Buck Stienke

Coming Soon

MILITARY ACTION/TECHNO

BLACKSTAR MOUNTAIN - by T.C. MILLER

HISTORICAL FICTION WESTERN

BASS and the LADY by Ken Farmer & Buck Stienke

HISTORICAL FICTION ROMANCE
THE TEMPLAR TRILOGY

THE CRIMSON AMULET by Adriana Girolami
TEMPLAR REDEMPTION by Adriana Girolami

TIMBER CREEK PRESS

CHAPTER ONE

NEMOURS CASTLE

The citadel towered over a vast and barren countryside, its ghostly image shrouded by the silvery shadows of an autumn night and a pale gibbus moon. Silence and darkness came to life when the massive palace walls began to echo the sounds of two mounted cavaliers galloping across the rolling hills toward the stronghold.

The cavaliers, Phillip and Duccio, were returning from a long and difficult journey, but neither was gladdened by the sight of the stately castle. The drawbridge had been lowered to welcome them across the surrounding moat, but they reined back their horses and stopped short of its dark waters for a few private words.

"We have reached our destination, Philip," Duccio began. "…and we had no evil encounters even though his grace had strong apprehensions about our safety."

Philip shook his head. "I am not consoled that everything seems to have gone so well. I fear something sinister is at work, something we have not yet discovered."

"Remove these thoughts from your mind, friend. For the moment at least, we are safe and Nemours castle is within our reach."

Philip reluctantly nodded agreement, and the two men spurred their mounts to the open drawbridge, crossed the moat, and entered the large courtyard beyond. Several guards awaited and quickly approached.

While the cavaliers dismounted, Duccio called out to the ranking guard, "We request an immediate audience with the Duke. It is imperative we see him at once."

Instead of challenging Duccio's claim, the guard bowed his head slightly and motioned for the two to follow him. Duccio flashed a satisfied grin at Philip and they followed the guard up several winding staircases and into the central hall, with its massive vaulted ceiling.

Banners with the Nemours coat of arms decorated the solid stone walls with bright crimson, lit from above by massive wrought iron chandeliers. In a less festive touch, armed sentries stood at regular intervals all around the stately hall.

The trio climbed the imposing central staircase and entered a long corridor. Here it was much darker, lit only by the weak yellow light of a few candles. They were finally escorted to an elegantly carved wooden door with an armed guard posted on either side. The guards threw back the doors, allowing Duccio and Philip to enter a large study where two gentlemen stood in apparent anticipation.

"Your grace," the guard announced. "The emissaries of the Duke of Lorengard-Lorraine."

"Come forth gentlemen," the Duke answered in a firm voice. "Welcome to my home."

Philip and Duccio each bowed before Alexander, Duke of Nemours, then respectfully approached. The Duke was tall and lean. He appeared to be in his fifties, and wore black from head to toe, topped by an ornate brocaded vest and a thick silver belt that gleamed even in the pale light. His thick hair was speckled with gray, shoulder length and meticulously arranged. The cares of office had lined his face, but he still was a strikingly handsome man. Visible on his left cheek was the long scar of a cutting wound.

"Good evening, your Lordship," Duccio announced in formal tones.

"Yes, good evening," Philip quickly added.

"Your names, gentlemen?" the Duke asked.

"I am Duccio Degli Uberti and this is Philip of Rohann. We are loyal servants of Arsenio, Duke of Lorengard-Lorraine."

"Gentlemen, we have been awaiting your arrival with some trepidation, since we have ruthless enemies in many places. You have truly taken a dangerous and difficult assignment in making this journey, and I admire your courage in executing it."

"The Duke Arsenio honors us with his trust," Philip humbly responded. "We have pledged our lives to him for the success of our mission." He produced a letter with the seal of Lorengard-Lorraine, but because he was uncertain of the identity of the second man, he hesitated before handing it over.

The Duke noticed and quickly spoke up, "Ah. This is my trusted ally and friend…Count William of Rozenberk."

The Count nodded to each of the knights.

"Forgive me, my Lords," Duccio answered, somewhat embarrassed. "…but Arsenio gave us specific instructions to guard the letter with our lives…and give it to you in private."

"I respect your loyalty, my young friend," the Duke responded. "Be assured the letter is secure in my hands. Now it is time for both of you to retire. You must be tired from your long and dangerous journey."

Without waiting for a response, he pulled a long velvet rope that rang a melodious bell. A young page immediately entered the room and bowed to the Duke.

"Extend to these gentlemen my hospitality and make certain you serve them our best food and wines. Make comfortable beds at their disposal for a good night sleep."

With those parting words, Alexander smiled to end the audience. Duccio and Philip realized they had been politely dismissed, so they bowed and left the room.

Although Arsenio's message was now in his possession, the Duke still felt heavy concern. He paced the room while Count

William waited for him to take the initiative. Finally, the Duke rang a bell once again and another page immediately appeared.

"Go inform lady Polyxena that I request her presence as soon as possible. She is to be dressed in hunting attire."

The young page looked confused by the request, considering the late hour, and hesitated for a small moment. It was enough to prompt the Duke's impatience.

"What are you gaping at?" Alexander snapped. "Haven't you heard my command? Make haste and call my daughter at once."

The intimidated young page bowed and quickly ducked out of the room. When they were alone again, the Duke broke the seal and read the letter.

My dear friend,

I thank you for the valuable allegiance you offer me. As you know, my Dukedom is in peril. We are threatened by mighty enemies who are planning to overthrow my government. If my cousin, the Duke Ludwig of Saxe-Hanover, succeeds at this, his evil intentions will destabilize Europe, threatening the precarious peace we presently enjoy. The unification of our two houses is the only beacon of hope available, to forestall the looming aggression. I wait impatiently to make your daughter Polyxena my bride as we have arranged, and have her acknowledged as the future Duchess of Lorengard-Lorraine. In this regard, I have taken steps to safeguard the union of our families and avert interferences. We will celebrate the marriage

by proxy, and a trusted friend will stand in the bride's place. The union will be blessed by the Cardinal of Lorengard-Lorraine, who has secured an alliance with the Pope to validate the marriage. Your daughter consequently will become the new Duchess of Lorengard-Lorraine.
Salutations,
Arsenio of Lorengard-Lorraine
DUX

Alexander exhaled with relief and handed the precious document to his friend, who immediately read it.

"The alliance is on, then," the Duke said. "It's time to inform Polyxena. We must hope she will grasp the importance of her cooperation and rejoice at being offered an entire Dukedom to share with a noble person."

"No doubt she will, my Lord," the Count concurred, while the sounds of approaching footsteps floated down the corridor followed by several urgent knocks at the door.

"Enter," Alexander called. The door opened without hesitation and a youthful figure emerged from the shadows and walked through the imposing entryway.

POLYXENA OF NEMOURS

Polyxena entered the room attired as her father had requested, in dark green hunting tights. She also wore a matching vest and cape—a brown leather belt with a golden buckle cinched her narrow waist. Her brown leather boots and gloves completed the ensemble. Even by the room's dim light, Polyxena was a beautiful young woman with a lovely face and athletic body.

Her masculine attire did nothing to detract from her femininity, but magnified them by contrast. Her appearance was crowned by a cascade of lustrous dark hair that beautifully framed her face. She walked with a confident stride, but bowed her head in deference when she reached the Duke.

"You wish to see me, father?" she asked in a voice that was soft and melodious.

"Yes Polyxena." The Duke extended his arms in greeting. "I have a pleasant surprise for you. Someone you hold very dear has come to visit." He gestured toward the Count of Rozenberk who had remained silent and discrete throughout, nearly invisible in the shadow of the massive fireplace. The gentleman stepped forward to greet Polyxena with a warm smile. Her face lit up.

"Dear Count William. We missed you during your long absence. Indeed, this is a great day that returns you to our house."

The Count appeared moved by her warm reception and eagerly approached her. He took her in his arms with fatherly affection.

The Duke of Nemours stood in silence and watched with mixed emotions. The Count of Rozenberk, sensing Alexander's uneasiness, approached his friend while still holding the young girl by the hand. "Do you remember, dear Polyxena," the Count asked. "…my promise to you that whenever possible I would always make it a point to be by your side during the special occasions of your life?"

The question puzzled her even more than the odd request to don hunting attire at this hour. "Special occasion, milord? You mean tonight? I don't understand."

"My dear child, I believe today will be important to you. And as promised, I am here to lend my support." He glanced over at Alexander and cleared his throat. "But it is your father's place to clarify the issues and answer your questions."

"Yes daughter," the Duke of Nemours agreed. "I have important news to share with you. And I hope sincerely you will be pleased."

"What news, father?" she asked, already feeling alarmed by the tone of the conversation. The Duke walked to her holding the letter with the broken seal and showed it to her. "I have a message from Arsenio, Duke of Lorengard-Lorraine requesting the honor of your hand in marriage. I have recently given my consent, after much deliberation and thought to the union, because there could have been repercussions that would put your life in danger if the negotiations had failed to work out. It was for this reason that you were kept in the dark about it until now."

Polyxena remained so silent and composed—it appeared that the news didn't faze her. Only a tremor in her hands betrayed her.

Her father failed to notice her distress and continued, "Arsenio is a noble and righteous person who justly governs his Dukedom. He is currently threatened by powerful enemies who want to bring down his regime. Because of the geographical importance of Lorengard-Lorraine, his fall could destabilize parts of Europe, including the Dukedom of Nemours. The specter of war could threaten our existence."

Now Polyxena's true thoughts came to the surface. "Is *this* the reason why he wants to marry me? To preserve his power with an alliance?"

"Yes daughter," her father solemnly replied. "Uniting our two houses is a necessary step to safeguard our future. Arsenio needs financial aid…in this case that means your dowry…to strengthen his army and add wealth to the empty coffers of Lorengard-Lorraine."

After a pause, Polyxena took a deep breath and steadied herself. "I understand. It appears that this union is necessary to protect our people and to come to the aid of a just Prince and valuable ally."

"Daughter, it isn't only to safeguard the alliance that you will become a bride. Why, I believe Arsenio will be a proper husband. And hopefully the marriage, even if politically motivated, could be blissful for you. You will become a Duchess…a position coveted by many. It will elevate your status and allow you to share the power to govern Lorengard-Lorraine alongside him."

"I will do as you bid, father," Polyxena answered, but now her resignation revealed itself. The idea of marriage to a total stranger filled her with trepidation. Nevertheless, political marriages were common in the aristocracy and she knew her only recourse was to obey her father. Still, she felt the need for solitude to cope with the powerful news.

She dreaded leaving the security of her home and the familiar places she loved. Most of all, she feared marrying a man she had never met, even if he was said to be noble and kind. In spite of her attempt at self-control, she felt her tears begin to flow, making it impossible to retain her dignity. She desperately wanted to hide in a dark corner of the study or quickly leave the room unnoticed. But etiquette did not allow a woman such small luxuries. She had no recourse but to ask her father's permission to retire.

"No," the Duke answered. "Remain here a little while longer. There is more you must learn on this fateful day. We talked about sharing a secret with you and you are worthy of our trust because you have a courageous and noble heart. Since your departure from Nemours is imminent, we must now tell you without delay."

"Father, I am exhausted and overwhelmed. I cannot absorb all these great changes taking place in my life. Whatever this secret may be, it is an unexpected burden in this moment."

"Daughter, it is essential that you trust me. What I am about to tell you is extremely important. If there was another way, I would not burden you. But we must include you in our plans and trust you with a vital task."

Polyxena was taken aback by her father's urgency. "Of course. Forgive me. You have always been my loving protector. I trust your judgment and will follow your lead."

Alexander smiled and lovingly embraced her, and then he took her by the hand and escorted her out of the study, followed by the Count of Rozenberk. Once outside, he dismissed the guards at the door and walked briskly with her through the corridors of the massive castle until the trio reached their destination. It was a chapel with two elaborate bronze doors decorated with religious effigies and biblical scenes.

The Duke firmly pushed the door handles and opened the imposing doors. The chapel was austere but beautiful in its simplicity, with massive vaulted ceilings and a white marble altar as the focal point of the room. Though the chapel was empty, it shimmered in the light of a hundred votive candles.

Polyxena felt at ease in the familiar room and crossed herself with respect and devotion, but wondered why they were there at that moment. Her father led her behind the marble altar and revealed a hidden stairway connecting the chapel to a crypt below.

Polyxena knew they were entering the castles' burial chamber, a sacred place she knew about, but had never visited. The ceiling was low and dimly lit by torches, which gave the area a gloomy appearance. Barely visible in the dark were stone plaques on the walls and floor, inscribed with the names of the departed nobles, and embellished with the house of Nemours coat of arms.

A granite sarcophagus crowned the center of the crypt, with a life-size bas-relief of a knight in repose sculpted on the top. The knight was dressed in full regalia as one of the Knights Templar. His armored right hand lay upon the handle of a mighty sword, which rested upon his body. His left hand was hidden behind the familiar emblazoned shield of the Holy Cross, depicting the nobility of the crusader's cause.

Sculpted on each corner of the knight's resting place was a remembrance of early poverty—the Knights Templar seal showing two knights on a single horse.

"Here rests our noble ancestor," the Duke told her. "Wilfred the Valiant, 3rd Duke of Nemours. He was a member of the Knights Templar, regarded by many as the greatest military order, because it played an important role in liberating the Holy Land. Unfortunately, after defending the Christian faith for two centuries, the order was dissolved by King Philip IV of France. Motivated by greed, he sought to destroy the Templars by confiscating their property. Under his direct order, the Templars were arrested on Friday, October 13, 1307."

Alexander solemnly approached the sarcophagus, followed by Polyxena and the Count of Rozenberk. He placed his hand on the cold stone and bowed his head respectfully. "They were tortured, forced to give false confessions, and then…burned at the stake. It was all done by the King for the purpose of confiscating their property."

"Was Wilfred the Valiant burned at the stake?" asked Polyxena.

"No," the Duke answered. "Our ancestor, Wilfred the Valiant, escaped with other knights. They suspected the King's treachery and abandoned extensive properties to save their lives and protect the future of the order, hoping one day to enact revenge."

The Duke of Nemours and the Count of Rozenberk flanked the sarcophagus and placed their hands over their hearts.

"We are Knights Templar, Polyxena," the Duke somberly told her. "We have sworn a holy oath to perpetuate and protect the survival of the order. You are to play an instrumental role in this."

"I?...What can I do, father?"

Alexander remained silent for a long moment, hoping to conceal his turmoil. Finally, he touched Polyxena's face with a loving caress, trying to calm her anxiety as well as his own.

He began, "King Philip IV was known for his cruelty and greed. He had dealt a devastating blow to the Knights Templar but did not succeed in destroying the order. The Count and I are not only Knights of the holy order of Templars, we possess a mighty secret that grants us power."

"This is true, Polyxena," the Count affirmed. "We are sworn to protect the Templar order and we alone have this secret knowledge. Today we have no choice but to share it in spite of the danger it may represent to you."

"I am humbled by the honor, my Lord," she answered. "May I be worthy of the honor and your trust."

With that, the Lord of Nemours silently approached the knight's sarcophagus and after respectfully bowing his head, placed his right hand firmly upon one of the engraved seals. Under the pressure of his touch, the stone effigy rescinded and the upper layer of the sarcophagus stirred, moved to the right, and slowly rotated with a loud, grating sound. In a short time, it had moved enough to reveal a large opening.

Polyxena stood stunned, but the Duke gently took his daughter's hand and led her to the open grave, helping her overcome her fear. She peered inside the sarcophagus and saw not a knight's decayed corpse, but a long staircase that spiraled down into darkness.

The Count of Rozenberk removed a torch from the crypt wall and climbed into the sarcophagus with the agility of a cat. Once he entered the large opening, he signaled for Alexander and Polyxena to follow. Silently, the trio descended the stairway and carefully moved down the damp and slippery stone steps.

By the light of the torch, she could see the roughly finished walls and uneven steps. The circular staircase was treacherous and appeared to have been hastily built by unskilled laborers. They had to descend carefully to prevent a fall.

She suddenly felt helplessness and claustrophobic despite her father's comforting presence. She finally understood why she was asked to wear hunting clothes. A gown would have been impractical and dangerous there.

During the descent, the Count was able to light several torches mounted on the walls. Polyxena felt a little better in the faltering torch light and was relieved to finally see the end of the long staircase. She took a deep breath and stepped briskly onto a small platform at the bottom of the stairs.

The stone of the landing was rough and uneven. Several unlit torches ornamented the barren walls, mounted on rusty metal holders. A door, barely visible in the torch light, offered the only opening available to them. Like the stonework, it was simple and hastily constructed, of unfinished wood, and reinforced on each corner with iron plates and metal studs.

The Count of Rozenberk lit more torches on the wall, and then joined the Duke in trying to open the heavy door. Its hinges groaned under the effort. With considerable force, the two men opened the door and exposed a cavernous, darkened room with spider webs draping the walls. An icy draft burst through the opening and surrounded them with its chill.

Alexander was aware of Polyxena's distress and comforted her with his touch before entering the room and helping the Count light more of the wall torches. Little by little, the darkness was replaced by a reddish-orange glow, giving a less ominous appearance to the area. Despite her reticence, Polyxena followed the two men deeper into the mysterious room, avoiding the mice that squeaked and darted about the area. Ignoring her natural disgust, she moved forward to explore the unfamiliar surroundings.

Stacks of wooden coffers leaned against the walls in disarray, covered in more of the spider webs. They reflected the sinister light of the torches. On closer inspection, Polyxena was amazed to notice that the coffers were filled to the brim with gold coins and loose jewels, along with crosses and religious objects of solid gold or silver, embellished with precious stones. The treasures had obviously been pillaged during the crusades. Their splendor was so overwhelming that she was left speechless by the sight.

The Duke was first to break the silence. He approached Polyxena with a benevolent smile. "This great treasure is the result of bloody battles lasting throughout the crusades. Many people died violent, horrible deaths for the sake of it. The greed of the knights who accumulated it brought dishonor to the proud order of Templars. The shame of it remains."

"How did this treasure get to be here, father?" asked Polyxena.

"Our ancestor, Wilfred the Valiant, was a noble knight who fought fearlessly and believed in justice. He despised the dishonor brought to the order by greedy Templars. These evil knights with their brutality and lust for blood had plundered Churches and Temples alike to obtain this incredible wealth. Thus, this great treasure is forever stained with the blood of murdered Christians, Jews, and Muslims. That is why I tell you it has brought shame to the proud name of the Templars.

"War exploded within the ranks of the Templars, who remained divided in their quest by good and evil, knight against knight fighting to the death. Wilfred of Nemours was victorious, and with the help of other righteous knights, took possession of the treasure and secretly transported it to the castle of Nemours.

"They built the passage directly below the false tomb above us, for the sole purpose of concealing this treasure. The great architect, Benvolio Dei Cerni, was also a Knight Templar and created the mechanical device used to open the tomb above us."

"Where is Wilfred buried, father?"

"His body rests within these walls, according to his wishes," he replied. "It is beneath the altar of our chapel in an unmarked grave, his name known only to God."

The Count of Rozenberk joined them. "Polyxena, there is much for you to learn in a short time. Wilfred and the Knights Templar swore a holy oath that none should seize or profit from this treasure…tainted with innocent blood. We can only protect the treasure and use it to aid the helpless against tyranny. This secret was passed down with extreme care from father and son…if the son was deemed worthy of the knowledge. We who know of this treasure agree it would be better if it were forever lost, rather than fall into the wrong hands and used for evil purposes."

"Who else knows about the treasure?" Polyxena inquired.

"No one else but us." The Count smiled. "Which is why we have no trouble sustaining a consensus. You, my dear child have been chosen as the next protector because you have a kind and noble heart. You have been trained for years in the use of arms by your father and I with this specific purpose in mind…And you have proven to be an adept pupil with remarkable fighting skills, even if you lack brute force. However, our chief problem is that regardless of your abilities, according to the laws of chivalry a woman can never be a Knight Templar because she must be constantly be willing to fight to the death."

Her father added, "That is true my, daughter, but destiny ordained a loftier role for you, that of custodian and protector of the Templars treasure. Should death befall me or the Count, your judgment will be the only recourse available to restore the honor of the Knights Templar." He took her face in his hands and solemnly added, "In such a case, remember only you can dispense the treasure."

Polyxena remained silent and closed her eyes, battling her thoughts to order. The responsibilities placed upon her in the course of a single night were highly taxing. It took all of her training and strength of resolve to call her own sense of gallantry and nobility to the surface. In this manner, fear and doubt were replaced by determination and resolve. Her lovely face took on a peaceful aura of acceptance. She stood tall before two men she now understood so much better than a single day earlier. She placed her hand over her heart.

"My Lords," she proudly said. "…you have given my life a purpose. May I prove worthy of this honor. According to the laws of chivalry, I pledge my life to protect the treasure and guarantee that its sole purpose will be to restore the honor of the Knights Templar."

✝✝✝

CHAPTER TWO

A MOST UNUSUAL WEDDING

In the faraway Dukedom of Lorengard-Lorraine, intense preparations had been made for this wedding. They were strange preparations for a wedding, however. In place of the throngs of elegantly dressed guests and beautiful floral arrangements that would ordinarily mark such an occasion, the exquisite chapel in the castle swarmed with armed guards.

Their presence made the place seem more like a military compound than a place of worship. An emotionless Cardinal stood before the altar, waiting to officiate the ceremony. He wore exquisite crimson and gold robes and kept his eyes solemnly closed as if in deep meditation.

The wedding couple kneeled before the Cardinal, flanked by witnesses and ready to take their vows. The tall patrician bridegroom, a man in his twenties, was dressed for the occasion with great elegance and style. His handsome features were framed by perfectly coifed blonde hair and his intense dark eyes depicted a strong character. His commanding demeanor signaled his rank as Lord of the manor, though he appeared calm and composed, he instinctively grasped his sword. That detail alone was like a sour note in a concerto.

Another sour note sounded with the visage of the bride. Instead of the expected young princess, a much older woman kneeled next to him. She dressed in understated elegance, a bit too severe for a wedding, but nevertheless the attire of a refined and aristocratic woman of her age.

"Arsenio, Duke of Lorengard-Lorraine," the Cardinal began. "…do you take as your lawful spouse, the Lady Polyxena of Nemours, represented here today by Amelia, Countess De Vargas? Do you promise to honor and endow the Lady Polyxena with all your heart and material possessions for the rest of your natural life?"

"Volo! I will," responded the Duke.

"And you Amelia, Countess De Vargas, representing Lady Polyxena of Nemours, do you take on her behalf as her legitimate spouse, Arsenio, Duke of Lorengard-Lorraine? Do you hereby represent her promise to honor and obey him above all others for the rest of her natural life?"

"I do," the Countess answered. At this pivotal moment in the ceremony, the Cardinal, with aplomb, consecrated the couple as man and wife-by-proxy, ending the Ceremony.

"Thank you, your eminence," the Duke said, relieved and grateful. He kissed the aristocratic hand extended by the prelate. "The last few months have been filled with danger and uncertainty. Because this marriage and the alliance are threatened by mighty enemies, who fear the unification of our powerful houses, we would not have been successful in our endeavor without the help of your eminence and his Holiness the Pope."

"You may rely on my support, your grace," the Cardinal somberly answered. "I have been a friend of the house of Lorengard-Lorraine and of your noble father for many years. And now you, following his honorable lead, are leader of a government that is just and which protects your people against aggression and war."

"That is my aim, your eminence," Arsenio responded. "But unfortunately, my wealth is greatly depleted and I can't sustain this precarious peace. Large expenditures were required to protect the Dukedom against the predatory aims of my ruthless cousin, Ludwig of Saxe-Hanover. More than anything else, it was his voracious thirst for power that made this alliance necessary and vital."

The Cardinal lowered his head in tacit consent. Meanwhile Arsenio addressed the lady next to him, "Dear Countess, there are no words to express my gratitude for your loyalty toward me. You have placed yourself in a perilous position by coming to my aid at this dangerous time."

The Countess replied with maternal affection, "Dear Arsenio. Your mother was my benefactress. I hope to repay my debt to her by aiding your quest."

Arsenio valued the courage and loyalty of his friends. He was young and inexperienced, thrust into power by his father's premature death. As the leader of an important Dukedom, heavy responsibilities weighed upon him. He craved wise counsel and felt especially grateful for the support of the few people he could truly trust. He addressed them with concern.

"It would be wise for you to leave the palace my friends," he said. "We can no longer risk your prolonged presence here. I have ordered my guards to escort you safely home, praying that the blessings and protection of God will follow you both during your journey."

The Duke signaled for his guards to escort his guests from the palace. Without hesitation, the Cardinal and Countess left the chapel.

Finally, Arsenio breathed a sigh of relief. Everything, for the moment, was going according to plan, with no threat to the vital alliance. The proxy marriage was successfully complete and the Duke was eager to depart from the confinement of the chapel.

He left surrounded by heavily armed guards, necessary after numerous attempts on his life. He entered a long and dark corridor followed by his armed escort, which led to another wing of the palace. After climbing several staircases and many winding passageways, he entered a well-lit area decorated with tapestries woven of silver and gold. He stopped before a doorway detailed with exquisite carvings, though entry was marred by another pair of armed guards. With Arsenio's arrival, the guards opened the doorway.

His magnificent bedchamber was decorated with lavishness and splendor. A large bed with an elegant canopy crowned the room, embellished with crimson draperies and emblazoned with Lorengard-Lorraine's coat of arms.

Arsenio was eager to rest after the ordeal of the day, and dismissed his valets. Alone in his bedroom, he sighed with relief while he removed his wide belt and heavy broad sword, depositing the weapon on a nearby chair. His cape and vest quickly followed, but overcome by fatigue, he lay down on the bed and closed his eyes.

He managed a few minutes rest before a sharp female voice woke him up from his slumber, "Is the bridegroom tired tonight?"

Before the surprised Duke could utter a response, a young woman appeared from the shadows in the corner of the room. By the yellow light of the wall torches, a mysterious and beautiful stranger came into view.

Her skin appeared as fine as porcelain and her cerulean eyes shined. She was beautifully shaped, with full, sensual lips parted in a seductive smile. Her crowning glory was in the deep golden tresses spilling over her shoulders.

She was immodestly dressed in a translucent gown that did little to shield her voluptuous form. The only stain on the image was her expression. She was cold with disdain. The air of contempt on her face distorted her presence.

"Flavia, is it you?" Arsenio asked in surprise. "I have missed you. And I was deeply concerned over your absence."

She ignored the Duke's caring words. "My dear Arsenio, I wouldn't be absent on your wedding day. I am here to extend my congratulations for the grand occasion in spite of the fact that I was not invited to the festivities."

His anger swelled. "You offend me with your sarcasm, Flavia. My marriage was a necessary tool, a political move to cement an alliance to protect Lorengard-Lorraine and my people's welfare. The ceremony was conducted with a woman my mother's age, and whatever the bride herself is doing at this moment, I am certain she knows the necessity of all this as well as I do."

"Ah, my Lord, your concern for your people is touching," she sneered. "What about all the empty promises you made to me? You falsely proclaimed your eternal love and devotion *to me*. I am the one you pledged to make your Duchess."

"I am sorry, Flavia. If I have hurt you it was unintentional. I wanted to marry you. But I had to protect my Dukedom with an alliance because I am in danger of being overthrown by a tyrant. You must understand my predicament and the duty I have to the people."

He softened his voice and spoke tenderly to her, "But despite everything, my love for you remains untarnished."

"You speak of love, Arsenio. But your new bride will be the Duchess of Lorengard-Lorraine, not me. The humiliation of a secondary role is my only recourse."

"She will have the title, but you will have my love, always," Arsenio responded. "My father loved you as a daughter and your place is secure as a respected member of my family. You will be treated with honor in Lorengard-Lorraine."

"And how will you treat Polyxena, your new bride?" Flavia asked angrily.

"I will treat her with all the respect and honor due to my wife," he replied. "...and you should understand that she is also a victim of circumstance. She is forced into a loveless marriage for political expediency. I don't know anything about her and even what she looks like is a mystery to me. The marriage is based on the fact that she is the daughter of a noble and powerful Duke."

Arsenio paused and remained silent for a long moment with an apprehensive look. Then he addressed Flavia in concern, "Who told you about my wedding and how did you learn my bride's name, Flavia? Only a few people were privy to that information. You were not one of them."

Flavia instinctively moved toward the back wall, intimidated by the Duke's suspicion. But in another moment, she regained her composure and haughty attitude.

"Arsenio," she proclaimed. "My loyalty toward you and the house of Lorengard-Lorraine is common knowledge to everyone. You offend me with your mistrust."

And yet Arsenio's suspicions were growing. "Where did you go while you were away, Flavia? You have not been in the palace for weeks and you didn't tell me where you were going. I was deeply concerned then and I demand an explanation now. Where were you hiding, my lady?…And with whom?"

Flavia had regained enough composure to respond in a mock playful fashion, "There is no place I wish to be where you are not, my lord. There is no joy for me, except near your loving embrace."

Without waiting for a reply, she encircled Arsenio's neck with her soft, rounded arms, planting a kiss upon his lips with such passion that she took his breath away. The nearness of her voluptuous body filled him with such desire that he was oblivious to everything except the ecstasy of the moment.

As soon as Flavia saw that she had achieved the upper hand, she pushed him away from her embrace.

"What are you doing?" the Duke asked, distressed.

"You won't make love to me in this room," she hissed. "Not in the same place where she will become your bride and Duchess, where she'll be triumphant and take you from me."

"You frustrate me with these ridiculous assertions. I told you my marriage is a necessary alliance. Please believe me Flavia. You above all have my heart. I will love you forever, even though I am obliged by my duty to act as a Duke rather than man."

Flavia seemed to believe Arsenio was honest about his loving feelings for her. His passion soothed some of her distress.

"My Lord," she said. "You promised me eternal love and call me Queen of your heart, but your mysterious new bride will be the Duchess, not me. I will only be your lover. Forever relegated into a subservient role, disgraced and shamed."

"That's unfair," Arsenio protested. "Your privileged place in the family is well established, and I give you my word you will suffer no disrespect at court and in the Dukedom." Hoping to convince her with reassuring words, Arsenio embraced Flavia with renewed passion and desire. But she pushed him away once again.

"Despite your protests, this is your wedding night, Arsenio. And I will not be a substitute lover in your bridal chamber."

"You're jesting," Arsenio said impatiently, "My bed is empty and I'm lonely for your company. The lady Polyxena is far away from us and she is not expected to arrive before a fortnight."

He again tried to embrace her without success or satisfaction. She faced him with defiance.

"I am going to my rooms, Arsenio. If you wish my company, join me within an hour. But I beg you to be discreet. Come alone, without your guards."

Arsenio felt frustrated and confused by her disrespectful behavior and answered in anger, "Go back to your rooms Flavia, and fear not. I won't disturb your sleep tonight." He turned his back on her, blind to his own fatal mistake.

Flavia's self-esteem was based on her beauty and sexual power. Arsenio's rebuff frightened her down to the core of her being. She responded by accosting him once again and kissing him with full ardor, actively seeking his sexual arousal. As soon as she sensed it, she removed herself from his embrace and donned a velvet cloak, then swiftly retreated toward the door. She stopped there and seductively addressed him, "Please come to me. I shall wait for you."

FLAVIA De BREZZÉ

Arsenio stood silent for a long while. His head throbbed with racing thoughts, but his main focus was on Flavia's sensual beauty. His desire was so overwhelming to him, he had to work hard to avoid following her like an obedient puppy. He reminded himself that he was the Lord of the manor, and her rebuff in the face of his terrible situation was humiliating. He was all too aware it would be foolish to give in to her demands and cast himself in a weak role inside his own castle, but youthful passion overwhelmed him. His mind filled with memories of Flavia starting with the day she first arrived in Lorengard-Lorraine as a little girl.

She was the daughter of the Count Henry, a once influential and wealthy French nobleman who suffered a reversal of fortune in the power struggles and prolonged wars. He escaped France to save himself and his family. His close friend, Edward, Arsenio's father, welcomed them in Lorengard-Lorraine. Yet Count Henry fell ill and died within a year of his exile and his unfortunate wife was so grief-stricken by her beloved husband's death that she soon followed him to the grave. The tragic couple, mercifully united in death, had left behind an orphan daughter. This was the young girl, Flavia.

Through Edward's kindness and generosity, Flavia was raised with all the advantages and privileges he would have bestowed upon his own child. Tutors schooled her in writing, reading, arts and music, privileges available only to females of the highest aristocratic strata. She was sent to a finishing school for patrician ladies to complete her education, making her eligible to enter the high station in life for which she had been groomed.

Arsenio remembered when she returned from boarding school at the age of fifteen. Even then, she was so sensual and stunning that he was instantly and helplessly attracted to her magnetic appeal.

Even at that early age, her great beauty was diminished by a cold and aloof expression that often radiated from her. Having known life as the poor orphan who received charity from the Duke of Lorengard-Lorraine, Flavia had grown to have a voracious need for grandeur and wealth. The lack of it was so humiliating and degrading to her that she covered her insecurity with a haughty nature.

In her eyes, the world had cheated her family by taking away wealth and privileges that she had been born with and was entitled to possess. Thus the only emotions she could muster toward the benefactors who had showed her such kindness was her deep-seated resentment and jealousy. Gratitude and appreciation were alien to her, but she had long concealed her true feelings from him. He mistook her beauty for sincerity and her seductiveness for love. In his youthful eyes, she was a trustworthy family friend.

But on this strange wedding night, the young Duke was filled with his longing for the only women he loved. He buckled on his sword and casually draped a cloak on his shoulders, then took a deep breath and marched out of the room.

He ignored the armed guards at the door and entered the long corridor. His guards rushed to his side as usual to protectively flank him, but he signaled them to remain behind. In his impatience and desire, he felt as if he no longer needed protection. The surprised guards were reluctant to obey the order, and Luca, the eldest of the guards, even dared to question the command.

"My lord…It is unwise for you to go unescorted. There have been too many attempts on your life. Please allow us to keep you safe."

The Duke placed an affectionate hand upon the old guard's shoulder. "Luca, I refuse to be afraid to move about in my own palace. Besides, I am well-versed in sword play and can defend myself."

"But your safety, milord," Luca insisted. "…is most important for the welfare of Lorengard-Lorraine. Should any harm befall you, the repercussions could be devastating for everyone."

Luca had gone too far in challenging his master's order. "I am the lord here," Arsenio replied with displeasure. "And I am fully aware of the dangers. In my judgment, I have taken proper precautions. Therefore, it is my express desire to move about unescorted. My order stands and you will all remain here."

Arsenio turned and strode down the long corridor, descended the central staircase and disappeared into the shadows of the center hall.

The disconcerted old guard remained silent, unable to reconcile the Duke's reckless behavior. Luca's long service to Lorengard-Lorraine had commenced decades earlier, when he was brought over from Italy because of his great skills with the sword. He had served as the personal bodyguard for Duke Edward, Arsenio's father, and quickly gained enough of the Duke' trust to be promoted to head guard.

His duties not only included the protection and guardianship of Arsenio, but also that of instructing him in arms use as the boy grew older. A relationship of mutual respect developed between them, and in addition to the great deference, Luca held for his lord, he also came to feel fatherly affection.

Left behind now, he paced the corridor. According to the constraints he lived under, his obligation was to serve and obey his master without question. He had never even contemplated disobeying a direct order, but his dread over his lord's safety dictated otherwise. While precious moments elapsed after Arsenio's hasty departure, Luca found himself paralyzed by his concerns. Finally, with a commanding gesture, he ordered several guards to follow him and started off through the long corridor.

"My dear Arsenio," Luca muttered. "...your loyal servant will follow you in spite of this misguided order."

Arsenio was well ahead of his guards when he arrived at Flavia's rooms, located in another wing of the palace. He stopped before the elegant wooden door to her rooms just long enough to push firmly on the handle. The door yielded and opened to him. He peered inside and smiled when he saw her standing in the center of the room waiting for him.

It struck him once again that she was supremely beautiful, even more so now in an exquisite blue gown tightly gathered at the waist. The garment was open in the décolletage, allowing her white shoulders and breasts to be visible, shielded only by transparent fabric. The effect greatly enhanced her power over his attention.

Arsenio's desire intensified. When Flavia flashed a seductive smile at him, he approached her with ardor and took her into a passionate embrace. She allowed him to kiss her and responded in her usual way, igniting his unbridled passion. Then she once again freed herself from his embrace and pushed him away with a flirtatious laugh.

He was so frustrated by her rebuff that he spoke in desperate tones, "My lady, please stop this cruel and vindictive game. I understand your anger and actions may be justified, but you are truly avenged, since you have made me into a sex slave. I am forced to succumb without dignity to your wishes and commands."

She showed him another small smile. "My lord, I no longer harbor hostility toward you. It's merely that the sharp edge of your sword injures my flesh and bruises my body when we embrace."

"Ah." His confusion betrayed him. "My, uh, deepest apologies."

"Thank you. But if you truly apologize, my lord, then give me your weapon. Place it in my hands with complete trust, and let me have, for just a moment, power over your life. I will accept the sword as a pledge of your fidelity."

Arsenio retreated in surprise, gripping the sword. Flavia's sneer dripped sarcasm. "If you please, my lord, do I read fear in your eyes? Because vengeance is alien to my nature. I am a faithful and loyal member of Lorengard-Lorraine. Of course, I must admit your unexpected secret marriage distressed me, after you promised to make me your Duchess. But I understand your predicament and the challenges you face in protecting the Dukedom. Therefore, because of my great love and devotion… I forgive you."

Arsenio desired to hear those words so much that he missed the irony in the tone. His heart filled with joy and overruled his brain, and he removed the sword to place it in his beloved's hands. Flavia took it and paused to admire the intricately engraved designs.

She erupted in laughter and threw the sword onto the stone floor. It struck with a resounding metal clang. Then she broke into a strange and alluring dance that emphasized her sensual curves.

Arsenio was so beset by passion that he ignored his sword on the floor while he remained captivated by her, irresistibly attracted while she continued her magnetic dance. After a few more moments, she leaned against a heavy tapestry separating the anteroom from the bedchamber and with a graceful motion opened the tapestry and walked away from him and into the room.

"It is time to stop this tortuous game," Arsenio cried out.

He followed Flavia into the room, forgetting his sword on the floor. She sat invitingly on the bed, shrouded by shadows, with a look of intense longing. The sight of her desire set loose his passions and he hungrily embraced her. She fairly smoldered while she responded to his advances, making Arsenio oblivious to everything except the elusive enchantress, finally captive in his embrace.

In the dark behind him, a sharp blade reflected the orange flames from the surrounding torches. An assassin leaped from the shadows and brutally assaulted helpless Arsenio, striking from behind. He cried out in shock and pain, then fell onto the floor, draped at Flavia's feet. It was that easily done, and Arsenio was no more.

She fixed a cruel stare at his motionless body, unmoved by his murder and feeling nothing more than contempt for him. The loathsome assassin, with his weapon still in hand, proudly stepped forward and stood before her.

Her smile of welcome bled the beauty from her face. "Well done," she whispered. "Everything worked according to plan. It was easier than I thought to defeat this 'mighty' Duke. The ingrate blindly followed me to his slaughter."

Her triumph was abruptly silenced by the clatter and clang of approaching armed guards. A moment later, they aggressively entered pushing their way in the anteroom. Flavia recoiled in fear when Luca Morosini burst into the bedchamber, followed by his guards. At the sight of Arsenio's motionless body, Luca's eyes widened in horror.

"My lord Arsenio!" he cried. "I am too late. I could not save your life." He faced Flavia and the assassin with fire in his eyes. "But the vile traitors who were instrumental in your demise will pay with their lives."

Boundless rage filled Luca's heart with the need for personal vengeance. It was not enough for him to order the guards to seize them. He fell upon the assassin with agility that belied his age, forcing the younger man to retreat until Luca disarmed him and plunged his blade into the traitor's chest.

The assassin emitted a bloodcurdling scream, fatally wounded and gasping, then fell to the floor next to his victim, the Duke of Lorengard-Lorraine. Luca spun to Flavia, who retreated to the rear of the room covering her face as if that might shield her from his blows. She screamed and became hysterical. She began to plead for mercy, but Luca spoke over her.

"Accursed woman!" he cried. "Pay with your life." He ignored her pleas and raised his sword, preparing to dispatch her in a single blow.

A moment passed. Then another.

Luca shook his head contemptuously and lowered his sword, unable to kill an unarmed woman, even a loathsome one responsible for Arsenio's death. The Code of Chivalry was embedded in his thinking, and it prevented him from exacting his revenge. He turned in frustration to his guards, but at the same moment realized, their behavior during his fight with the assassin. In absolute defiance of their strict training, they all held back at a safe distance and did nothing to aid him.

"What are you gaping at?" he demanded. "Seize her." The guards immediately responded and entered the room with swords drawn. But instead of apprehending Flavia as ordered, they turned against their leader and attacked him together, outnumbering him four to one.

Valiant Luca bellowed, "Traitors." And with all his strength, waved his sword in a menacing fashion, prepared to fight the disloyal mercenaries to the death. He did not doubt he was about to die, but he attacked them with a master's skill and the fury of a wounded lion.

Blades flashed and glinted in the firelight, clanging like sour bells. Within seconds, Luca managed to kill one of the guards and then seriously injure a second. He spun on the ball of one foot and faced down the other pair, carving a deadly steel web in the air and advancing behind it. Step by step, he moved forward, shielded with a whirling blade.

His wild offense forced the men into retreat, but they preferred cowardice to courage and used his age against him, dancing just out of his reach and waiting for him to tire, as they knew he must quickly do.

After a few more moments of powering his sword in wide figure-eight moves, Luca was sweating profusely and barely able to breathe. Instead of backing down, however, he defiantly shouted at them, "So you were paid to betray our gallant Duke? It is easy to guess who is responsible...Ludwig, Duke of Saxe-Hanover."

"You called me, Morosini?" a familiar voice rang out from the shadows.

The sound filled Luca with dread, even though the guards reacted by halting their attacks and backing away. Safe for a moment, he slowly lowered his weapon to rest his aching arm.

"As you can see," he continued. "I'm promptly responding to your call even though I know full well your low esteem for me." Ludwig, Duke of Saxe-Hanover stepped through the dimly lit bedchamber and into a dim patch of red firelight.

His features revealed a young man in his late twenties, slender with a patrician appearance. He wore his dark hair unusually long, but had a light and rosy complexion. His lips were surrounded by a meticulously manicured mustache and beard that emphasized the disdainful turn of his mouth. His whole appearance reflected affluence, but whatever good looks he might have put forth were diminished by the scornful look in his light gray eyes and an exaggerated air of superiority.

"You killed him," Luca gasped, shaking with rage. "It was your bloodstained gold that paid these vile assassins. And you did it with the help of that cursed woman."

"Don't be unreasonable," the duke dispassionately replied. "Why blame me because I have more wealth at my disposal and am better equipped to pay mercenaries than my poor departed cousin? Besides, dear Luca Morosini, you killed a couple of my best guards and even dear Flavia was in danger of dying by your sword. You are a most unwanted guest here. Your intrusive presence nearly disrupted a well-coordinated plan to commit a perfect coup and end Arsenio's power for all time."

The Duke walked toward Flavia, still cowering and lifted her chin. Even in her distraught condition, Flavia was a beautiful and desirable woman. "You couldn't possibly have desired to kill someone as lovely as this?" he asked with a sardonic smile. "What a waste of beauty."

Luca ignored the scornful words and glared at Flavia with fiery eyes. When he spoke, he did not raise his voice, but used a deathly quiet none of them had ever heard from him before.

"Cursed woman! I always believed you were cruel and arrogant, but I did not think you could betray the people who were generous to you." He dropped his voice to a whisper that somehow slid into her brain and rested between her ears.

"May your death be a thousand times more violent than Duke Arsenio's. And may his sacred blood be upon on your head."

Flavia recoiled instinctively from the terrible curse, cold beads of sweat permeating her brow. She felt herself overwhelmed by a feeling of dread and a terrible sense of doom.

The Duke walked with menace toward Luca. "It is time to stop your foolish discourse, Morosini. Your empty threats have no place here. I suggest you show proper deference to those in charge if you care to live another day. Arsenio, your beloved Duke whom you worship and revere, was a foolish and weak man. He was unworthy of command and sealed his own fate.

"Under his misguided leadership, the taxes of the Dukedom were too low and the demands of his worthless subjects too steep. In desperate need of help, he entered into a secret marriage with an heiress to enrich his state and fortify his political power with an alliance. I had knowledge of the situation…and had the capability to stop it."

"Why then did you allow the marriage to happen?" asked Luca.

Ludwig smiled with satisfaction. "Our new mysteriously elusive Duchess, who is perhaps ugly and deformed, will bring great riches to Lorengard-Lorraine. She is one of the wealthiest heiresses in Europe. That's the only reason my dear cousin requested her hand in marriage. She will arrive in Lorengard-Lorraine in a fortnight, with her fabulous dowry that under the present circumstances…will be mine. And the lovely lady will be my hostage."

The Duke ended with a sinister laugh that devastated Luca. The older man dropped his head forward in resignation.

Flavia's bedchamber was like a morgue, dead bodies everywhere on the floor. Despite of her innate cruelty, she found their presence terrifying and unsettling. She made her way swiftly toward the door, but a gentleman who entered in haste and claimed to have important news for the Duke prevented her exit.

His casual greeting lacked the usual deference and implied his high rank in the Duke's regime. Baron Frederick Van Halt was in his forties and heavy in the middle. He proudly carried a shiny sword with the panache of a warrior, but looked like a man who enjoyed a good meal more than sword play. He dressed predominantly in black to emphasize his flaming red hair and beard as well as to minimize his corpulence. He was a close ally and confidant of the Duke, equally ruthless and cruel. Their relationship was based on a mutual lust for power, and this alliance had proven successful in the takeover of Lorengard-Lorraine.

"Great news!" the Baron announced. "The palace and Dukedom are completely under our control. We had minimal opposition from the mercenaries except for a few foolish loyalists who preferred an early death to the thought of joining us."

Luca moaned desperately when he heard the Baron's account of mass betrayal. "Calm down, Morosini." the Duke said with scorn. "You're fighting for the wrong side. You wasted your considerable martial prowess on an imprudent and naive Lord who trusted too easily."

For emphasis, he pointed to Arsenio's motionless body, while the lady Flavia moved back suddenly, intimidated by the Duke's words. But fearing reprisal, she wisely kept her displeasure in check.

"I have a proposition, Morosini," the Duke continued at a deliberate pace. "Since I am victorious, I find myself predisposed to be magnanimous. You are a valiant warrior despite your age. Time has bent you a little, but has not broken your fighting spirit. You wield your sword with amazing strength and ability."

The Duke went on in a softer voice, almost friendly in its tone, "I will reward your talent and spare your life, despite your stance against me. You can be my head guard and be in charge of training my soldiers in the proper use of arms. For this service you will be highly honored and richly rewarded."

Luca silently lowered his head and once again took in the sight of Arsenio's body. He raised his head again and answered in a serene voice, "I won't live in the world you offer, my lord. It lacks honor. The greedy thirst for power has unspeakable cruelty as the only recourse. It would be an abomination for me to train your hired assassins, enabling them to murder and pillage innocent, helpless people. Fate has ordained my birth into servitude and I bowed to my inescapable destiny. But I always retained my honor by following the chivalrous code. It has empowered me and given meaning to my existence. I cannot and will not live as a traitor in whatever time I have left."

"Then die a fool and join your beloved Lord in death," Ludwig furiously gave the order to his waiting guard, who immediately plunged a sharp sword into Luca's chest. With a final desperate cry, Luca fell down and died next to the body of his lord Arsenio.

The Duke stared at his latest victim with contempt, unable to understand Luca's enormous sacrifice in defiance of his generous offer. "Fool," he said to the body. "You were as misguided and imprudent as your precious Lord."

Finally, tired of looking at death, he ordered his guards to remove the corpses from the bedchamber. He smiled with sinister pleasure when Arsenio's body was dragged from the room.

"Baron!" he called. "...Make certain our beloved Duke Arsenio receives a proper burial," he spoke without a trace of irony.

"It will be done," Baron Van Holt replied while he led the gloomy procession of dead bodies out of the bedchamber.

Finally alone, Ludwig turned his lustful attention toward Flavia. His erotic nature was stimulated by witnessing the violent spectacle and the euphoric victory.

He seized her and hungrily drew her to him. Even though Flavia was traumatized and fearful, she kept her wits about her well enough to respond with equal ardor to his passionate embrace.

✝✝✝

CHAPTER THREE

THE DEPARTURE

In the castle of Nemours, far from Lorengard-Lorraine, great preparations were made for Polyxena's departure. She was unaware of the tragic events in Lorengard-Lorraine or the treachery awaiting her, and because no one at Nemours knew of Arsenio's assassination or about the violent overthrow of his government by Ludwig, Duke of Saxe-Hanover, the task of sending Polyxena on her way proceeded.

Once everything was ready for her departure, the castle courtyard bustled with life. Many servants carried large trunks filled with her wardrobe and necessities, placing them carefully upon large, horse drawn carts. Polyxena's many servants were lined up and patiently waiting to bid her farewell. An elegant coach, covered with green damask and embellished with the Nemours coat of arms, waited for the distinguished traveler.

She finally entered the central portico, escorted on one side by her father, the Duke of Nemours, and on the other, the Count of Rozenberk. Four ladies in waiting followed to accompany the young bride to her new residence and bring the comfort of home to Polyxena's new surroundings. Also lined up in perfect symmetry was a regiment of fifty heavily armed guards entrusted with responsibility for her safety and guardianship of her valuable dowry.

Polyxena traveled in simple but elegant clothing, wearing a long, flowing mantle and hood. Her face remained shadowed by the garment and was difficult to see. This only reinforced the sense of enigma surrounding her. She had always been solitary and mysterious in spite of her status as a wealthy and eligible lady, and close friends were the only ones allowed in her presence besides necessary and trusted servants.

Life in the Dukedom of Nemours was austere, lacking excitement or festivities suitable for showcasing the beautiful young heiress. But rather than rail against the quiet life, this played into her nature because she favored either solitude or the hunting and sword play at which she excelled.

Her father's best friend, the Count of Rozenberk, who trained her in the use of arms, was also a man of great intellect. He tutored her in a vast field of knowledge traditionally withheld from women in that era.

The elder gentleman became her chosen companion, preferred to people her own age. In time, word spread throughout the realm that she was a recluse and with nothing but idle speculation to fill the vacuum of knowledge about her, rumors began to spread about Polyxena's appearance. They suggested that she was ugly or that she suffered from some physical deformity. In truth, Polyxena was beautiful and had the capacity to be quite charming when she chose to do so, but because of her isolated ways few people knew that about her.

When the sad moment of her departure arrived, Polyxena concealed her distress to the world with dignity and cultivated serenity within herself. She approached the servants who stood waiting to say good bye and greeted each one with warmth and kindness.

The Count of Rozenberk was saddened by her departure and spoke to her with loving affection, "My dear child, may your life be filled with joy, and truth and honor always be your path. Go forth with my love and blessings."

The old Count embraced her, then silently stepped away to allow his old friend the Duke of Nemours to be alone with his daughter.

The proud Duke guided Polyxena to the coach, keeping to protocol for a military man. He retained his habitual decorum until the last moment, then tears began to flow down his face. Polyxena was stunned and deeply moved by his show of emotion. She had never seen her father cry. She lovingly embraced him in complete disregard for staid conventions of etiquette.

"I shall miss you with all my heart, father," she whispered in his ear. "I will always love and honor you."

He spoke with a sad smile. "Forgive me, daughter, for all the pain I have caused you in this life."

"What? There is nothing to forgive," she protested. "Cruel destiny dictated these events. You have remained a loving and caring father to me at all times. May God grant me the joy to see you again."

Polyxena embraced him one last time, then entered the coach followed by her ladies in waiting. The Duke resolutely closed the coach door and signaled for the coachman to go.

"My precious daughter," he whispered while the coach pulled away. "My precious daughter."

The escorting regiment swiftly moved through the large courtyard arcade, and then through the main entrance and across the lowered drawbridge. With clear passage ahead, they speeded up and entered the surrounding countryside at a fast road trot, quickly distancing themselves from the castle. They soon disappeared from the Duke's sight.

He slowly walked away, looking like a man feeling helpless and alone.

Polyxena's journey to the Dukedom of Lorengard-Lorraine was difficult and slow, even though they remained free from attacks by bandits. Weather and terrain made formidable enemies and delayed the journey by several days.

Finally, the day's sunrise revealed Lorengard-Lorraine ahead of them. The walled city formed a picturesque vision, shrouded by a morning mist and perched atop the hilly countryside. The beautiful landscape was surrounded by acres of verdant forest favorable for hunting and outdoor sports. The Dukedom presented such a welcoming appearance that for the first time since her departure from Nemours, Polyxena relaxed and smiled in approval.

Within minutes, the entourage reached the summit and entered Lorengard-Lorraine through a passageway in the protective surrounding walls. Duccio and Philip knew the way and guided the group through the winding streets, surrounded by curious inhabitants trying to get a glimpse of whomever the important person traveling in the elegant coach might happen to be. But the curtains were drawn in the coach windows and no one could see inside. Still the crowds swelled and gathered around the coach, creating difficulty for the escorting guards while they attempted to clear the way.

However, this display of public curiosity was the only fanfare on exhibition. There was no welcoming committee in attendance and it was soon clear that the realm had no plans to honor the arrival of their new Duchess. Philip and Duccio felt their warriors' intuition vibrate with a sense of dread.

Another concern for the travelers was the unusual presence of threatening armed guards who seemed to be posted everywhere. By the time they arrived in the large plaza crowned by the magnificent Ducal palace everyone in the entourage looked nervous. The coat of arms of Lorengard-Lorraine decorated the structure's central portico, and the clear water of the splendid palace fountain reflected the majestic beauty of the edifice. But still there was no sign of a formal reception.

The large palace doors opened and several pageboys assembled on each side of the entry, elegantly dressed in blue and gold striped uniforms emblazoned with the coat of arms of Lorengard-Lorraine. They each carried a long, shiny, trumpet and began to play in unison. The music reverberated throughout the square, and here at least was some measure of welcome.

The entourage moved on into the vast courtyard, with Duccio and Philip acting as Arsenio's ambassadors and taking direct responsibility for Polyxena's safe delivery. The group resolutely climbed to the summit of an imposing staircase, where an elegant gentleman backed by heavily armed guards approached the young knights. The presence of armed guards was definitely outside of the expected protocol. Duccio paled at the sight of this ominous welcome. His tension rose again when he recognized the man. *The Baron Frederick Van Halt. Why is he here? This is an accomplice of Ludwig, Duke of Saxe-Hanover.*

The Baron pointedly ignored the surprise on the faces of the young knights and approached with a deliberate stride, speaking up in a voice tinged with sarcasm. "Well then, here you are. I hope your long trip has not proven too tiresome, sir knights. And of course that the lovely bride has arrived safely."

"Step aside milord," Phillip responded, gripping the scabbard of his sword for emphasis. "I do not understand your presence here and we expect to see the Duke at once."

"Ah! The Duke. Yes, yes, easily done, my young travelers," the Baron replied, though his tone still mocked them. To the entire entourage he announced in mock-formal tones, "One and all, Ludwig, Duke of Saxe-Hanover awaits you."

Philip raised his voice and spoke in a stronger tone, "You should know I am not referring to him." He moved his hand up to the pommel of his sword. "I refer to the legitimate lord here…Arsenio, Duke of Lorengard-Lorraine."

The Baron responded with a poor imitation of sadness and spoke quietly so the rest of the party would not hear, "My young friends. It is my sad duty to inform you of tragic news. The Duke has died." He paused to let the impact settle in, then added, "Several weeks ago, actually."

"What?" Duccio cried. "I do not believe you. Is this some cruel and vicious game? Beware of lying to us or you'll taste steel."

Before the palace guards could interfere, Duccio put his sword point to the man's throat. "We have seen no signs of mourning in Lorengard-Lorraine. I do not believe Arsenio is dead."

"Calm yourself," the Baron insisted in a snide tone. "Remove your blade from my throat, I am speaking the truth. We kept it a secret out of respect for the sensitivities of the intended bride. It is part of my function here to inform you, and her, of the Duke's untimely departure." His solemn frown did a poor job of covering a sneer.

Duccio lowered his sword, bewildered and distressed by the news. He turned to Philip and the two men stepped close together and began to whisper.

The Baron ignored them and walked toward the coach. Without asking permission, he opened the door and looked inside. Seeing several female passengers, he asked, "Which of you is Lady Polyxena of Nemours? Please come forward. I request an audience."

The other women gave him no indication of their identity. They also took care not to point out Polyxena, who sat with her mantle shrouding her head and effectively obscuring her features. However, she took the initiative.

"I am here, milord," she responded, and gracefully stood up from her seat and stepped down from the coach. In contrast to the implied shyness of her shrouded features, she spoke in a voice that left no doubt about her regal persona. "But since the day of my marriage to Arsenio, my true name is no longer Polyxena of Nemours, but the Duchess of Lorengard-Lorraine. Please keep that in mind, sir."

"Yes, yes. And with regard to that very point...Unfortunate news. Difficult times indeed. I fear I must bring you evil tidings, since you may not have heard me a moment ago. To repeat... Arsenio, whom you call your spouse, is no longer alive. I do not wish to whittle too fine a point on the feather, but he died unexpectedly weeks ago and molders as we speak...My condolences, of course."

Polyxena swallowed a gasp and braced herself against the coach. "How can this be possible, milord? I want to know how he died. A man so young. Only a few weeks ago, I was told he enjoyed perfect health."

"True, but a mysterious malady killed him quickly. Very quickly indeed. I may fairly say his physicians could do nothing to prevent it. However, I am not as well-versed in this matter as others here. My first duty is to welcome you to Lorengard-Lorraine. No doubt you'll receive the specific story regarding Arsenio's passing. Meanwhile, please allow me to invite you to be the honored guest of Ludwig, Duke of Saxe-Hanover. Ludwig was Arsenio's closest living relative and he has journeyed here to ensure his cousin a proper burial."

Polyxena felt her anxiety tighten at the sound of Ludwig's name. She had heard many stories about Ludwig of Saxe-Hanover and none of them were good. She willed herself to hide her concern and retain her dignity. "I wish to retire as soon as possible," she said. "I am weary from my journey and distressed over this sudden news of my husband's death. I trust you will allow me to mourn in privacy."

The Baron bowed, then turned and signaled his guards to escort Polyxena to her rooms. She and her ladies in waiting were escorted to acceptable accommodations and left undisturbed there for several hours, during which time there was no communication from the palace. It was impossible to tell whether this was a show of respect or a sign of indifference.

Late in the afternoon, a messenger brought an invitation from Ludwig. There was to be a banquet followed by a grand ball that very evening in honor of the memory of Arsenio. It was a disorienting invitation, since armed guards also accompanied the messenger. Apparently, she was invited to come at that very instant and the soldiers were there to see to it. The messenger moved like a nervous mouse and assured her that he had only been told to inform her that the Duke eagerly awaited this opportunity to meet Polyxena of Nemours. He barely placed any emphasis at all on the use of her former name.

The great banquet hall sat in the heart of the palace, a vast and majestic space with vaulted ceilings hung with iron chandeliers that illuminated the entire room with yellow-orange torch light. Splendid tapestries of hunting scenes covered the walls, along with a variety of polished weapons and pieces of elegantly displayed armor. Three massive horseshoe-shaped tables filled the center of the room. They were covered with heavy brocade tablecloths and laden with solid gold dishes and cups that reflected the beauty of the lavish display of food and garlands of fresh flowers.

The Duke of Saxe-Hanover sat on a regal high-backed chair, brimming with self-satisfaction. Lady Flavia perched at his right side, clearly enjoying the position. She wore a magnificent crimson gown richly embodied with gold and her blond hair was artistically styled beneath a golden net entwined with pearls.

Ludwig stood up and signaled for silence, raising his golden goblet. "Milords," he cried. "Today we celebrate a new government in Lorengard-Lorraine, one with renewed power and strength. We will destroy anyone who opposes our victorious path. I promise to fill the Dukedom's empty coffers with gold and restore Lorengard-Lorraine to its former glory."

The Duke provided the opportunity to cheer, which the assembled crowd wisely accepted while he took a drink from his cup. "I drink to you, dear cousin Arsenio, so conveniently disappeared. And moreover I drink to the riches currently in my possession from the dowry of your lovely bride."

The Duke laughed at his own jest and provided the opportunity for the rest to join in, which they did without delay. He rewarded their enthusiasm by inviting everyone to join him in a drinking fest. Once again the obedient crowd gladly enthused, rapidly emptying cup after cup of spiced wine. The drink was said to be especially conducive to debauchery and drunkenness. With that expectation in mind, the attendees soon became shrill and strident, falling under the spell of the wine's reputation.

The Duke continued his drinking with great gusto, stimulating his senses and spurring him to cast off all self-restraint. "I drink to you, dear friends...You who were instrumental in my triumph are entitled to share the elation of this faithful day. And this evening our greatest entertainment will be the arrival of our new Duchess, who will finally unveil her ugliness or deformities to the world." The crowd laughed and roared in appreciation.

"And finally, I drink to you, dear Flavia, our lovely Queen of the feast. You, my lady, are more pleasing and desirable than ever." With that he forcefully embraced her, holding her tightly about the waist, and kissed her with abandon. He found himself feeling not at all shy about groping her body for all to see.

Flavia responded equally, melting into the Duke's passionate embrace and showing no restraint or shame. The erotic spectacle stimulated the drunken crowd, who quickly joined the royal pair in a sexually driven bacchanal. An orgiastic atmosphere took over the room while everybody rubbed and caressed anything that wasn't theirs.

They became so loud in their revels that the Lord Chamberlain had to raise his voice considerably to announce the arrival of the guest of honor. It was all he could do to make himself heard above the din. "Her grace arrives…The Duchess of Lorengard-Lorraine."

Immediately, complete silence descended upon the banquet hall. Here before them was to be the evening's main entertainment. The less intoxicated ones tried to regain some dignity by adjusting their attire and rising in a show of respect for the honored guest.

They stared at the graceful woman who descended the central staircase and advanced toward them. They saw that she was elegantly dressed in a purple gown with loose fitting, oversized sleeves lined with golden silk. She wore a tall and ornate hat that made her petite frame appear taller, and her long flowing veil reached the floor to form an elegant train.

She proudly advanced with her face visible to all. Her general appearance lacked physical beauty, but there was nothing odd about her features. An aura of kindness and gentleness graced her, although while she descended the staircase her expression turned to one of dismay at the scene in front of her.

When she drew close enough for all to see her well, relentless taunting of her looks rose from the drunken mob, who had been primed to expect ugliness in Polyxena of Nemours just as they were primed to expect the wine to drive them mad. They made certain she could hear their scornful comments.

"If I had a face like that, I'd conceal it too," one impudent drunk shouted.

Everyone laughed loudly, mocking the helpless visitor without mercy. Nevertheless, she bravely walked directly up to the Duke, in spite of the fact that he made no attempt to hide his sadistic pleasure at the crowd's disrespect.

Flavia felt elation over the uninspiring appearance of her rival and savored the pleasure of the moment. Only when the woman approached the dining table did the Duke finally stand to welcome her. He stared at his guest with disgust he was already primed to display and gave her a mock bow.

"My *beautiful* Duchess," he cried out for all. "Despite our sadness and sorrow, welcome to the Dukedom of Lorengard-Lorraine. Unfortunately, my poor cousin has died and cannot revel in your inspiring presence." His words drew laughter from the unruly crowd.

Overwhelmed by the insults, she struggled to keep her dignity while the Duke continued heaping scorn.

"Unfortunately, milady, early death was Arsenio's destiny. All of us who loved him have come to honor his memory at this great banquet. Therefore, dear Polyxena of Nemours, please come and sit by my side so I can luxuriate in your beauty." He laughed again at his own little joke.

"Your grace," she answered in a firm but humble voice. "There is a misunderstanding. I am not the Duchess of Lorengard-Lorraine…"

"Neither is the Duchess," he interrupted. The remark earned guffaws from the sycophants.

She lowered head like a woman leaning into a strong wind and continued, "Sire, I am Lady Davina of Devonshire, in service to her grace. I have been singly honored to bring you a message."

At this, the crowd finally fell silent.

"Message?" parroted the Duke. "What 'message' is necessary from the Duchess that she couldn't come and tell me herself?" His anger was already rising at having his little joke ruined in front of all.

"She is tired and distressed by the tragic news about Duke Arsenio's death. She begs your pardon, but under the circumstances she could not accept your invitation to the banquet."

"Refuse my invitation?" the Duke cried out. A wine-fueled rage instantly rose in him. "And we are not all here to pay her homage? Her refusal is a marked insult to my person and my guests." His cheeks were bright crimson. "You will tell your lady she must make an appearance at this funerary banquet. Refusing is offensive and unacceptable to me."

Davina tried to respond in spite of the intimidating circumstances, but was silenced when the Duke called out, "Come forth, Baron Van Halt."

The Baron immediately appeared and the Duke continued, "Escort Lady Davina back to the Duchess' rooms. Make certain lady Polyxena comes back with you voluntarily...*or otherwise*. I will not accept any further delay."

The Baron bowed his head and extended his arm to Lady Davina, who took hold of it regardless of her preference in the matter. They exited the great banquet hall.

When they arrived at Polyxena's rooms, Davina asked the Baron to remain in the antechamber. He consented, but ordered Davina to leave the door open.

In the rear of the room, Polyxena sat on a chair with her back to the door. The Baron only saw her lustrous dark hair and a white delicate hand on the armrest. When Davina entered the bedchamber, she saw that Polyxena was dozing in the chair, so she gently cleared her throat to wake her.

"Oh...Davina. I hope you gave my message to the Duke, because I am terribly tired this evening. Please help me undress and prepare for bed."

"Forgive me, my lady," Davina exclaimed in distress. "I cannot fulfill your request. Your message was rejected by Ludwig. He yet awaits your presence in the banquet hall."

Polyxena was taken aback by the Duke's offensive response and resolutely answered, "He will not have any choice in the matter, since I shall not attend. I desire rest and need to sleep. I do not intend to see anybody on this day."

"My lady." The Baron stepped into the room and revealed that he had been eavesdropping. "Your refusal is unwise. I suggest you change your mind and honor the request. I have been sent by the Duke to escort you to the banquet hall without regard to your opinion."

In response to this insolence, Polyxena turned angrily toward the uninvited guest. It was the first time anyone of royal line in Lorengard-Lorraine got a clear look at her face. Even flushed with rage, she displayed beauty such as the Baron had never seen.

He was momentarily silenced by the sight of her and could only stare. Polyxena's features were magnificent, with sparkling green eyes framed by long, dark eyelashes and arching brows. Her perfect oval face was crowned by lustrous ebony hair.

"It is quite apparent milord," she spoke with regal dignity. "...that the so-called invitation is in fact a direct order and a sign of great disrespect toward me. However, I will accompany you of my own volition because I am suddenly eager to meet this arrogant Ludwig, Duke of Saxe-Hanover, whose claim to nobility appears to lie only in his title."

The Baron was fascinated by her self-possessed behavior. Such a thing was rare among the submissive women of his day.

She stared at him for a silent moment, then brusquely spoke again, "Milord. I wish to properly dress for the banquet. You must leave my room at once and wait for me in the antechamber. Hopefully, you will cease your disrespect and grant this small request, will you not?"

Her dignity in the face of his intimidation caught the Baron off guard. He bowed with deference and left the bedchamber.

Finally alone, Davina spoke up, "My Lady, I witnessed the behavior of the dinner guests and I am still embarrassed by the shameful sight of them. It is not appropriate for you to appear at such a spectacle. I beg you, leave this evil place tonight and return to your father's house."

"I am afraid that would be unwise, Davina. We must be vigilant to safeguard our rights and seek the most advantageous way out of our difficulty. I will meet this 'Duke' and assess his character."

Regardless of Davina's misgivings, she and two chambermaids began helping Polyxena into a magnificent gown of green brocade. The beautiful garment enhanced her eye color with its precious stones and showcased her height and well-formed figure. The neckline displayed her full breasts and slender waistline. The women placed a golden diadem, encrusted with jewels and pearls above her brow, and left her flowing hair loose upon her shoulders. The overall effect greatly enhanced her stunning beauty.

By the time she and the escort party arrived at the banquet hall, the atmosphere was considerably more subdued than it had been before Lady Davina's appearance. Most of the guests now found that their curiosity outweighed their need to misbehave and quietly waited for the arrival of the mysterious and elusive

Polyxena. When she finally appeared on the central staircase, everyone in the room was dazzled by the vision she presented.

She slowly descended the steps surrounded by the admiring glances of the crowd. The gleaming lights of the hall enhanced the splendor of her presence and sparkled on her beautiful, bejeweled gown. She held herself with dignity, regal in spite of the frightening moment. Her face flushed and she could feel her heart wildly beating, but she allowed nothing to betray her turmoil.

The Duke found himself shaken by the sight of her. Nothing in his expectations prepared him for this. He slowly stood, mouth open in surprise at the sight of this magnificent creature who walked toward him with such a graceful air. His eyes did nothing to conceal the desire already burning within him.

Meanwhile, Ludwig's sudden fascination with his new guest did not escape Flavia's jealous eyes. She felt herself filled with rage.

"My Lady," the Duke greeted Polyxena, kissing her extended hand. "My heart bleeds for my cousin Arsenio, both for his premature death and for the loss of so magnificent a bride."

Polyxena ignored him and responded coldly, "I am here at your command, my lord, since apparently my presence is essential."

"I beg pardon my lady, but I wanted the pleasure of your company to honor your dead spouse at this funerary banquet."

Polyxena remained silent, aware that the Duke held all the power in that moment. But while she gazed across the drunken crowd surrounding her, she saw no respect for her departed husband. In spite of her youth and inexperience, she understood how dangerous her situation was, with her powerful father too far away to help her. At that moment, her only strength lay in her beauty and the lure it held over the Duke.

She instinctively knew that she needed to stall for time and try to gain his friendship and trust, so she decided to play a dangerous hand. Without further ado, she gave the Duke a seductive smile that hid her disgust even as it captivated him.

"I beg your indulgence, my Lord," she began. "The difficult day has overwhelmed me, and I ask your kind permission to retire. I hope my request will not inconvenience you during my husband's funerary banquet, since I know we have a great deal to talk about. Tomorrow, after a proper rest, I would be honored to meet with you in private at your earliest convenience."

"Of course my lady," the Duke cried loud enough for all to hear. Her appearance of receptiveness greatly pleased him and her beauty so excited him that he stood and he extended his arm to her. "It is my pleasure to escort you to your rooms." He threw a wink at the crowd. "Tomorrow, we will have ample time to converse in a leisurely fashion."

"I am very much honored." Her smile hid her perfidy as she placed her hand on the Duke's arm.

Without delay, the royal pair left the banquet hall with lewd salutations from the guests.

Flavia was left standing alone to watch them depart with no more regard for her than for a chambermaid. She felt publicly humiliated by the cruel and capricious Duke and fought back bitter tears. She knew in that instant that her fantasies of ascending to power in Lorengard-Lorraine had just been defeated. *But only for the moment,* she assured herself. *Only for the moment...*

Polyxena successfully manipulated the Duke into dropping her off at her temporary rooms and leaving her in peace for the evening. Now safely away from him, she finally relaxed and threw herself onto a chair. She closed her eyes, trying to gather her thoughts and decide upon her best course in this precarious situation. When she finally opened them, again she saw loyal Davina looking at her with a puzzled expression.

"Yes? What is it you wish to say?"

"Forgive me my lady. I have been in your service for many years, but I never had the opportunity to see you dressed in such magnificence and splendor. You look so beautiful tonight, and I wondered why you never..." She stopped, embarrassed by her own daring.

"What are you trying to say Davina?"

"I am ashamed of my boldness, my lady. It is not my place to ask personal questions."

"Perhaps your questions are based upon devotion you have for me, rather than curiosity?"

"That they are, my lady."

"Then you have my permission to ask. If it is within my power, I will answer."

As a deferential woman, Davina was uneasy, but continued, "I have often wondered why you have been so solitary, hidden from sight. Because of that, rumors have been spread about possible physical deformities and tonight I had an unrestricted look at the effect these rumors have in the minds of the people, or at least in the minds of the people surrounding the Duke.

"It has always been difficult for me to understand why someone of your great beauty would live in solitude. I found it especially difficult to understand since nature has gifted me so little."

"I am sorry if I caused you sorrow in any way, Davina. It's true that beautiful gowns and glamorous banquets have never been part of my life, and I can understand why this behavior must seem strange, since I was born to that privileged life."

"It has been difficult for all of us in your inner circle to understand."

"The reasons are intertwined with my family's history and have been buried in my heart for years," Polyxena answered with an odd sadness that Davina did not understand.

"It is not my place to question you, my lady. I do not wish to hurt you. Please forgive my curiosity."

"There is nothing to forgive...Perhaps it is time for me to remove this great burden from my mind. For far too long, it has taken the joy of living from me and I wish to finally be free of its secrecy. I will gladly confide in you, my loyal friend.

†††

CHAPTER FOUR

THE DUCHESS OF NEMOURS

"My father was the elder of two brothers and became the new Duke of Nemours at the age of twenty-three following his father's death. Dynastic protocol dictated that only the elder son would inherit the Dukedom, so as not to diminish the house's power. His younger brother, Roland, received only a modest estate and a monthly allowance. It was truly an unfair situation for him, and I am sure Roland must have been jealous and competitive.

"Fortunately, since great affection existed between the brothers, their love was not undermined by the financial situation.

My father was generous toward his sibling and increased his inheritance, proclaiming Roland as the most valued Nemours citizen, a man second only to himself.

"During that period, Nemours enjoyed a peaceful, stable time and the Dukedom flourished under my father's benevolent rule. In time, more was expected of the young Duke. He needed to marry to secure the dynasty, providing an heir for the house of Nemours. Many princesses of Europe vied to marry the handsome Alexander and become his Duchess. My father had ample opportunity to choose from many wealthy heiresses who could bring advantageous alliances to his Dukedom. But none of the ladies in question suited him. Therefore, he refused to buckle under the political pressure of his ministers and advisers and continued his search for the proper bride.

"Shortly after, the woman of his dreams finally arrived. It was during the yearly celebration of Saint Justin, the patron Saint of Nemours…And she would change his life forever.

"To honor the festive occasion, entertainers from different parts of the countryside performed at the castle and public squares. There was a carefree aura throughout the Dukedom, and the Ducal palace was resplendent with lights and cheerful decorations. The guests in attendance were treated to a bountiful feast that included exotic entertainers who had performed throughout Europe.

"During the festivities, my father's eyes were attracted by one of the dancers, a young girl who skillfully performed graceful and intricate moves. Her dancing emanated a strong sensual aura and a special radiance that captivated everyone. My father had never met anyone quite like her and was instantly attracted to her beauty, coupled with her undeniable magnetism. He became oblivious to everything except his attraction to that woman who had so captivated him, and he decided to make inquiries into her background.

"But the other members in her dance troupe were able to reveal very little about her. She was known only by her first name, Chantal, because she was an orphan who did not know her lineage…At the age of seventeen, she had already been traveling with the dancers for years, living the life of a gypsy while performing in Nemours and adjacent realms.

"My father's youthful impulsiveness overtook him and at that point he refused to inquire further into her background. His fascination with her made it feel morally wrong to examine her background for any other virtue besides great beauty. He chose to ignore his wise advisers' concerns over her unsuitable lifestyle.

"He could have possessed any female companion he wanted, but because of his great love for Chantal, he decided instead to make her his bride.

"He had many obstacles to surmount before the wedding could take place, because Chantal was not a noble and therefore was forbidden by existing law to marry a Duke, but his determination remained fixed in his heart.

"He stubbornly used his power to change the laws concerning royal marriage to accommodate her status and make her eligible as his bride. Special dispensations were also obtained from the Pope with intervention from the Cardinal of Nemours, who was a dear friend of my father…Thus, the final obstacle was removed.

"Chantal was invited to court, where she was taught the proper etiquette befitting the future Duchess of Nemours. She responded with great enthusiasm and gratitude for the opportunity.

"She realized it was an unheard-of honor to be chosen as the bride of such a powerful man and was equally captivated by the handsome Duke himself, who made a grand show of his affections for her.

"The wedding occurred with all the pomp and circumstances my father's great wealth could provide. Music and festivities lasted for days and Chantal was the most beautiful bride anyone had seen. She was enthusiastically welcomed by their subjects, and eagerly accepted as the new Duchess of Nemours.

"Chantal was my mother...I was born during the first year of their marriage. My father remembers this time as the happiest and most peaceful in his life, because he was with the woman he loved and who bore him the child he wished for. His delight was not diminished when a daughter was born to them because in Nemours women are equal to men in dynastic succession and can rule.

"During this idyllic time, there was peace at the Dukedom and prosperity was enjoyed by the people. But those special years of tranquility did not last. Disruptive forces were already at work in Europe.

"To prevent a looming war from spreading, my father left Nemours at the head of an army sent out to protect the Dukedom. Unfortunately, such missions were frequent and my father was forced to be absent from home for long periods in those days, sometimes on campaigns that lasted for months at a time.

"But my mother was restless by nature. She very much disliked the continued separations and found them disruptive and unbearable. In his absence during these times of war, life at court was somber and gloomy. The lavish balls and festive banquets she loved were considered inappropriate absent the household ruler, and she was bored with the restrictions imposed by royal etiquette.

"Because she was self-centered and immature by nature, she found that her illustrious position placed burdens upon her that she never anticipated and did not want to fulfill.

"My mother was canny enough to refrain from revealing her true feelings to her husband, but severely missed the excitement and freedom of her former life and its lack of enforced structure. As a result, she left me in the care of a nurse and servants and began to capitalize on my father's absence by living a duplicitous life dictated by her lustful nature.

"Her servants were replaced by new ones, whose loyalty she could buy. Lavish parties were reinstated at her command, with no regard or respect for my father's absence. During festivities, she wore many sumptuous gowns, showcasing her great beauty, and loved the attention it brought her. Endless revelries lasted throughout the night, while she recklessly surrounded herself with handsome young men and indulged her lust and need for adulation. No one dared intervene for fear of her reprisals, and the courtesans were well paid to protect her privacy. During my father's brief visits home, she would behave in a loving and attentive fashion, easily misleading him.

"But there was no end to her uncontrolled desire for pleasure. Her wild nature had only been temporarily stifled by the court etiquette and restrictions. In the end, they ignited an overwhelming desire for the unrestricted freedom of her nomadic early life.

"She became even more daring in her search for diversions outside the palace walls. She found it entertaining to disguise herself and visit the many inns in the Dukedom, searching for the sorts of male companionship a woman of beauty and wealth can easily obtain. However her endless infidelities became increasingly difficult to conceal and despite efforts by my father's loyal friends, who wished to spare him the dishonorable and painful knowledge of her indiscretions, the Duke inevitably heard about the rumors.

"At first he scoffed at the reports. He would not believe the woman he loved would be so loathsome and dismissed the stories as idle gossip. But he was nevertheless a highly intelligent man and the seeds of doubt had been planted. Eventually he found it impossible to ignore them. He decided to investigate, but in hopes of exonerating his wife rather than confirming her guilt.

"He returned unannounced from one of his frequent outings and, in complete secrecy, chose to enter the castle alone late at night and sneak into my mother's rooms.

"He entered his own castle beset with anxiety, sword in hand, prepared to combat a possible betrayal. He reached his wife's chambers and saw several handmaidens posted in the corridor, guarding the door. They appeared terrified by his sudden arrival, but before they could deliver a warning, my father silenced them and threatened dire repercussions to any who made a sound.

"Swiftly and silently, he entered the dark bedchamber and saw two bodies on the bed, entwined in a torrid and passionate embrace. He gasped in outrage, overwhelmed at the sight.

"My mother and her lover heard him and recoiled in terror to the far corners of the room. Their faces were hidden by the darkness, but the Duke heard their labored breathing.

"'Make yourself known,' he cried. "'...you vile and dishonorable person, who steals another man's wife. Take up your sword. I do not need to fight an unarmed man."

"He retrieved the man's sword from the side of the bed and hurled the weapon into the corner. Instead of accepting my father's chivalrous offer, the man refused to reclaim his sword. He threw a chair at my father in hopes of opening the way to safety, but it proved useless and he could not get away. His only choice was to take up his sword.

"A violent fight ensued. My mother's lover displayed poor fighting skills and soon retreated in a futile attempt to avoid my father's superior strength, but in doing so, he stumbled forward and impaled himself upon the Duke's sword. He fell mortally wounded. When my father approached the dying man and got a good look at him, he discovered to his horror that this illicit lover was his own brother...Roland.

"Grief stricken at his brother's death in spite of the betrayal, he cradled his body. With his final breath, Roland begged my father's forgiveness.

"My father was devastated by Roland's death as well as the betrayal that caused it. The situation was so unreal to him that he was too horrified to think. He held the lifeless Roland in his arms and he remained motionless, paralyzed by his pain.

"My mother had hidden in the shadows during the struggle and was terrified by the reprisals facing her. She desperately tried to escape the bedchamber by taking advantage of my father's exhausted condition and darting with feline speed to silently retrieve my uncle's sword for herself while my father's back was turned. With ruthlessness in her heart, she was ready to plunge the lethal weapon into his back.

"But the Duke was a man of arms, trained as a Knight, and his heightened sense of self-preservation alerted him at the last moment. He moved into a defensive stance and deflected the fatal blow, receiving instead a deep gash on his left cheek. It is the wound that created the scar still etched upon his face.

"My mother was overcome with terror and recoiled from my father, who was bloodied both by his own wound and from Roland's body. She grabbed her hooded mantle and fled the bedchamber, leaving my father too stunned and miserable to bother chasing her. She ran toward the stables, mounted her favorite horse, made a dash across the drawbridge and charged into the countryside at a full gallop.

"The tower guards saw her flee and because of darkness and the shield of her hooded mantle they failed to recognize their

Duchess. Naturally, they commanded her to stop, but she took the gamble of ignoring their warning. As a result, one well-placed arrow ended her wild and misguided life."

Polyxena paused and tears streamed down her face while she finally released the pain that had haunted her throughout her life.

"Maybe it's better she died that terrible night, sparing my father the need to condemn her to death. Our laws make death the final justice reserved for adulterers as well as those who commit murder. These are the circumstances that destroyed our family.

"My father had fearlessly faced death on the battle fields but couldn't cope with the betrayal from those he had loved and trusted. He quickly found Nemours to be an unbearable and cruel reminder of the happy youth he shared with his brother and the joyful marriage he once had.

"His peace was gone. His ability to concentrate on governing his Dukedom was so impaired that he was forced to make a drastic decision. He decided it would be best for the welfare of his people if he left Nemours for an indeterminate amount of time. Perhaps, he thought, he ought to join the Holy crusades and travel to distant places in search of peace.

"The Count William of Rozenberk was my father's most trusted and loyal friend and so was made regent in the Dukedom and my guardian during my father's absence. My father traveled to many faraway places in Europe and Palestine. During that time I had no other communication with him than through messages relayed via courier.

"The Count of Rozenberk was a wonderful substitute father to me. Ironically, it was he who gave me the love and affection I had always craved but couldn't get from my parents. He was a noble and knowledgeable man who taught me wisdom, and he helped me understand my family's tragic history.

"He encouraged me to avoid placing blame or harboring resentments toward my father over his painful absence, and encouraged me to have compassion and understanding for him. The Count was also a valiant knight, who trained me in the use of arms even though this was not ordinarily done for females. So you understand why I love and honor the Count of Rozenberk, second only to my father.

"Finally, the long separation came to an end and a courier arrived with the message that he was returning home. I remember that fateful day so well, waiting to be reunited with him. My heart was filled with joy.

"I ran toward my father to embrace him, and although he responded with warmth, I could see torment in his eyes when he looked at me. I knew the reason, because during his absence, my features had matured and come into their own and now my face had become identical to my mother.

"Ever since that time I have been uncomfortable with my appearance, knowing that my looks caused my father's anguish. I was a constant reminder of the woman he loved and who deceived and betrayed him in such a terrible way. I felt irrationally guilty and responsible for the woe that befell my family.

"Since my father and I never discussed the tragic situation, there was nothing to dispel the pain. I became reclusive and a loner, uncomfortable about meeting new people and surrounded only by close friends. I played down my appearance by wearing simple garments. I often favored men's hunting clothes to make my appearance different from my mother's audacious feminine style.

"Most destructive of all for me was my deep fear that I might have inherited her destructive character. The fact that I resembled her so closely amplified the fear that sooner or later her perverse nature would manifest in me... "

"No, my lady," Davina interrupted. "You only look like your mother. The resemblance is merely skin deep. In every way, you are your father's daughter. You possess his gallant spirit and honorable nature. Your heart is filled with love, not hate."

"Thank you Davina, my loyal friend," she replied. "Your kind words give me hope. Today, for the first time in my life, I appreciated my physical appearance, not for any reason of vanity but because it was the only power I possessed over the Duke of Saxe-Hanover. Beauty is the only gift my mother gave me besides life, and I am finally aware that I am a different person than her in every way. Above all, at last I am free from that terrible guilt."

"Of course my lady," Davina responded with compassion. "You are a victim in this situation, just as your father was, and not the perpetrator. I had no idea that such a terrible history of blood existed in your family. But it is my fervent hope that you can be free from the shadows of the past and go on with your life in the spirit of optimism and hope."

"You are right, my friend," Polyxena answered with gratitude. "I feel better now, thanks to your understanding nature. It was time to free myself from those poisonous feelings of guilt."

Polyxena and Davina embraced. They both felt that they were sisters of a sort, now. Confined in an alien palace, both existed at the mercy of a ruthless and evil despot. Davina was the first to address that dangerous issue.

"My lady, we must leave this evil place. Perhaps he can be convinced to set us free and return us to the honor and safety of your father's house, since the Duke is favorably predisposed toward you."

"No Davina, " Polyxena answered. "Life only moves in one direction, and I am a married woman now, even if only in title. Since I believe in destiny, I feel certain that I am here for a reason. Now I intend to find out what that reason is.

"I am sure my husband was murdered and it is my responsibility to avenge his death. It is also my duty as Duchess to protect the people of Lorengard-Lorraine, who tragically lost their benevolent leader and are now in the hands of that ruthless man."

Polyxena remained silent for a long moment. "Maybe he will show me the way."

"Who, my lady? Your Father?"

"No Davina. The Duke of Saxe-Hanover."

It was late in the afternoon of the next day when Polyxena was informed the Duke of Saxe-Hanover had come to visit. For the occasion, she wore one of her most beautiful gowns made of ruby red velvet and embroidered with pure gold. Her hair was artistically styled in an upsweep and entwined with pearls and precious stones. The effect was enhanced by her tall, shapely figure and rendered her more beautiful than ever.

She greeted the Duke in the antechamber and for once allowed herself to revel in the admiration and desire she saw in his eyes. She was not so young or inexperienced that she failed to grasp how powerfully her appearance influenced him.

The trick of it was to appear receptive to him while curbing his romantic advances without puncturing his vanity. It felt like she was performing a high-wire walk, but it was vital for her to gain his trust and have a stronger hand in the dangerous game she was about to play.

After a moment of hesitation, the Duke bowed his head in an imitation of chivalry. It was obviously driven by his attraction to her.

"My enchanting cousin," he exclaimed. "Your loveliness and your radiant smile brighten this sad day."

"You honor me with your presence, my lord, and I thank you for your gracious words," Polyxena answered.

She extended her hands to Ludwig, who hungrily kissed them. She made it a point to appear pleased by the Duke's attention and invited him to sit by her side in a nearby divan. There she continued her discourse with him in private.

"My lord, I am compelled to rely once more on your tolerance in allowing me to seek answers to the many questions that lay heavy on my mind."

"I bow to your request my lady," Ludwig gallantly answered. "But permit me to share some plans I made for the future, where you could play an important role if you're willing to participate…my dear cousin. I firmly believe that our meeting was predestined and ordained by a superior power and I hope you will be receptive to my suggestions."

"Cousin, since that is the name you wish to be called by me," Polyxena answered. "I am eager to learn your ideas and will give them the respect and value they richly deserve. But I hope you will indulge my need to learn the circumstances of my husband's death and to be told of the whereabouts of his remains."

Polyxena remained silent for a moment, saddened by the words she uttered, but she quickly regained her composure and continued with the task at hand. "I have another question, my lord, which I find disturbing."

"Feel free to ask, my lady," the Duke responded, eager to keep her happy.

"I want to know the reason why the citizens of Lorengard-Lorraine have no knowledge of Arsenio death. When I entered the Dukedom, I saw no signs of mourning anywhere."

The duke took a deep breath. "The time has come, my lady, for me to explain the present situation and to make recent occurrences clear to you. It began when my cousin Arsenio joined political forces with your father by way of your marriage contract.

"According to their plans, the union was to be a secret to protect the alliance against any opposition. Others would fear such an alliance of two strong houses because their combined powers could destabilize control over large parts of Europe. I was aware of the repercussions and possible dangers inherent in the situation, but I chose to feign ignorance and allow the situation to evolve unobstructed while I remained vigilant in the shadows.

"Thus I awaited my time to take control. I knew about your father's power and wealth as well as my cousin's desire to free himself from the impoverished condition he inflicted upon himself with his reckless ways.

"Arsenio lacked the ability to lead. It hurts me to say it, but that is the truth of it. He proved himself unworthy of the power he possessed by foolishly lowering taxes to retain favor with the people. He bought their enthusiasm in that way but foolishly avoided restricting his lavish and reckless lifestyle. While he claimed to be a 'man of the people,' he drained funds designated for his army and his government's necessary expenses, to compensate for the diminished tax revenues. Thus, both the army and his government itself were soon ready to collapse.

"Finally, to rid himself of debt from his misguided reign, he sacrificed himself by entering a marriage with you, a wealthy and powerful heiress. He completely disregarded the woman he loved and whom he had promised to make his Duchess. Thus he deceived the Lady Flavia De Brezzé even though she had always been faithfully by his side and shared a long and intimate relationship with him."

"My lord!" Polyxena erupted, abandoning all caution. She could not contain her feelings of being deeply offended by the barrage of hateful words directed toward her husband. "I find your words unworthy of a gentleman of your standing." She fumed. "I hope you will spare me further discourse, since I have no desire to be the recipient of your disparaging words toward my husband simply because he is tragically unable to defend himself. Any illusion on my part about loving or being loved by Arsenio would have been impossible for me because the union was arranged and I didn't know him.

"We had mutually agreed to enter in the marriage, hoping to ultimately develop feelings of affection and respect for each other over time. Now, because of his premature death, I will never know if our marriage could have succeeded. But I respect his memory and honor him in death and I will not allow anyone to speak in judgment of him in my presence."

She defiantly faced Ludwig, fully aware of the danger she was in but which her noble nature would not allow her to consider, regardless of the consequences.

But instead of taking offense at Polyxena's defiance, the Duke was impressed by her courage. Her self-assurance made her even more attractive and desirable to him.

He smiled, feeling both bemused and benevolent toward her and addressed Polyxena in a friendlier fashion out of respect for the ethical courage she displayed.

"As you wish my lady," he replied. "I will weigh my words more carefully now, since you are a strong and self-assured person who wishes to hear the unvarnished truth.

"You have been informed that Arsenio died from a mysterious disease that was unknown to the court's doctors. You were also told that the tragedy ensued the same day your marriage was celebrated by proxy to assure your position as the Duchess of Lorengard-Lorraine.

"However, I am afraid that the Catholic Church, even with the intervention of his holiness the Pope, decrees your union to Arsenio invalid, not merely because you were not physically present at the marriage ceremony, but because your husband passed away weeks before your arrival. Forgive my indelicacy cousin, but since the marriage was never consummated, the union is considered null and void."

Ludwig paused and moved closer to Polyxena, then lowered his voice to a whisper, "Since Arsenio's death has remained secret and only those who are loyal to me are aware of the circumstances, I could announce that his death occurred after your arrival, allowing you to become the legitimate Duchess of Lorengard-Lorraine."

This came as a complete surprise. "You would do that for me?" Polyxena asked. "I am confused by your decision, my lord. By allowing me to become Duchess you disinherited yourself. Since you are Arsenio's closest relative, you will become the legitimate heir if my marriage is declared invalid. It's difficult for me to understand why you choose to forgo power and sacrifice your ambitions for someone you just met."

"Cousin," the Duke answered with a smile of false warmth. "Let's put our cards on the table. I will play a secondary role in appearance only. If I were to openly take control of the Dukedom, I could be considered a usurper by the population, who have been notoriously unfriendly toward me. However, I believe you will be readily accepted as the new Duchess since your marriage was celebrated by the Cardinal of Lorengard-Lorraine. He is a man trusted and beloved by the people.

"Since he regards you as the new Duchess, they will accept your claim as legitimate. You will enjoy all the honors and benefits of your lofty role, while I will be in control and govern from behind the scenes. Therefore, the true power will be mine, only it will have been implemented in a more diplomatic way."

"According to your suggestion my lord, I will be used as an enabler, for you to archive control and power," she said. " I will not be the real Duchess of Lorengard-Lorraine, but a figurehead and tool used at your pleasure and discretion. That position lacks dignity and self worth." Frustration burned in Polyxena's green eyes and she could no longer contain her anger.

"Calm yourself dear cousin," responded Ludwig, aware of the young woman's indignation. "It is apparent my words are misunderstood by you. I made my proposal in good faith, hoping you would accept my offer. But let us be clear about this. I am powerful, presently in charge, and I do not fear the populace of Lorengard-Lorraine…I will squelch any revolt and destroy anyone who dares to oppose me.

"My proposition was dictated by the great affection I have for you, rather than any need. I find you fascinating and I am overcome not only by your beauty, but by your remarkable self-assurance and dignity. As I mentioned, I believe our meeting was ordained by a superior power and we were meant to be together. Therefore, my desire is to request, after a proper period of mourning we owe your departed spouse, your hand in marriage. So you see, I never wanted to use you, but I wanted to share the Dukedom and my life with you."

She felt overwhelmed with an impulse to refuse the proposal. But common sense prevailed. She understood that he was in charge and it was necessary to remain in his good graces, but the compromised position made her feel confined and helpless. The only potential solution was that the proposal offered a possible way out as a means to stall for time and regain control over events that had spiraled downward ever since her arrival.

"My lord, your offer and your affection are most welcomed. As you can imagine, this is a difficult time for me. Having had the misfortune of being widowed before I had the opportunity of becoming a bride, I am reluctant to get married again so soon. I must rely on your tolerance of the simple fact that I cannot respond too quickly to your proposal. However, after the space of a year, which I consider a proper time for mourning, I will gladly honor your offer and become your bride if you still desire to marry me."

"My lady," Ludwig joyfully responded. "I am divided between your affirmative answer and the prospect of a long wait." With that, the Duke who had respectfully restrained his longing to passionately hold her in his arms, approached Polyxena and elegantly kissed her hands instead.

Polyxena made her greatest effort to appear receptive toward him and to conceal the dread and turmoil she experienced at his touch. She breathed deeply to regain her composure, then retreated from him by feigning shyness.

"My lord," she began, hoping to change the subject. "Where are Duke Arsenio's remains? I desire to pay my respects and give my late husband a final farewell."

"As you wish my lady," Ludwig answered. "I have no objection and you may see him whenever you wish. But let me advise you in the matter. Your husband has been gone for weeks now. His body is decomposing. Why would you subject yourself to that sight?"

His sobering words powerfully affected her and she moaned at the thought of her tragic Prince lying cold in his shroud. She lowered her head and placed her hand on the back of a chair to steady herself. The Duke approached and placed his arms around her waist to comfort her. The unwelcome closeness brought her back to reality and she instinctively recoiled, but quickly regained her demeanor.

"I thank you for your valuable advice, my lord, and I shall heed it. However, I wish also to know the whereabouts of my escort party. I have received no news from them since we arrived in Lorengard-Lorraine and I am concerned."

"No need to worry, my lady," Ludwig replied. "They have been treated as honored guests and await your disposition before joining the palace guards. I might also add that your dowry is safe within these walls. No one has touched it and you can take possession of it whenever you wish."

"Thank you so much, my lord," she said. "Your generous behavior toward me is deeply appreciated. May I beg your indulgence for a last request? Where are the two knights, Duccio Degli Uberti and Philip of Rohann, messengers from my late husband to my father in Nemours?"

Ludwig's expression darkened when she mentioned the names and he coldly responded, "They are where they should be my lady. It would be wise to leave them to their destiny."

But Polyxena had no intention of failing to intervene on their behalf. Relying once more on her tantalizing beauty as her only power over the despot, she presented an inviting smile to him while she affectionately touched his arm. "My lord, I beg clemency for those young knights who have met your displeasure. They were loyal to my late husband and were obviously held in great esteem by him. The situation places a heavy burden upon me and I must intercede for their lives on his behalf. Freeing them will be my final gesture of respect and honor for my spouse."

While she spoke, Polyxena allowed her lustrous and perfumed dark hair to caress his face. The Duke responded to her overture by holding her hands, kissing them with ardor while he gazed deeply into her enigmatic eyes and tried to read her hidden thoughts. But her loveliness left him beset by passion and unable to think clearly.

She noted his vulnerable condition and continued her plea for mercy, "My generous lord, it's your future bride who requests this favor. Please be magnanimous. Spare the young knights' lives and allow them to serve me as my bodyguards. I give you my word of honor that I will use all my powers of persuasion to convert them into subjects loyal to you."

Polyxena added a tempting smile worthy of the most seductive enchantress. "Be merciful my lord and you will have my eternal devotion…"

The Duke was unable to repress his desire and felt so strongly enticed by Polyxena's closeness that he encircled her waist with a muscular arm. "And what else besides devotion will you give in exchange, my lady? It seems that a reversal of judgment against enemies of my regime requires a more tangible reward. What do you offer to make my refusal impossible?"

She carefully disengaged from the Duke's embrace while also taking care to avoid causing offense. She knew how important it was to save two innocent lives, but she also felt terrified by his ominous demand for a 'reward'. She felt her heart beat wildly in her chest.

Ludwig remained oblivious to Polyxena's revulsion and was only concerned with his carnal needs. He addressed her in a voice filled with desire, "A kiss will be my reward, enchanting lady…A kiss from your ruby lips will seal the agreement and your request will be immediately granted."

He seized her and held on with a grip so tight it took her breath away. Polyxena could do nothing but acquiesce and save her two valiant knights. Blushing violently, she surrendered to his desire. He kissed her with such force that when he felt her tremble in his arms, he confused her distress for passion. However, she experienced only horror and revulsion. When he finally released her, he gave her an elegant bow and left the room, satisfied that he had made a conquest.

Finally alone, Polyxena felt shaken and revolted by the dreadful first kiss of her life.

†††

CHAPTER FIVE

DUCCIO DEGLI UBERTI
And PHILIP of ROHANN

As promised, the Duke of Saxe-Hanover ordered the release of the two knights. The young men had been confined in a dark cell within the gloomy palace dungeon, resigned to their fate. As military men, they faced death without showing their fear and remained stoic in the face of their circumstances.

Therefore, when an armed guard entered their cell, they assumed he was there to escort them to the executioner. Both men quietly rose to follow him and meet death with dignity, but neither could conceal his astonishment when they were told they were free to go and were given back their swords. Their instructions were to present themselves to Polyxena, who waited for them.

Both knights had been born to noble families that were powerful and wealthy at one time, but had fallen on hard times and financial ruin. Thus forced by economic circumstances to become soldiers of fortune, they relied on their acquired expertise in the use of arms for their sustenance. Nevertheless, each of the knights had carefully chosen their masters. It did not matter that they were temporarily impoverished—they favored serving Lords with noble aims like Arsenio over ruthless despots who could pay their weight in gold.

Philip was the oldest at the age of twenty-three. He stood at medium height, but had a well-developed warrior's body. His ruddy complexion complimented his blonde hair, which he wore unusually long for a gentleman of the time. The focal point on his chiseled face was the blue of his eyes. They shone with innate intelligence and revealed a reserved temperament.

Duccio was three years younger and much taller than his friend, with an athletic body that gave him an intimidating appearance. His perfect features and golden skin color afforded him great masculine appeal. The handsome face was framed by shoulder length brown hair and his eyes expressed his restless nature.

They found themselves delivered to Polyxena's rooms, where Davina warmly welcomed them. The handmaiden offered them comfortable chairs so they could rest after their ordeal, but they gallantly refused, in order to respectfully welcome their benefactress while standing.

Polyxena soon joined them, and for the first time both young men saw her face without her customary hooded cape. Her unexpected beauty and grace stunned them. Philip blushed and stepped backward, completely intimidated by her loveliness.

Duccio was beset by an even stronger attraction to her. The intensity of it confused him, even if mixed with his more acceptable feelings of gratitude to her for saving their lives.

Polyxena noticed both knights were tense and hesitant, so she offered a welcoming smile and extended her hands in greeting. They immediately knelt in her presence and kissed her hands in gratitude.

"Welcome Sir Knights," she said. "Please sit and make yourselves comfortable after your recent ordeal."

"My lady," Duccio replied, "You honor us with your graciousness. Please let us remain standing to give you the respect you deserve."

"As you wish," Polyxena replied with a smile. She knew better than to attempt to unwind the awkwardness that most men seemed to fall into in her presence. She sat on a nearby divan and went on, "You both look as if you're in good health, and I'm grateful for that. When I became aware of your unworthy accommodations, I hastened to change them. I know my late husband relied on your trustworthy loyalty, so it was essential for me to come to your aid. I am told Arsenio respected and admired you both, as did my father. Such qualities deserve reward. So for my part, I request that you stand by my side as my protectors with the same loyalty you gave my spouse. The recompense for both of you will be my friendship and protection from the Duke's vile temper."

"Your grace," Philip responded. "Your generosity touches us deeply, because our lives and loyalty belong to the noble house of Lorengard-Lorraine. We're here with our swords to serve you with devotion. And if faith wills it, we will gladly give up our lives to serve and defend you."

Polyxena smiled in approval and stood as a sign of farewell. Philip bowed, retreated toward the door, and quickly exited the room, while Duccio knelt once more before her to take the hand she extended in friendship. He kissed it once more.

"My lady, your intervention on our behalf was instrumental in saving our lives. You placed yourself in grave danger by the generosity of your action and we are forever grateful."

"As the new Duchess of Lorengard-Lorraine I will be duty bound to protect the good people of the Dukedom regardless of personal danger to me. It is a matter of honor." A proud look flashed across her face as she spoke, and with that, Duccio bowed to her in gratitude and exited the room.

After their meeting with Polyxena, the Knights spoke at length about their employment as her personal guards. Despite their sincere sorrow for the death of Duke Arsenio, they were elated that their new lady presented herself to be so noble and kind.

Philip noticed with some apprehension that Duccio spoke with a bit too much enthusiasm about her. Though he was only a few years older than Duccio, Philip had a more reflective and thoughtful nature and was the more insightful of the two.

"Hear me friend," he warned. "I see a strange light burning, in your eyes and I must confess it worries me. From the moment you saw the Duchess, you appeared to be taken by her presence. I am also impressed by her, but she carries a superior status in life and I cannot forget who I am. An inaccessible barrier divides our worlds and we must not covet the unreachable. The lovely lady who saved us from the hateful Duke of Saxe-Hanover is also the daughter of a powerful Duke and a Duchess in her own right. We are her humble servants."

"Your words wound me, Philip," protested Duccio. "I request nothing beyond my reach. No one will know my inner thoughts."

"You are wrong to speak like this, Duccio," Philip answered sternly. "Fantasizing is for poets and children. We are men of arms, and our destiny is as cold as the weapons we carry."

The warning touched Duccio. He remained pensive and silent. Philip was moved by his friend's tacit dejection. He patted Duccio on his back. "Come friend. A miracle set us free today and snatched us from certain death. Now life unfolds before us. We shall honor it by living with enthusiasm."

Duccio smiled in response, then a roguish look came over his face and he placed his hand on his sword. "On guard," he cried, playfully pretending to attack.

Philip grinned and took a defensive stance against the pretend assault.

They commenced a fierce mock duel, one of their favorite forms of exercise. Duccio moved with agility, attacking and retreating with the power of a wild cat. Philip responded with his own considerable expertise.

Since both were expertly trained, the duel was prolonged and exciting and soon attracted a curious crowd with their skilled swordplay and fighting capability. To the onlookers, the combat looked so real that the crowd began to choose sides and pick favorites for the final kill, shouting encouragement for their chosen knight.

Finally, Duccio, with exquisite finesse, dislodged Philip's sword from his hand. The excitement from the crowd reached a tumultuous roar.

"I am dead," Philip shouted.

"Well, my friend," Duccio triumphantly cried out. "You have proved yourself unworthy of my exceptional strength, and your defeat was simple child's play."

"My lord," Philip cried, feigning offense. "I say it was obvious to everyone I allowed you to win. Your expertise is comparable to a clumsy ox."

Despite the offensive words, both knights laughed and sheathed their swords. Arm in arm, they walked away from the fighting scene, leaving it to the stupefied spectators to explain the outcome of the unusual duel.

THE FUNERAL

When the news of Arsenio's death was released to the populace of Lorengard-Lorraine, the Dukedom went into mourning for their well-loved leader. However, the tragedy left them unsettled and confused, with a thousand unanswered questions. Most important among them was the question of the manner of the Duke's death. And who was this new Duchess who married him under such mysterious circumstances?

Since no answers came forward, a rancorous mood developed in the population. Ominous rumors sprouted and grew.

The only official response was to send heavily armed guards roaming everywhere, ready to crush the smallest uprising. But the people's disposition was like rope stretched nearly to its breaking point, ready to snap at any moment.

Black and purple silken blankets were draped from balconies and windows. The local taverns, usually filled with rowdy and hard-drinking crowds, closed down for the event. The stately palaces were adorned with banners depicting the coat of arms of Lorengard-Lorraine to signify mourning for the departed Arsenio.

The main square in the Dukedom was chosen for the stately funeral. The gothic cathedral of Saint Justin dominated the vast area with its magnificent facade and ornate bell tower. The entire area was alive with activity in preparation while carpenters built a platform where Arsenio's body would be displayed in repose for his faithful subjects.

The podium was a simple rectangular shape surrounded by stairs on each corner of the structure. In its center, a box-shaped funerary platform was covered by an exquisite purple brocade drape adorned with the coat of arms of Lorengard-Lorraine.

Directly behind the podium, a makeshift altar was erected so the Cardinal of Lorengard-Lorraine could celebrate the funerary mass while also accommodating the huge crowds expected to say good bye to their beloved Duke. After many hours of relentless work, everything was ready for the solemn occasion.

The people were allowed to enter the vast piazza and silently assembled in the open space. The crowd soon engulfed the entire area, where they waited impatiently to see the young leader so mysteriously taken from them.

Finally, the funerary entourage approached the crowd, moving at its somber pace to the muffled funeral drums and accompanied by the mournful chiming of the cathedral bells. Two companies of uniformed soldiers marched in time to the drumbeats. A young page heading the entourage held a large banner with the Lorengard-Lorraine coat of arms.

A congregation of nobles followed them, wearing black hoods over their faces to keep their identity hidden from the crowd. They carried an imposing statue of Saint Justin, the Dukedom's patron saint.

The entourage continued with a chorus of young children dressed in flowing white lace garments. Their voices were beautiful and filled the square with hymns.

The Duke's body was welcomed by the crowd, carried in on the shoulders of his personal honor guards. He rode in an open casket decorated with beautiful flowers and Lorengard-Lorraine coat of arms.

But strangely, the body itself was covered by a black shroud and could not be seen at all. Only the outline was visible, with his hands resting upon his sword, laying supine on the center of the body in the tradition of honoring a fallen warrior. But some of the people could not help but notice that it could have been anybody under there.

The Cardinal followed, holding an elaborate crucifix decorated with precious stones. The prelate moved along in silent prayer, flanked by children holding votive candles and white flowers.

Now the crowd began to openly murmur in reaction at the sight of the concealed body. Their voices became noticeable above the commotion and threatening in their tone. Their distress was not only at being denied a final look at their beloved Prince, but because they feared that the shroud might be disguising the mysterious cause of his death.

The crowd's restlessness grew. It was only when Polyxena appeared that the disturbance gave way to curiosity. She followed the Cardinal in the funerary procession, her lovely features exquisite even in sorrow. Her face was visible through a transparent veil that flowed gracefully down from her jeweled headdress over an elegant black brocade gown with oversized sleeves trimmed in ermine. The strength of her appearance was so great that the observers were filled with admiration for their new Duchess.

The Duke of Saxe-Hanover shared Polyxena's place of honor in the entourage, walking by her side. However, his demeanor was the opposite of hers, disdainful and contemptuous of the crowd, so much so that after the momentary distraction caused by Polyxena's striking appearance, the crowd resumed their threatening sounds. Some were more daring than the rest and raised their voices in protest.

"Why is our beloved Duke, concealed from our eyes?" one brave man cried out. "We demand the removal of the black shroud so we can all witness how the Duke died."

Guards promptly silenced the impudent man. The procession continued uninterrupted.

Duccio and Philip acted as Polyxena's bodyguards and followed her closely. They were stoic men of arms and they did not show their emotions. But the knights felt genuine sorrow over Duke Arsenio's death because of their respect and admiration for him. However, they were unsure about their new duty. Although they were grateful to the Duchess for saving their lives, they did not understand her friendliness toward the Duke of Saxe-Hanover, whom they were certain had been instrumental in killing their lord.

They began to question her loyalty to her deceased husband, regardless of her benevolent public demeanor. Their devotion to Arsenio remained even in death and they despised serving the Duke of Saxe-Hanover, the enemy of their lord. However, the new Duchess was noble and kind, and Philip and Duccio realized she had placed her life in jeopardy to save theirs. They decided to trust her judgment, believing that she might have good reasons to behave that way toward the Duke.

Duccio's great attraction to Polyxena remained and he had difficulty performing his duty while helplessly witnessing the tyrant's loving overture toward her. He was troubled and mystified by his deep feelings and bewildered by his inability to suppress the desire he had for her. He knew it was hopeless to covet someone so far above his station. Despite his knighthood, he was only a soldier of fortune. Their worlds could not have been more distant and he realized his dreams of love were hopeless.

When the funerary procession reached the square, the Duke's body was ceremoniously placed upon the platform. Polyxena, her entourage, and Ludwig took their honored places on the upper tier facing the altar. The Cardinal approached Polyxena to express his sympathy, then turned to introduce her to a noble, dignified lady who accompanied him.

"Your Grace. It is my pleasure to introduce you to the Countess Amelia De Vargas, a great lady and loyal friend of long standing to Lorengard-Lorraine."

"Your Grace," the Countess said. "...you have my condolences for the untimely death of your noble spouse and I am saddened that we meet under such tragic circumstances. Your distinguished father, the Duke of Nemours, has always been my esteemed and valued friend and I am sure you are worthy to be his daughter.

"Arsenio, your late husband, was dear to me as my son, and I grieve to have lived long enough to witness his death. He was the last member of a noble family and his death heralded a distinguished blood line's tragic end."

"That is not accurate, my Lady," the Duke of Saxe-Hanover rudely interrupted. "You are misinformed. Arsenio was my first cousin and his blood flows in my veins. Therefore the blood line is alive and will continue to flow unhindered, in me and my future heirs."

"I beg pardon, your Grace, if I have offended you," the Countess De Vargas answered. "Possibly you misunderstood my words, since I was talking about the dynastic end of Lorengard-Lorraine with Arsenio's death. You, my lord, are related to him through his mother and the distinguished house of Saxe-Hanover. For years, I prayed fervently that the benevolent house of Lorengard-Lorraine would survive and I hoped that it would endure its difficulties and challenges.

"Unfortunately, today we bring it to a final rest. If you permit me, my lord, I will gladly pray for your success and your illustrious house, that prosperity will continue and you will provide a benevolent and just government to the people."

"I thank you my lady," Ludwig sneered. "But, I prefer tangible measures other than simple prayers to guarantee success. Prayer is a weapon for the weak and incompetent who aimlessly toil, a panacea for expendable members of society. The sword is my weapon of choice because it guarantees supremacy by decimating those who oppose it."

The Countess bowed her head in tacit consent, aware of the Duke's displeasure, but continued undaunted, "Your supremacy is undisputed, my lord, and I concur that the sword is a mighty weapon capable of bestowing victories over the weak."

The Countess met Ludwig's intimidating gaze with dignity and pride. "In my opinion, this is not the chosen weapon for the brave, but a tool for aggressors and tyrants. Prayer is a glorious and mighty weapon, a refuge for those who have no defense but who are ready to die for a just cause strengthened by Faith."

"Milady," the Duke responded. "...I concur that prayer can be valuable to a person in peril, perhaps someone like yourself, a privileged matriarch from a rich and powerful family. I suggest you pray fervently to the lucky star that protects you, and hope it doesn't suddenly fade."

The Countess simply bowed with deference, but her point had been made and she turned to rejoin the crowd.

Polyxena was impressed with the noblewoman's courage. Although she could not show her feelings at that moment, she wished to get better acquainted with the Countess and decided to become her friend at the first opportunity.

The angry murmur from the crowd grew louder and more intimidating and did not cease when the Cardinal commenced celebrating the funerary mass. Polyxena remained stoic and impassive during the ordeal of the funeral, but eventually felt demoralized and overwhelmed by the oppressive atmosphere in the square.

The venerable Cardinal ignored the tumultuous crowd, but his words were drowned out by the rising uproar. He tried to control the crowd by raising his voice. Still, his words could not be heard over the turmoil. Finally, one daring and reckless young man shouted with contempt.

"Remove that black shroud from our Prince. Let us see how he died. Let us see if it was ordained by God or by a vile assassin."

The youth was violently accosted by the Duke's soldiers, who forced him to the ground, beat him mercilessly, and stabbed him with a dagger, inflicting a deep gash in his side. The wounded youth's cry of pain incited the crowd.

As quickly as that, the angry people became a mob. They ferociously broke the defensive barrier and ran toward the center of the square, bowling over any guard who opposed them. Screaming, clenching their fists, they reached the platform edge where Arsenio's body lay in repose.

Most hesitated at the sight, unsure of their next steps. Only three among them dared to climb a few steps to the podium to reach the summit and see the Prince's body. But once there the daring trio was unable to advance further. Having emerged from the mob, they lost the mob's momentum. They needed something or someone to force them into action.

The Duke of Saxe-Hanover clenched his teeth, frustrated by the unexpected events and of his mortal peril. The unruly crowd now overflowed the square and was apparently in control. No power at his disposal could stop them.

One rebellious man suddenly regained his purpose and climbed the platform to approach Arsenio's body.

Polyxena secretly applauded the people for rising up against the tyrant, but she was aware that the revolt was premature and might precipitate the Duke's vengeance. His reprisals would undoubtedly be bloody and merciless. It was also paramount in her mind that she needed to secure her position as the Duchess of Lorengard-Lorraine, a necessary step in her quest to help the people of the Dukedom and to avenge her husband's death.

However, she also knew that the sight of Arsenio's decomposing body should not be seen by the citizens because they believed in his recent death. Her anxiety and concern was evident to Duccio, who interpreted her reaction as the desire for someone to prevent an alarming situation. He moved with catlike speed to reach the platform, draw his sword and plant himself between Arsenio's body and the patriot.

"Step aside, my lord Degli Uberti," the patriot cried. "I have no grievance with you. You have always been known as a faithful and loyal defender of our Prince, so you should let me remove the shroud from his sacred body. Let me reveal to all the manner of his death. It is an imperative step for justice to be done. You should consider the people's right to know."

"My lord," Duccio proudly responded. "...I am indeed a loyal servant of our revered Duke and my obligation to him continues whether he is dead or alive. Therefore, I will allow no one to defile his body, even for the best of reasons. If you persist in your unholy endeavor and try to uncover his sacred remains, I will regretfully take you down with my sword."

Having uttered those threatening words, Duccio accosted the man, forcing him to retreat. But suddenly, the man was flanked once more by his two reticent companions and with their help, he regained his daring.

"Well then, my lord," he cried out. "Kill me! It will be an easy task. However, many of us here are ready to die for our just cause. You will be overpowered and killed. So step aside in the name of justice, my lord, and live."

Duccio did not move. There was a slight tremor in his body, but he maintained a determined look designed to intimidate and garner respect. When he turned to Polyxena, her grateful gaze reinforced him.

"Come forward, if you want to die," he cried loud enough for all to hear. "Before I fall, I will kill many of you, regardless of your well-meant intentions. It will be an honor to die defending my lord, whom I respect and love."

Duccio was relieved that his words had the desired effect in deflating the challenging situation. The aggressive patriots grew calmer and began to look uncertain of their task. He was encouraged by their retreat and continued, "It was our Duke's desire that his body would be shrouded from public view to spare his people from seeing his corpse in the stillness of death. To allow them to remember him as he was…young, strong, and handsome. Do you dare defy his final wish?"

Duccio was known by the populace for his honest and chivalrous nature and the leader of the revolt was moved by his determination. He lowered his head in sign of consent.

"Sir Knight, you win," he said. "Your eloquent words have touched my soul. I make no further demands and only seek permission to pay my respects and say a final good bye to my beloved lord."

Duccio stepped aside and allowed the three men to approach Arsenio's body and kneel before it, reverently kissing the shroud. Then the patriots left the funerary platform and disappeared into the crowd.

Polyxena was greatly relieved to see a peaceful end to the perilous situation, and was deeply moved by Duccio's valor. She admired the noble knight who placed his life in danger without hesitation. She also noted his ingenuity and skill at persuading the patriots to retreat.

She felt a sudden attraction to the splendid and heroic knight, whose presence was clearly admired by everyone. Strong emotions surged inside her when reverently he knelt to kiss her hand.

She shivered at his touch. A crimson glow tinted her cheeks. Controlling her emotions by avoiding Duccio's luminous stare and obvious charm, she invited him to stand and thanked him for his valuable service.

The Duke of Saxe-Hanover joined her in celebrating Duccio's heroics. He was truly grateful to Duccio for his fortuitous intervention, which saved the day and perhaps his life.

This was a strange situation for Duccio and he felt troubled to be cordially conversing with a man he secretly regarded as his most hated enemy.

A great silence reigned over the crowd. The Cardinal of Lorengard-Lorraine, who had stayed aloof in silent prayer, now decided to use the peaceful moment to his advantage. He invited

Polyxena to join him on the platform near Arsenio's body, then turned to the people and addressed them in regal tones.

"Citizens of Lorengard-Lorraine. It is my distinct honor to introduce you to Lady Polyxena of Nemours, beloved Arsenio's chosen bride and new Duchess of Lorengard-Lorraine."

The crowd was confused by the announcement but deferential to his words, since they respected the Cardinal for his kindness and honesty.

"I was privileged to marry them," the Cardinal continued. "...and I hoped and prayed the marriage would be blessed with longevity. Sadly, destiny ended the union too soon. The noble Duchess Polyxena is our only reason to rejoice here on this tragic day. I request you to join me in prayer that she may be inspired by the Lord to perform the difficult tasks ahead of her in this hour. I ask that you welcome her with the same respect and affection our beloved Arsenio gave to her."

The Cardinal lifted Polyxena's arm triumphantly and cried, "God save Polyxena of Lorengard-Lorraine! Long live our new Duchess."

That cry was welcomed by a thousand people who joined with him in a chant, "Long live our new Duchess! God save Polyxena of Lorengard-Lorraine. Long live our new Duchess."

An atmosphere of gaiety soon replaced the crowd's mood of anger and despair. Polyxena found herself overwhelmed by the warm and loving welcome she received from the good people of Lorengard-Lorraine and gratefully waived to them with affection.

She touched the shroud covering her husband's body and silently prayed on behalf of a new purpose that now filled her heart. "God guide the new Duchess. God enlighten and strengthen the new Duchess…May God help me."

IN THE CASTLE

That evening found Duccio restless and unable to sleep. He decided to walk alone in the vast Ducal Palace gardens. But once there he was startled by the sound of footsteps and realized he was being followed. He turned suddenly and saw his friend Philip, who approached him with a somber air.

"Why did you do it my friend?" asked Philip.

"Do what, Philip!"

"I keep thinking about it, but I don't understand why you interfered with the valiant patriot who wanted justice for our lord. I was also tempted to remove that black shroud and prevent it from concealing proof of his violent death."

"Apparently, you have forgotten that we are servants to the new Duchess," Duccio responded. "She generously saved our lives and we have pledged supreme fealty to her. While I was near the coffin, she signaled me with her eyes to stop the patriot from removing the shroud. I assumed she had good reasons and decided not to question her motives."

"I witnessed no such request," Philip answered, though he continued in his usual soft-spoken way. "Since you are obsessed and oblivious to everyone but her, I understand why you assumed she wanted you to act. I also understand we are indebted to the Duchess for saving our lives. But we must not forget that he who rests lifeless beneath the shroud, according to the laws of chivalry, is still our responsibility, and we need to protect his honor against treachery. This responsibility endures beyond the grave."

Philip paused momentarily to gather his thoughts, but avoided Duccio's eyes while he continued, "I also question your statement about being willing to die defending our Duke. Since I saw what happened, I believe otherwise...I observed your eyes when she smiled at you. You were beset with desire and it was strong enough to make you ready to die. However, if in that moment you would have sacrificed your life, it would have been for her and not for our lord, Arsenio. My dear friend, it is clear to me that you are in love with our new Duchess."

Duccio recoiled. "You offend me by suggesting I was dishonest to the memory of our departed lord. Many times, you have witnessed my devotion to the Duke. But the lady who we serve now is noble and kind and she must have had valid reasons for the strange request to cover her husband's body. My friend, spare me your cruel words. They unjustly offend my honor."

Philip sorrowfully looked at Duccio and tapped his shoulder as a sign of farewell, then began to walk away.

Duccio followed and grabbed his arm. "Forgive me, my friend. It is useless to deny what is evident to you. Hence, I admit it to you when I have not dared admit it to myself. I love her. I love her and my desire paralyzes my judgment. I have tried to control my emotions…but I cannot. There is no reprimand you could give me that I have not given myself."

He sadly shook his head. "I am aware the situation is hopeless, since I am her servant and unworthy to covet a Duchess. But I tell you my friend, she has an indefinable lure over me, far more than her great beauty. It's a spell that entices me and makes me believe we were meant to be together. So you can see how distressing my thoughts have been."

Philip saw Duccio's torment and was moved by his sorrow. "Forgive me if I appear insensitive to your pain. I tried in vain to prevent you from becoming a victim to your own obsession. But I understand that love cannot be controlled and that it can be the strongest and most beautiful emotion, but only when it is reciprocated. Sadly my friend, the situation is impossible, even if you believe it is ordained by God. It's also dangerous. Did you notice how the Duke of Saxe-Hanover watches her? His desire is apparent. He wants the Duchess and I fear he will soon have his way with her."

"He is an accursed man," Duccio raged, gripping the hilt of his sword. "If he touches her using force or blackmail, I shall kill him with my bare hands."

"My poor friend you are delusional. Don't you realize if the Duke suspects you love the Duchess, he will have you killed? You count on your sword, but no matter how skilled you are with it, he has a thousand assassins. Duccio, a man's life is the most precious of God's gifts. Please, my friend, guard yours well."

Duccio offered his friend a sad smile. "I thank you for your concern, and for your words of wisdom. You are my true brother and the only family I possess. I always have admired your judgment, but today I am at the mercy of my emotions and unable to change course. I love the Duchess, but to no purpose, and only death can diminish my pain."

"Let us not talk about it anymore, Duccio. I sympathize with your situation and I understand your need to follow your heart. Therefore, I wish you good fortune in this dangerous state of love. Your heart is too soft and your head is too hard."

Duccio laughed at that and the two friends embraced. They departed in separate directions and disappeared into the night.

LUDWIG

When he returned to the palace from the funeral, the Duke of Saxe-Hanover was filled with rage. He locked himself in his rooms and aimlessly paced the floors consumed with the desire for revenge for the day's terrifying experience and its threat to his life. A thousand violent and cruel thoughts against the people ran through his mind.

"Despicable peasants," he said out loud, as if they all could hear him. "You behaved like wild beasts and dared to threaten my life. But I will suppress your daring and show you no mercy! A river of blood will cleanse you of audacity."

These words released the rage consuming him and he threw his knife fiercely against a wall. The sharp blade penetrated a tapestry and stuck there, but before he could vent more aggression, he was interrupted by the voice of a palace page.

"Your grace. The lady Flavia De Brezzé is here, as you have requested," he announced with a deep bow. The page then stepped aside, allowing Flavia to appear in the imposing doorway.

The Duke found himself staring at a blonde vision. She was dressed in a dazzling and audacious blue gown encrusted with jewels. Ludwig smiled with excitement and went to greet her, gallantly kissing her hand.

Flavia felt nothing but coldness toward his overture, but wisely decided to temper her displeasure and responded with a pleasant smile. "You wished to see me my lord?" she asked. "It is an unusual privilege to be invited into your rooms, since I have been diminished in your eyes and replaced by a more desirable attraction..." Flavia took a deep breath, then continued, "Milord, your neglect has caused me deep sorrow because of my devotion to you."

The Duke already expected her to be upset by the situation. She had been openly ignored and humiliated because of his attraction and fascination to the beautiful new Duchess. Knowing she was proud and easily insulted, he could imagine how bitterly jealous she felt about Polyxena's eventful arrival, but he also had no desire to endure a resentful tirade.

What he needed from Flavia was the burning passion she exuded during their sexual encounters. Flavia was petite and well-endowed, and she displayed her voluptuous curves with sophisticated skill. She realized the ploy was essential to obtain the Duke's favors and turn his sexual desires toward her quest for power.

Her ultimate goal was to become the Duchess of Lorengard-Lorraine and she felt entitled to the position as the only cure for the humiliations she experienced for her years as an impoverished recipient of charity. Despite the great privileges generously lavished upon her, Flavia knew the Duke of Saxe-Hanover was the only one who possessed the power necessary to fulfill her dreams of grandeur.

"My dear Flavia. Please understand that the present situation required all my attention, regardless of my desire to be free from it. However, you always were present in my mind, and I could not forget your beauty and your alluring embrace. Therefore, abolish these foolish recriminations and be satisfied with my sincere apologies for any sorrow I have caused you."

"Beautiful words, my lord, but words nonetheless. They fail to explain the unexpected crowning of the new Duchess of Lorengard-Lorraine, which was unopposed by everyone, including you. Arsenio's widow had no legal claim to the title of Duchess, because she arrived in Lorengard-Lorraine weeks after his death. Therefore, the union ought to be null and void in the eyes of the church." Her voice faltered when she uttered those words, but with effort, she retained her composure and continued.

"On that fateful banquet day, I thought I had attained a place of honor by your side. The name of Polyxena of Nemours was touted by you with ridicule. But when she made her entrance in the banquet hall in all her radiant beauty, you were enthralled.

Your desire for her was evident. I was publicly ignored and humiliated."

Flavia was too angry to control her rage. The Duke attempted once more to appease her in spite of his waning patience, but shrewdly ignored her probing questions.

He moved to embrace her. "My lovely girl, please forget your discontent. If I have inadvertently offended you, I humbly apologize. Let us overlook our grievances."

By then she was so enticingly close to the Duke that his frustrated passion tormented him. He was reluctant to engage in further discourse, but Flavia's resentment had taken control of her. She continued to speak with indignation.

"My lord, I finally understand why I suddenly regained favor in your eyes. You already know I am well-versed in the art of love and that I can make you forget your unfulfilled nights of lost passion with her. For it would seem the reticent lady who is our new Duchess is too pure to succumb to your charms. She has undoubtedly locked the doors to her bedchamber, leaving you outside."

"Cease the chatter, my lady," Ludwig fumed. "You are an ingrate. All the more so, since I apologized even though I'm free from blame. You ought to be pleased. Yield to this moment and to my embrace."

After speaking with such ardor, he placed his arms around Flavia and attempted to kiss her on the lips. But she was overrun by her jealousy and once more rejected his advances. She twisted herself out of his arms.

"You say you have an overwhelming passion for me. But what about the Duchess, in spite of your denials? I need you to ease my burden of uncertainties. I am being tormented by lingering doubts. I have my pride and I will not be passed over by someone else. Therefore, tell me if you are in love with her, and if you desire her more than me."

Ludwig did not hesitate for an instant before he snapped his reply, "Very well, if that is your wish, I will admit it." His sadistic nature was pressed to the limit and simmering with ire. He needed to hurt Flavia for her petulance.

"You want to know the truth?" he continued. "You shall have it. The Duchess excites me more than any other woman, including you. Her allure is capable of igniting passion in any man. I wish to possess her with all my being. But I do not love her.

"This thing you call 'love' is alien to me. I acknowledge only my pleasure without regard to the people involved, as long as the experience satisfies me. In this matter, I differ from my foolish cousin whose life ended so tragically because he most unwisely fell in love with you…"

His skill at dealing this blow to her left Flavia livid with jealousy. Her response was driven by anger more than caution.

"You will never possess her," she hissed, simmering. "I know the Duchess is truly different than I am because she lacks the passionate nature you so deeply desire. The lady is cloistered in her shroud of decency, appearing virginal. In reality, she is cold and remote. You will find her passionless."

Ludwig barely swallowed his rage and nodded. "Your words ring true, my lady. The Duchess is truly different from you. She is pure and chaste and even though those qualities obstruct my desires, I respectfully bow to her wishes. Her uncommon reserve arouses me. Therefore, since I can't have her as a lover, I asked for her hand in marriage. To my delight, she has accepted my proposal and will become my bride."

The news struck Flavia like a spear. In a flash, it was revealed that her ambition was to remain unfulfilled. She would never possess the Duchess crown. It had been twice within her grasp, but was now forever lost. She leaned on a nearby chair for support, feeling faint, and took a deep breath to steady herself.

"And what will happen to me, my lord? You have recanted on all the promises you made? I destroyed Arsenio, who truly loved me. I helped you acquire the power you wanted, which you promised to share with me."

"Why, my dear Flavia, I was certain the only reason you betrayed my poor cousin was because you loved me, not for any reward."

"You promised to make me Duchess." She was beset with despair and threw caution to the wind. "As a gentleman, honor your words, my lord, or I swear you will pay in blood for this vile betrayal."

Those reckless words sent Ludwig into a fury. He seized Flavia's flowing blonde hair and mercilessly snapped her head backward, causing her to scream.

"Listen well, viper. Hear your last warning. If your objective is to be venomous, you would be wise to deter or I will crush your poisoned head without mercy. Never forget who is the absolute ruler here. I make no promises...I give orders. I share my power with no one, least of all you. I have witnessed how you betrayed my cousin and I know, if the occasion should arise, you would betray me too. Therefore, my lady, if you care to live, I advise you to obey me without question. You have survived this time only because I find you physically pleasing. Hence, if you be discrete and abandon your desire for glory, I will always welcome your passionate embrace. So long as I find you desirable."

The Duke released Flavia's hair. The blond tresses fell over her white shoulders and she still trembled with fear at his violent rage.

Ludwig's reaction was the opposite of hers. Wrath had rekindled his desire and he became oblivious to everything except Flavia's sensual beauty. He embraced her and forcefully kissed her lips.

This time Flavia was wise enough to accept his embrace and return his passion. She did her best to make amends in the hope that the Duke could be soothed into forgetting her impudence and somehow reward her for it.

†††

CHAPTER SIX

DUELING WITH ATTILA

Six months passed following Arsenio's funeral and a welcome springtime warmth reigned over Lorengard-Lorraine. Splendid flowers blossomed under the crystal blue skies. However, only nature rejoiced in the season. The sunshine, the blooming flowers, and the verdant trees did not console the people. Despair now reigned supreme. The just government of the late Duke appeared to have been buried along with him and the tranquility that the people once enjoyed had vanished under the tyrant's menacing forces.

The Duke of Saxe-Hanover remained the true power behind the throne and ruled the Dukedom with a cruel fist to satisfy his ambition and thirst for power. Tributes and taxes were raised so high that the Dukedom was becoming impoverished. The people barely had enough food. The poorest ones who lacked the funds to pay were routinely imprisoned or put to death. Even the wealthy and powerful aristocracy, once loyal to Arsenio, was forced into the ranks of the impoverished when their estates and proprieties were confiscated.

Polyxena was sadly aware of the terrible situation, but could not alter the course of events. Her dilemma increased as the dreaded day of her promised betrothal to Ludwig approached.

She realized that she had become hated by many of the citizens, who knew nothing of her kind heart. Their aversion was based upon her apparent complicity with the villainous Duke of Saxe-Hanover. His clever move of leaving her in place as a figurehead meant that the people blamed her for the calamities that befell them, deflecting their resentment and hatred from himself.

He ordered that Polyxena be closely watched. She could not move about the palace without being escorted by his personal guards and mercenaries. The Duke had all of her correspondence meticulously scrutinized and censored. As a result, she was prevented from any true communication outside the palace. She found herself in complete isolation, a prisoner in her own apartments.

Polyxena accurately guessed that the controlling Duke would read her letters to her family, so all her messages to her father contained only harmless information and no explanations for the conditions in the palace. Nor could she explain her true intentions to him. If he knew the truth, her father might question her judgment. Though he was kind to her, he was also rigid in matters of chivalry. He might determine that Polyxena's decision to marry the tyrant, regardless of her good intentions, would bring dishonor to the noble house of Nemours and the memory of her husband, Arsenio.

She envisioned his displeasure when he received her drastic announcement of possible marriage to a man her father abhorred. Later, when no answer came back to her, her sense of isolation and despondency increased. The inability to communicate with her father caused her to fear he might be preparing for war against the Duke of Saxe-Hanover. She knew it would be a terrible last resort. Both sides were equally powerful. Their confrontation would be bloody and devastating.

At the funeral Polyxena had been deeply impressed by the love and respect the people displayed toward their departed Duke. She knew how much Arsenio cared about his people, even without having known him herself. She was proud to honor his wish to protect the people of Lorengard-Lorraine.

For that reason Polyxena knew she had no choice but to continue her deception, keeping a friendly relationship with the Duke of Saxe-Hanover and hoping her receptiveness would bolster his belief in her loyalty and allow her greater freedom. It was only in freedom that she could find a way to undo him and his corrupt reign.

On one bright Sunday morning, she received an invitation to join the Duke in a hunt. She consented, eager to participate in a stringent physical activity. She summoned her ladies in waiting to help prepare her for the hunt and requested Duccio and Philip to serve as her bodyguards.

The Duke awaited for Polyxena's arrival in the palace courtyard. He was relaxed and happy to be going hunting and was stylishly attired for the occasion. He appeared to be surprised by the unexpected arrival of three well-dressed gentlemen.

The men approached him in greeting, and upon closer inspection he recognized Duccio Degli Uberti and Philip of Rohann. To his great surprise however, the third 'gentleman' was the new Duchess Polyxena, dressed in masculine hunting clothes.

She was lovely, tall, and striking in ankle-length boots over black tights with leather inlays, topped with a short waistcoat bearing the Nemours coat of arms. She carried an elegant dark green cloak draped over her shoulders. Her elaborate silver belt held a beautifully chiseled sword that glinted in the sunlight. Her flowing dark hair was hidden under a black velvet cap plumed with a matching ostrich feather.

The effect she created was splendid and most alluring, even in masculine clothes. Ludwig was more attracted than ever to this mysterious female who could hide her true thoughts behind an enigmatic smile. The challenge of possessing this elusive and exciting creature greatly excited him. He had come to deem her the most beautiful woman he had ever known and in his heated dreams, he gratified his lustful desires with her at last.

For now, the Duke approached Polyxena with an approving smile and he gallantly kissed her hands through her elegant chamois gloves.

"My enchanting cousin, your presence is exceptional and surprising. I must admit that all Lorengard-Lorraine has never seen a more attractive gentleman."

"Thank you, my lord. I am pleased my attire meets your approval. I dressed for the hunt like this in Nemours, also for long rides in the forests. Feminine attire is far too cumbersome on horseback."

Ludwig gazed down at her shiny sword and smiled. "Is that exquisite sword dangling at your side a simple adornment? Or is it a truly menacing weapon?"

"It depends on the occasion," she answered with a bright smile intended to confuse him. "Let me say that, for now, it complements my riding outfit."

The Duke grew tired of his own questions and without further adieu he helped Polyxena mount her horse, then quickly joined her on his own magnificent stallion.

Duccio Degli Uberti and Philip of Rohann joined with the imposing hunting party in mounting their horses, and then riding in a deliberate stride through the exit of the palace courtyard. In a short time, they were in a verdant countryside, riding through lush forests.

The hours began to melt by and the Duke's spotty temper was rendered affable under the brilliant sun, the warm weather, and the presence of Polyxena. He shared stories of his hunting prowess and she responded by recounting her experiences in the hunt for wild boars back in Nemours, where her father possessed land favorable to the hunt.

"Cousin," the Duke called out to her. "Today, I will introduce you to my special friend. He is a rare, elite, white-tailed eagle and a magnificent specimen of his royal breed. He will join us in the hunt, in his unique way, and I hope he will amaze you with his great intelligence and ability. A Muslim Sheik who is a friend of mine gave him to me. He trains these unique birds for the hunt in his spare time."

Polyxena responded with what she hoped was a fair imitation of an eager smile.

Ludwig spurred his horse to a faster gallop. Suddenly, a small animal appeared in the path of the hunting party, scurrying across the dirt road. When he saw the little creature, the Duke was suddenly overwhelmed with dread and terrified. He forcefully reigned his horse, pointed toward it and ordered his guards to kill it before the animal had a chance to escape.

The source of his fear was an ordinary black cat, with piercing green eyes and a shiny pelt. The terrified cat tried to escape into the thick shrubbery flanking the road, but with lightning speed, a guard's well-placed arrow pierced and killed it instantly. The Duke quickly dismounted his horse, sword in hand, and struck it eight more times, spreading bloody parts over the dirt road.

Having finished the gruesome task, Ludwig finally appeared to calm down and regain his composure. Without further delay he remounted his horse and continued galloping through the bucolic hills as if nothing had happened.

Polyxena felt herself deeply upset by the Duke's cruelty. She rode up next to him. "Forgive me if I appear tactless, my lord, but I am astonished by your attack on that helpless cat. It was a harmless domestic animal, not a coveted hunting prize."

"Dear cousin," he exclaimed. "I understand your curiosity...therefore I will share some powerful knowledge with you. A remarkable mystic who possessed great wisdom and knowledge of the supernatural tutored me as a young child. She showed me ways I could protect myself against evil signs heralding calamities and disasters.

"You must already be aware that a black cat is a creature endowed with dark powers. Its ominous presence in one's path signifies incumbent destruction. According to the legend, the cat possesses nine lives. Therefore one death is not enough to destroy the evil it disseminates, and this is why I was forced to inflict the eight additional blows to be certain that I annihilated his curse."

"My lord," Polyxena answered, stunned by the Duke's strange explanation. "...your words mystify me. I find it hard to believe that a cultured and intelligent man like you can think an ordinary cat could possess ominous power over humanity."

"I believe it earnestly, dear cousin, in spite of your skepticism. I know through extensive study as well as personal experience that there are great occult powers, which direct and control our lives. It would be wise to familiarize and enlighten yourself with them. The insights will eventually guide us to great power and success.

"My grandmother was the amazing mystic who foretold my life path. She also predicted many other events in my life that have come to pass as she described, and she prepared me for my great destiny. However, I was forewarned that to fulfill her lofty prophecy, I had to scrupulously follow her instructions by familiarizing myself with the occult and dark powers. I bowed to her wisdom, treasuring her advice, and as you see from my present position, everything has occurred as she predicted."

Polyxena listened to Ludwig's response, aware of his displeasure at her skepticism. She knew it was unwise to challenge him further. Secretly however, she rejoiced at the Duke's fanatical superstitions and recognized them as a great flaw in his character. An Achilles heel such as that could possibly hasten his downfall.

"Please forgive my skepticism," she said. "I expressed myself poorly, my lord, because I am uninformed in matters of the occult. I would be grateful if you could impart your esteemed grandmother's teachings to me and expand my horizon."

"It will be my pleasure, dear cousin," Ludwig answered, pleased by the girl's receptiveness. Her affirmation caused him to regain a more pleasant attitude.

The hunting party continued toward its destination and in a short time it reached the summit of a wooded hill that crowned the valleys and country side. The hunters took in the breathtaking views of verdant forest and an unusually large clearing visible from the hilltop, drenched by sunlight.

The group spurred their horses toward the clearing at a full gallop, and soon reached the edge of it. The Duke dismounted from his horse and gallantly assisted Polyxena's dismount, clutching her in an ardent embrace before depositing her on the ground.

Duccio viewed the Duke's overture with distress, helpless to react. He burned with rage and jealousy when he saw Polyxena's apparent receptiveness to the Duke's lustful attention.

Several palace soldiers were already posted at the clearing edge, awaiting the hunting party's arrival. They guarded an imposing metal cage that contained a magnificent eagle. It was a splendid specimen, much bigger than the usual white-tailed eagle known in Europe. The bird moved restlessly on his perch and emitted loud, piercing screeches.

A beautiful young doe was tied to a tree near the eagle, clearly terrified by the presence of the menacing bird. The doe tried to escape by yanking violently at the restraining ropes, but she was hopelessly entrapped.

Polyxena gasped at the sight, envisioning a bloody game about to unfold for Ludwig's amusement. Although she was a valiant and capable huntress, she despised unnecessary torment inflicted upon the helpless creatures of the forest. She was also upset by the Duke's frequent and menacing sexual advances.

Hers was a difficult and dangerous game. The Duke was

becoming more unbearable and difficult with each passing day. She felt herself to be as trapped as the gentle doe.

He remained unaware of her turmoil and proudly escorted her to the eagle's cage. "Here is Attila, dear cousin. He is a shining example of his noble species. I named him to honor the King of the Huns, whom I greatly admire. Like him, this noble bird is innately ferocious and has been trained to kill upon request."

Ludwig signaled his guards to open the cage and free the eagle. The splendid bird immediately leaped out and spread his powerful wings to fly high into the crystal blue sky. After a short freedom flight, he circled the clearing and awaited a signal for action from the ground.

The Duke signaled to release the doe and the gentle creature ran with incredible speed toward the open space, as if savoring her unexpected freedom. He waited for the doe to enter the vacant area and distance herself from the protective shelter of the surrounding trees. Then he blew a silver whistle and the eagle instantly responded by lowering his flight pattern and descending toward the clearing. Its ominous shadow streaked across the ground.

The doe became aware of the danger and panicked, running aimlessly in a desperate desire to escape. Attila flew in a restrictive pattern that forced the doe to run to the center of the opening, leaving her exposed to attack from above.

The Duke laughed, savoring the coming kill, while the eagle dove with the speed of an arrow and landed on the doe's exposed head, digging deadly claws into tender flesh. The doe screamed and fought valiantly to save her life, with desperate leaps to dislodge the vicious assailant. But Attila plunged its beak into her eyes and blinded the poor creature. Mortally wounded, she rolled on the ground and convulsed.

When the silver whistle sounded, Attila stopped mutilating the doe's corpse, released the carcass and flew to a great height, returning to its circular pattern in the sky.

"Well cousin," he said, satisfied. "What do you think of my pupil? He is an amazingly talented bird with a keen intelligence, as you have witnessed. But he would have ripped the doe's carcass to shreds if I had not stopped him. We shall enjoy roasted venison for dinner tonight."

Polyxena forced herself to smile in approval and disguise the dread that filled her. It was apparent that the Duke had no desire to hunt in a sporting way. He wanted only to witness the torture and suffering of helpless animals. For the moment he had been placated by Attila's masterful kill and happily engaged Polyxena in animated conversation about his chef's exceptional skill at cooking wild animals.

Loud voices abruptly interrupted him when several guards appeared, restraining a man and a child who were fighting desperately to free themselves from their captors. "Who are these people, and what do they want?" Ludwig angrily demanded.

"They are impudent citizens, my lord," a guard answered. "…who dare to demand an audience with the Duchess."

The Duke ordered the prisoners brought before him and gazed contemptuously upon their disheveled appearance. The man was in his forties, poorly dressed, gaunt and malnourished.

In spite of his fear he maintained his dignity and stood tall before royalty. The child was between eight or nine years of age, with golden blond curls framing an angelic face. Like the man, he was also frail and malnourished, and his blue-gray eyes were distressed.

"Well sir," the Duke coldly addressed the man. "What brings you here at this inopportune time? And your answer had better be a good one, or you will pay a heavy price for your effrontery."

The man looked around for a friendly face and was relieved when he saw the new Duchess. Her loveliness and air of benevolence gave him the courage to speak, "My lord. My name is Antoine Roussell and this child is my youngest son, Derek." He then turned away and directly addressed Polyxena.

"My Duchess. You who are the custodian of our Dukedom and the protector of its people, have pity upon your servant. Poverty and sickness have plagued me and my family! And in our impoverished condition, we are unable to pay our taxes. The tributes are too high for the meager earnings of my family. I have too many mouths to feed and there is not enough bread on our table to ease our hunger."

The man stopped momentarily, overwhelmed by raw emotion. "I have lived a long life and I am ready to face whenever destiny wills for me. But my unhappy children grow hungrier each day. They have a right to live. Derek here is my youngest child and only son, but as you see he is sickly and frail. I fear he will soon die without proper food. Be merciful, my powerful and gracious lady, and allow me a little more time to pay the tribute. Take pity on a helpless father."

After his emotional plea, the man remained silent before Polyxena and the Duke, afraid to raise his eyes and unable to hold back his tears. Polyxena felt herself beset with sorrow by the wretched man's suffering because her hollow position made her little more than a figurehead with no power to help. She agonized for the unfortunate father, but before she could think of a response, the Duke spoke out.

"Sir! You are a vile, insolent person who dares disturb and intrude upon our leisure time with your complaints. Your request is denied. And if you want to live another day, you will pay your taxes without delay."

"Mercy my lord. Take pity on my children. Kill me if you must," he pleaded. "...but spare their young lives. Do not let them suffer and die."

To emphasize his plea, he unwisely touched the Duke's leg in a helpless gesture. It was a fatal mistake.

"Miserable beggar," Ludwig cried. "You dare place your filthy hands upon my person?" He brutally kicked Antoine in the stomach, sending him rolling onto the ground and moaning with pain. Unsatisfied with the punishment, the Duke removed a small whip from his belt and began to ferociously inflict blows upon the man's face, marking it with bloody red welts and forcing agonized screams from his victim.

Young Derek lunged forward in a desperate attempt to help his father. With the recklessness of youth, he picked up a rock from the ground and threw it at the despot, striking his left cheek and cutting his face.

"Run Derek! Run!" Antoine screamed. The child responded immediately to his father's command and with great agility mounted a horse at the edge of the forest. He rode away at full gallop but entered the vast open space, exposed to danger. The guards aimed their deadly arrows at the young fugitive, who could not hear his father's warning screams.

"Do not shoot!" Polyxena cried in her strongest voice.

The mercenaries ignored her, but held off their attack when the Duke also commanded them to lower their weapons. It was not the gesture of mercy Polyxena hoped it to be. With an evil smile, Ludwig brought the silver whistle to his lips and blew it until it reverberated throughout the forest.

Polyxena screamed, but Attila responded immediately to the whistle and he flew toward the oblivious child, landed and sank his powerful claws into the shoulders of his victim. A desperate scream reverberated throughout the clearing. The horse bucked in terror of the predatory bird, throwing the young rider to the ground, where Attila continued the attack. Within seconds, the youth succumbed to the predatory bird's awesome power.

The deadly talons sank into the child's stomach and the powerful wings easily lifted him from the ground and flew him to a great height. The horrified father screamed and tried desperately to free himself from the guards, to no avail.

Attila flew higher, still holding Derek's limp body. Polyxena could only pray that a merciful God had already taken his innocent soul and spared him further agony. Attila glided freely for a few moments, then abruptly released Derek's body and allowed him to fall to the ground and crash into the grassy meadow.

The poor father was overwhelmed by anguish and screamed incessantly until despair and grief finally silenced him. The eagle was ready to finish his gruesome job and mutilate his victim, but Polyxena was no longer able to stand helplessly by and watch the dreadful spectacle. Disregarding any dire consequences for displeasing the Duke, she swiftly removed her mantle and leaped onto her horse. "Quickly men," she called to one of the guards. "…give me your shield!"

"There is no need to interfere my lady," the Duke called out. "Justice has been served." He blew the silver whistle again and Attila obediently flew away, leaving Derek's remains untouched.

But Polyxena's outrage overwhelmed her. She turned to the Duke with a determined look and raised her voice to full strength. "My lord, I wish to challenge Attila to a duel."

"A duel?" Ludwig questioned, bemused. "Attila is a powerful and aggressive killer. It would be unwise and dangerous to tempt fate by challenging his power."

Polyxena retained her determined stance. "As the Duchess of Lorengard-Lorraine, I have expressed my desire to challenge Attila to a duel. I hope you will agree with my decision, my lord, and once more blow your whistle, signaling the new challenge."

Polyxena's unyielding demeanor fascinated him. She was so different than the submissive women of the time that he found himself disarmed by her boldness and charm. But he was also concerned over the possibility of losing a female he intensely desired.

Polyxena continued, "I demand no special privileges or safeguards. It will be me against that infernal bird."

Duccio and Philip stood prepared to protect her, and Polyxena noticed Duccio's deep concern. She responded with a comforting smile.

In spite of the Duke's personal concerns, he blew the silver whistle and Polyxena galloped into the clearing, guiding her horse to the center. She reached young Derek's body, where she was exposed to danger, but defiantly showed no fear of Attila's attack.

The bird immediately responded to the challenge and dropped down from on high, falling straight toward her.

Polyxena's only defensive weapon was her sword, and without her bow, she was in great peril. The eagle plunged onward, while Polyxena held the reins tight. By that time her horse was also aware of the danger and bucked, trying to flee toward the shelter of the trees.

She restrained the reluctant animal and remained in the path of the eagle's attack. Just as Attila was about to strike, she slid to the horse's right side, retaining her hold on the mount with a handful of mane, reins and her strong legs. This made her invisible to the bird.

Polyxena held onto the horse's mane and placed her shield against its head. Attila attacked with all the speed his powerful wings could reap. But his potent talons could not pierce the empty saddle. The awkward impact propelled Attila forward and the bird crashed forcefully against the metal shield protecting the horse's head.

The stallion bucked fiercely to deflect the invasive bird, which threw Polyxena to the ground. With acrobatic agility, she rolled on the grass and leapt to her feet, shield and sword in hand.

Attila struggled to regain his balance, but he was impaired by his massive wingspan. A bright light blazed from Polyxena's shining sword and with a precise and awesome strike, she severed one of the bird's talons. The wounded eagle shrieked in pain as he bled copiously. Overwhelmed by the crippling wound, he bounced several times on the ground, trying to reach Polyxena. But she swung her sword and deflected the attack, then raised her sword once more and crushed the bird's right wing with a precise strike to the dorsal area.

Using her weapon as a javelin, she impaled the bird on her sword and took him out of his misery. She stared contemptuously at Attila's carcass, angry and outraged by the horrific murder of an innocent child. This was as close to proper revenge as she could get.

"May the evil rulers of the world succumb to a violent and ignominious death like yours," she muttered under her breath quietly enough so the evil Duke could not hear her.

Then she approached and knelt next to Derek's body. Attila's gruesome handy work was apparent on his mangled and bloodied corpse. But the boy's angelic face, framed by golden curls, remained miraculously intact, retaining its beauty even in death. Derek's large blue eyes stared peacefully at the sky in sharp contrast to his violent death.

Polyxena fought back the bitter tears that clouded her vision. She sobbed and with trembling hands closed the lids of those splendid eyes. For a long moment, she remained on her knees in silent prayer.

The moment was interrupted when the Duke speedily approached Polyxena followed by Philip and Duccio. She hastily rose to her feet, preparing to greet them with her customary poise and dignity. Ludwig dismounted and approached Attila's remains, ignoring the little boy. He gazed with wonder at the incredible metamorphosis of the beautiful, powerful bird who had been reduced to bloodied feathers. He removed Polyxena's sword from the bird's remains and mocked him.

"You finally found a worthy opponent, dear Attila, in our beautiful Duchess. She has proven to be the most valiant huntress and warrior I've ever seen."

The Duke then moved away from the carcass and turned toward Polyxena with an approving smile. He placed the bloodied weapon in her waiting hand. "Dear cousin, you are an incredibly talented equestrian and fearless with the sword. I've never witnessed ability like yours in a woman or even in a man, I must admit. However, you caused me consternation and I feared for your safety because you are dear to me and irreplaceable. Therefore, my lady, please spare me such anguish in the future and do not expose yourself to unnecessary danger."

"Thank you, my lord," Polyxena replied, repressing once more the revulsion she felt in his presence. "I greatly value your opinion," she said perfidiously. "...and I am humbled by your praise."

Ludwig noticed that the heated conflict had tinted Polyxena's cheeks with bright crimson and her raven hair had become loose from under her cap. It flowed freely onto her shoulders like a lustrous mantle, enhancing her stunning beauty and making her more desirable than ever to him. He passionately seized her hands. "My lady, I believe it is time to end this depressing period of mourning in your life, and since your late spouse is finally buried, I propose to revive the doldrums with a great feast honoring your victory. We will end the pervasive gloom in the Dukedom. I will also stage a great joust, to commemorate your triumph over Attila, and you will reign supreme as the Queen of grace and beauty."

"I thank you again my lord," Polyxena answered, doing her best to imitate joyful excitement. "I accept, and I am humbled by the honor."

The Duke was so pleased by her response that he happily smiled and kissed her hands.

"I am overwhelmed by your generosity my lord," she continued. "But may I request a different reward instead?"

"Certainly my lady," he beamed. "If it is within my power, I will gladly oblige."

"Set free the citizen who disrupted our hunting party and allow him to give his son a Christian burial."

His retort was curt and angry, in vehement disapproval of Polyxena's benevolent nature. "It is dangerous to show weakness in dispensing justice. Death is the only suitable punishment for nonpayment of taxes. For this one, the noose is waiting to snap his worthless neck while the jackals consume his delinquent son."

Polyxena retained her composure and continued her request, "I beg your forgiveness my lord, for it was not my intent to criticize your judgment. I concur with the need for discipline. But I also believe that the father's daring has been adequately punished by his son's death. Besides, if he does not comply and pay his taxes, he will be executed with the rest of his family according to your law. Therefore, I believe justice was done."

"You are much too tolerant, my lady," Ludwig answered sternly. "We must send a strong message to the populace to eradicate this impertinence. It is imperative that the man die without delay."

"I respect your authority," insisted Polyxena. "But in this case, I believe this man can be a great messenger for us. If he is left alive, he can dissuade anyone to follow in his foolish footsteps by challenging the power of your laws. He is far more politically valuable to you alive."

Polyxena ended with an enchanting smile, hoping to minimize his anger. The ploy appeared to bear fruit because the Duke grew less stern and became more focused on her than his desire for revenge.

"Very well," he finally said. "I defer to your desires and wishes. Perhaps it would be wiser to allow the man to live and convey our message to the rebellious masses."

Polyxena was greatly relieved by the Duke's response and bowed her head while he ordered his guards to release the man.

The unfortunate father quickly ran to his son's body. There he fell upon the pitiful remains with anguish. He surveyed with agonizing pain the injuries incurred by his innocent son, and noticed by his right hand a small leather pouch. With trepidation he seized the mysterious parcel and removed the restraining cord. Suddenly, a multitude of ducats fell upon the ground like a golden rain. Antoine was stunned at the sight of the small fortune. He raised his eyes to the sky in silent prayer of thanks. Miraculously, the sacrifice of his precious child saved the life of the entire family.

The following evening Duccio met his friend in the palace gardens in response to Philip's request earlier in the day. It was difficult for the young knights to communicate freely during daylight, since Ludwig mistrusted them and used his mercenaries as spies. Since Duccio was the first to arrive, he used his time there to scout the area and be certain they were alone.

When Philip appeared on the far end of a tree-lined path, he swiftly approached with the moon light eerily making his blonde hair ghostly white. When Philip drew close, Duccio saw a concerned look on his face. When Philip spoke his anxiety was evident.

"Duccio my friend," Philip sadly told him, "I am here to say good bye to you. I must leave tonight and I won't return. Therefore, after all the years we shared as friends, these are our last moments together."

"You are leaving?" Duccio asked, stunned. "What happened to cause you to make this resolution? Do you have a dangerous mission that will prevent your safe return?"

No, my friend," Philip replied. "I leave of my own volition. I have been considering such a step for some time, but with our present situation being as it is, I have been reluctant to leave you or I would have departed sooner."

Philip took a breath and continued, "However, I no longer see any recourse. The Duke's sadistic nature has no boundaries. Yesterday we witnessed the cold-blooded murder of an innocent child and nothing I tell myself prevents me from being filled with rage. I have come to believe that know I can serve our lady better from a distance, away from this palace where we are nothing more than honor guards."

Philip leaned in close enough to whisper the next dangerous words, "Come with me my friend. This place is worse than a prison, for honorable men. It is time to become noble knights again. We have one right in this life, but it is paramount. That is the right to brandish our weapons with pride and, if willed by destiny, die an honorable death. There must be many patriots who remain loyal to Duke Arsenio. Certainly, it must be true that somewhere within this oppressed Dukedom…a nascent uprising is already underway. Duccio, I am determined to find them and join in that quest."

For a moment, Duccio did not respond. He felt the truth of his friend's words, along with a flush of guilt about not following him in the endeavor. But in the same instant he knew that his need to be near Polyxena and protect her with his life dwarfed any other course of action.

"I cannot come with you, Philip. I believe in the honor of your quest, but I cannot leave our Duchess alone amongst her enemies. Her father repudiated her when he discovered she was going to wed the Duke of Saxe-Hanover. Since then, there has been no further communication from Nemours. If you go, I will be all she has, and if I go, she will be left here alone among conspirators…"

"Hear me, friend. The invitation was sincere, but I already knew your answer. You are impaired by your love for her. You are made stupid by love. You wander naked in the forest and live on scavenged berries, all for your dearest love."

Duccio laughed in spite of the bite in the words.

"However," Philip went on. "…you are courageous and gallant, even if you are a bit of a love-struck fool and I have decided to trust your judgment in this. It appears destiny has decreed that we take separate roads from this point. If this should turn out to be the last time we are together, I want you to know that you are my family and my true brother. May the good Lord protect and guide you."

Philip warmly embraced his friend, then abruptly stood and walked away. Duccio knew it would be a waste of energy to call him back.

†††

CHAPTER SEVEN

THE JOUST

The joust proposed by the Duke of Saxe-Hanover in honor of Polyxena's victory over the hunting eagle was one promise he intended to keep. His motives became clear when took the initiative of announcing that the event would officially represent the 'end of mourning' for the woman he permitted to be addressed as 'Duchess.' Rather than concern himself with the impact of such blatant disrespect for the memory of the deceased young leader, he ordered spies to permeate the palace and report any grumblers to the palace guard.

Preparations for the joust proceeded feverishly under the Ludwig's command—in a short time the facilities were constructed, and Lorengard-Lorraine was ready for the event.

The entire Dukedom was lavishly decorated with large colorful banners inviting the surrounding realms to send their best champions to participate in the joust. The Duke offered what he called 'a conspicuous prize' to the winner in addition to the honor of victory.

Several days were dedicated to elimination rounds, since numerous knights entered and challenged for places in the preliminary rounds. For an entire day, they charged their mounts toward one another at full speed along the two-way list, colliding in the middle with sickening impacts.

Only six among the most valiant and talented knights survived the elimination rounds to become finalists in the tourney. The joust was done on relatively friendly terms and while death or grave injury was possible, killing one's adversary was not required. The knight who was able to disarm and render his opponent helpless would be declared victorious.

The joust itself began with much fanfare, in warm weather that favored the occasion. Throngs of spectators crowded their way inside to secure the best viewpoints. A multicolored sea of family crests floated through the Dukedom on illustrious banners.

The most privileged guests were the aristocracy, who occupied elegant banner draped viewing stands on comfortable seats built for the event. The noble visitors were attired in their best finery, befitting one of the most important social functions of the time.

Women who were looking to marry, were jealously competitive among so many maidens of outstanding beauty. Dressed in exquisite gowns of brocade and silk, their extravagant headdresses complimented lavishly jeweled attire.

The males focused on the joust itself, regardless of rank. Hearty voices filled the air while they taunted one another, comparing their chosen Knights and predicting tournament winners.

The centrally located Ducal podium was crowned by a splendid canopy and decorated with the coats-of-arms of the houses of Lorengard-Lorraine and Saxe-Hanover. Two ornate chairs upholstered in a crimson brocade prominently awaited Ludwig and Polyxena, whom the despot had publicly declared 'Queen of the Joust'.

Festive trumpets played by a neat double line of pageboys announced their arrival, each elegantly attired in silver-blue tights and a waistcoat embossed with the fleurs-de-lis.

Polyxena and the Duke of Saxe-Hanover entered followed by Flavia De Brezzé and Baron Frederick Van Halt. However, in spite of all the pomp to the festivities, the crowd remained quiet and their reception was strained through sentiments of rancor and fear.

Defiant and richly dressed in a black velvet jacket detailed in gold, the Duke's aura of superiority was evident. He looked over the opulent scene and basked in his wealth and power, voluntarily oblivious to his muted reception by the citizens.

Flavia was beautiful in a dark blue satin gown that showcased her white complexion and exquisite form. The luxurious attire was sewn with precious pearls and her golden hair was artistically braided under a fitted net. She felt some small satisfaction in knowing she was admired and envied for her beauty, but it was not enough. For her, there was no overlooking the fact that Ludwig was completely enthralled by the enigmatic 'Queen of the Joust', *whatever that means,* she thought.

Her envy was not without cause. Polyxena's radiance was unparalleled on this day. Her green velvet gown harmonized with her eye color and enhanced her figure. Her flowing raven hair rested on her shoulders, under a splendid bejeweled crown sparkling in the sunlight.

But the people of Lorengard-Lorraine were perplexed by their mysterious Duchess, who appeared so benign and lovely, but who inexplicably allied herself with the devil's spawn who gripped their homeland. For many, the joust was nothing more than an opportunity to study their Duchess in an attempt to understand what drove her.

The opening ceremony and parade began as soon as the leaders were seated. The six Knights selected as finalists opened the occasion by parading on horseback before the Ducal podium, dressed in their finest armor. Their powerful chargers were armored around the head and eyes by a metal shield—called a chanfron—designed to obscure the animal's lateral vision and prevent them from panicking just before impact as well as protecting them from otherwise leathal lance strikes. The competitors rode with helmet visors lowered. Only the coats-of-arms on their shields revealed each knight's identity, while the particular colors of the bright helmet plumes signified the realms they represented.

The knights proudly acknowledged the ovations from the crowd while young maidens vied for their attention in hopes that one of the knights might accept a handkerchief as a favor and perhaps dedicate a joust to them. The few young women who accomplished this feat leaped ahead of the others in their status among them. The rejected maidens could only fume with envy deep enough to place them closer to being Flavia's sisters than they could know.

When the opening parade ended, the knights aligned themselves in the center of the field, divided into two groups, and moved in opposite directions toward the extreme ends of the jousting list. They faced each other and stood motionless for a long moment, acknowledging the roar from the crowd.

Squires carried out long jousting lances and placed them in the knights' gauntlet-covered hands. Each lance was tipped with a coronel, consisting of three or more blunted metal prongs that allowed the lance to catch onto the shield and unhorse an opponent.

The herald signaled the commencement of the joust. Immediately the first two knights lined up on opposite ends of the list, kicked their mounts to a gallop and barreled toward each other with their lances aimed. One of the knights was thrown violently from his mount and eliminated from the tournament to boos of scorn from the crowd. There would be other chances for each losing knight, to provide enough action to please the spectators.

For the next few hours, knights took position on the list, charged and unseated one another until their numbers dwindled. At last two knights remained in the competition, one fighting under a black plume and the other plumed in red.

The challengers approached the Ducal podium and offered the customary salute to the distinguished gathering before the final contest to determine the winner.

Polyxena, as Queen of the Joust, greeted them with an approving smile and threw her handkerchief emblazoned with Lorengard-Lorraine coat-of-arms onto the ground between the two champions. By the rules of the joust, only the tournament champion could claim it and dedicate his victory to her. As far as Polyxena could tell, this was the grand extent of her reign as Queen there.

The crowd had dropped their surly mood over the course of the afternoon and was openly elated when the final confrontation approached. The two knights faced each other from the far ends of the list and stood still for a few seconds before the herald signaled them to begin.

Upon his cry, they charged at each other with great speed and collided with a mighty impact. The crowd roared in approval when both knights somehow remained on their destriers even though the tips of their lances snapped off in the collision.

Maces quickly replaced damaged lances—long handles fitted with chains the length of a forearm, attached to an iron ball covered with spikes that could strike blows as devastating as a cannon ball. Here the danger level steeply rose, but without a moment's hesitation, the two knights spun their weapons and attacked each other using powerful blows. Their shields sustained the masterful clanging strikes while the knights relentlessly went after each other.

Then the red knight took a mighty blow from his adversary's mace and fell to the ground. A cry of disappointment rose from that part of the crowd who favored him to win. They screamed encouragement to their champion and roared in approval when the fallen knight rose to his feet with amazing agility in spite of the heavy blow he sustained and the weight of the armor he wore.

But the warrior on the ground always has a definite disadvantage to his adversary. Now the black knight attacked with renewed ardor, fiercely spinning the deadly weapon for a final victorious strike at his opponent.

But the red knight moved with acrobatic agility and wielded his mace with skill, entwining it with his opponent's weapon. He immediately capitalized on the black knight's forward position and pulled him from his mount to the ground. It was an even fight once again.

The spectators screamed for their favorites while the valiant fighters, now toe to toe, brandished their swords in hand-to-hand combat. Both champions impressed the crowd with their expertise.

The black knight, who had briefly enjoyed an advantage, was eager to overcome his opponent and claim victory. He took hold of his sword with both hands and swung it at the red knight, who swiftly moved aside, deflecting the assault. The missed blow upset the black knight's balance and he fell heavily to the ground. His supporters cried out in frustration.

When the red knight pointed his sword at his fallen opponent's throat and placed his boot on his chest in symbolic victory, the crowd roared with fanatical enthusiasm for the amazing skills of the champion. The red knight gallantly helped his opponent to his feet and finally lifted his visor, allowing everyone to see him.

It was Duccio, with his handsome face still flushed from the arduous challenge. He removed the helmet, placed it under his left arm, and then walked proudly toward the Ducal podium. His tall and athletic figure, so impressive in his shiny armor, attracted admiring glances from the surrounding crowd.

Spectators continued to applaud him, especially the young maidens, infatuated not only by his bravery but by his striking good looks. They threw flowers in his path and multicolored handkerchiefs, hoping for a look or smile from the champion of the day.

Duccio appreciatively saluted the crowd, while making his way to the podium. When he arrived, he picked up Polyxena's handkerchief, then climbed the podium steps and reverently knelt before her. Polyxena was delighted with her champion and placed a golden laurel ringlet upon his head, symbolizing greatness and triumph. She extended her hand to be kissed in a formal gesture of her approval.

Duccio overturned that routine bit of etiquette by kissing her hand with such tenderness that she was struck by the power of it. Strong shivers went up her spine. She glanced briefly into his dark eyes and he looked back at her with obvious longing. She was instantly uneasy, beset by powerful feelings she had never experienced and could not explain.

She immediately regained control and motioned for him to rise, then invited the knight to stand by her side and receive the adulation of the crowd. Duccio was enthralled by Polyxena's nearness and was so deeply moved by the warm reception that in spite of the solemn occasion, he could not keep the broad smile from his face.

THE MESSAGE

On the evening after the joust, the palace glittered with the lights of torches and candles, showcasing the magnificent structure in all its opulence. The many lavishly attired guests were treated to a sumptuous banquet, seated according to rank.

Following the great feast, a celebratory ball was set to begin. The banquet tables were set in a U-shape, with the Duke and Duchess at the center of the curve, flanked by selected guests of the highest strata. Lesser guests were seated at side tables, knowing that the closer they sat to their host, the greater their honor.

Each table was lavishly arranged with all the abundance great wealth could provide. Experienced chefs prepared the food in the most delectable and appetizing manner, more than enough to stimulate the refined palates of the guests. Pheasants stuffed with sweetbread and walnuts were displayed on huge silver platters, enhanced with each bird's brightly colored feathers.

Coveted hunting prizes of wild boar and deer were special favorites, roasted to perfection and glazed with honey and precious oils. Tender suckling pigs were stuffed with apples and berries, and a great assortment of salt and fresh water fish from the surrounding lakes and imported from the Mediterranean completed the lavish display. This abundance was decorated with exotic flowers and fruits, delighting the guests, who washed down the food with precious Rhine wines and imports from all across Europe.

Young pages stood nearby with great silver carafes filled with wine and made certain that the guest's goblets were never empty. The important guests from the highest strata saw nothing novel in the experience and amused themselves by drinking with abandon, allowing the liquid to flow unhindered down their necks and clothes. They indulged themselves in ravenously consuming the roasted flesh, staining their hands and lavish attire with the oils.

As the levels of drunkenness increased, the scene began to deteriorate into a frenzied orgy of consumption. Eventually many became nauseous after eating and drinking without restraint and had to make use of the large metal containers placed under the tables for the purpose. Loud regurgitation noises echoed freely through the hall, worthy compliments to the host for a successful banquet.

The Duke decided the time was right to invite his happy guests to the adjacent hall and begin the grand dance. Dozens of torches brilliantly illuminated the vast room, casting a reddish-orange glow over everything.

Polyxena and Ludwig sat together on a double throne hoisted on a platform and covered by a canopy upholstered in crimson velvet with gold trim. Minstrels and musicians were scattered about the hall, to entertain the multitude with lyres, flutes, and handheld drums.

The dances were performed in groups or in double circles. Young maidens occupied the inner circle, holding hands, while the men on the outside faced them. The ladies danced around in a circular motion to the music until it stopped, and coupled in the dance with the particular gentleman who faced them.

The dance was graceful and romantic and the young ones danced close enough for their eyes to reflect their amorous feelings. But the couples barely touched each other during the sequences of elegant pirouettes and formal curtsies. It was a coveted pleasure simply to spend the intimate moments together as a couple, relishing the sensual feelings of intimacy which was only approved after marriage.

The mood in the dance hall was different from the atmosphere in the banquet, soothed and softened by the alluring music. The majority of the dancers were appealing in their lavish attire and fresh faces and took to the romance of the occasion with enthusiasm.

Polyxena felt comforted enough by the surroundings to temporarily relax and converse with guests. While she danced in step with the rhythmic music, she was unaware that Baron Van Halt appeared in the hall and accosted the Duke.

The men engaged in a brief discourse before the Duke's face took on a stony cast. He thanked the Baron, who quickly departed, and then started toward Polyxena. She was still engrossed in amiable conversation with two young maidens and welcomed the Duke with a pleasant smile when he approached.

"My lord. This is a memorable day, filled with excitement. I thank you for your thoughtfulness in generously honoring me with such an opulent feast."

"It has been my honor to give you joy, dear cousin," he answered. "However, it is now my solemn duty to inform you that a messenger has just arrived from Nemours and carries a letter for you. He awaits in your rooms."

"From Nemours?" Polyxena jubilantly cried. "Is this news from my father? My lord, may I be excused at this early hour? I am eager to hear the news as soon as possible."

"Of course, my lady," Ludwig agreed with a bow. Now that he had her hemmed in, it did not pain him to be generous.

Polyxena hurried toward the exit, doing her best to move gracefully through the inebriated guests. She was followed closely by Duccio as her bodyguard and they quickly walked through the endless corridors of the vast residence. Her rooms were located on the opposite end of the palace, making it an impatient journey. When they finally arrived, the guards at the door stood aside for her. The messenger from Nemours stood waiting in the antechamber. He immediately bowed to her and handed over a sealed document. She took it into eager hands, so filled with curiosity that she failed to notice his somber look when he offered the letter.

She happily broke the seal, but immediately noticed that the letter originated from the Count of Rozenberk and not her father. This alone was enough to send an icy rush of dread throughout her body. Her joyful anticipation instantly gave way to anxiety. She looked at the envoy, who was prepared to respond and clarify the situation to the Duchess. But Polyxena feared she would not be able to remain stoic if she received dire news. She looked up from the letter, not wanting to absorb it in a stranger's presence.

Before the envoy could blurt any further information, she quickly spoke in a voice that broached no hesitation, "You must be tired from your journey, good sir. Eager to rest. You will be extended our hospitality. Tomorrow we will have plenty of time to converse. Therefore, you are excused and may retire. Thank you."

The messenger bowed and quickly left the room. Duccio felt his concern for her rising, but his intuition told him to stand by her side and remain quiet for the moment.

Polyxena stood still, suddenly reluctant to read the message. For a moment, Duccio feared she would send him away as well, but she expressed her appreciation for his presence by saying nothing and allowing him to remain. Although not a word passed between them, they both understood that a new bond of closeness had just been declared. Duccio understood that he was being privileged to share the terrible intimacy of this moment.

With effort, she broke the seal and read the letter. Within seconds, she grew pale and whispered in pain, "My father is dead. Duccio, they say he is dead. Dear Lord, how can this be possible?"

She was suddenly so beset with sorrow that Duccio placed his strong arms about her to save her from falling. Overcome with the shock of the news, all she could do was to rest her head upon his chest while he held her up. So much confusion and pain filled her that she felt an instinctive need to run, as if she could outdistance such a terrible thing. It was too much to swallow at once, because she understood that the loss of her father could change everything about her life for the worse.

She looked deeply into Duccio's eyes as if to seek some form of shelter in him. In any other moment she would have remembered her position, her obligations and the wrath of her sadistic husband-to-be. It would have been enough to cause her to keep her regal bearing.

Instead, she felt herself overwhelmed by such deep emotion that before she stopped to think at all, she gave in to Duccio's magnetic attraction and their lips met in a passionate kiss while their bodies melted into one another. It was such a sensual embrace that both of them fell into ecstasy together and immediately became oblivious to the rest of the world.

The bliss was short lived. Like a snap of static electricity, the danger of that moment struck her. She avoided daring to look into Duccio's eye again and instead moved away from him.

Duccio was just as aware that his actions were forbidden. Besides risking a very unpleasant death, his behavior sharply conflicted with the chivalrous code he professed as an honorable knight. He suddenly felt mortified by his recklessness.

He knelt at her feet. "Forgive me, my lady," he pleaded. "I am appalled at my impudence…especially at such a tragic moment in your life. I am aware that my daring dishonors you. My humble station is inappropriate for the attention of a Duchess, especially one I have promised my fealty. But God forgive me, my lady, I must say it. I love you desperately, Polyxena. The hopeless situation torments me. I no longer know what to do."

Duccio's despair was so apparent that Polyxena was shaken by the depths of his love. She cooed to him in a voice that caressed his ears, "Calm yourself, Sir Knight. Banish your despair. Forsake any death wish. Your love honors me. You are a valiant and noble person. In a world of artifice and falsehood, you are an authentic man. The passion you harbor means more to me than empty titles of nobility and their never-ending treachery."

She took his face in both her hands. "But Duccio, I confess to you that love has no place in my life, for now. I have great responsibilities and they guide me in a direction I cannot alter."

Duccio exhaled a long sigh. "Your generous understanding humiliates me and I finally appreciate Philip's advice. He warned me against allowing my feelings for you to interfere with my duty. Therefore, with respect for these obligations that bind you, it is time for me to leave your service. If I stay, I'm certain I'll do something to antagonize the Duke on your behalf and bring disaster down upon us both. Please, Polyxena, remember that no matter where destiny takes me, my love will always be with you."

Polyxena was moved by the passionate farewell, but she also knew they had just played a dangerous game with death. If the Duke had chosen to follow them out of simple curiosity about the letter and walked into their moment of intimacy, they would doubtless be dead already. There was nothing else for her to do except acknowledge what he had just confirmed.

She extended her hand in farewell to Duccio. He hesitated for a moment, then quickly reached forward to take her hand and lightly brush his lips across it. He was wise enough to avoid her eyes, so that he could remain strong enough to do the only thing there was to do to protect her and walk out of the antechamber without looking back.

Polyxena remained alone in the vast room, grief stricken and confused. She sat on a nearby divan and breathed deeply in an attempt to slow her tumultuous heartbeat. Then with the feeling that something had broken inside of her, a sob tore at her throat and she could no longer hold back her tears.

†††

CHAPTER EIGHT

THE DUKE'S INHERITANCE

Polyxena received a condolence visit from the Duke of Saxe-Hanover the following day. She welcomed him with dignity, dressed elegantly in a flowing black gown, void of embellishment, but exquisitely tailored. Her beauty remained even in sorrow.

"My dear cousin," the Duke greeted her in a voice that was haughty even as it feigned sadness. "I share your sorrow for the loss of your father. Please receive my deepest condolences. Sadly, your celebration was marred by tragedy. Therefore, I hope in some small way to bring you some comfort in your hour of need."

"Thank you for your solicitude, my lord. I am grateful for your consideration." Though she smiled, Polyxena noted Ludwig's hypocrisy. She did not want to engage in empty chatter at such a painful time. After greeting him, she walked to an elegant desk and retrieved a manuscript of fine parchment, which she handed to him.

"My lord, this message from Nemours was written by my father. The document contains his last will and testament. Perhaps you should read it. I am certain you will find it surprising and highly significant."

The Duke eagerly took the document, but his attitude quickly changed when he ran his eyes down the page. "I am shocked, my lady. According to this contemptible message, you have been disinherited and disowned by your own father. How is this possible? The Count of Rozenberk, with no dynastic claims, has been named sole heir to his fortune and declared the new ruler of Nemours. I can hardly believe my eyes, that your father behaved in such an unjust manner toward you in his final hours."

Polyxena expected his reaction and remained detached. "I agree the news is unsettling, but not entirely unexpected. I was aware of my father's great displeasure in my decision to marry you, since the antagonism between the two of you was long standing."

"But this is an absurd and reckless action," the Duke sputtered. "How can your father deny your inheritance? You are not only his daughter, you are the last descendent of the distinguished house of Nemours."

With his anger growing, Ludwig instinctively grabbed the hilt of his sword. "Well cousin, I will defend your rights against this injustice. Even if war is the only option."

Polyxena paled. "No my lord! I will not challenge my father's will. That is now sealed forever by his death. I bow to his wishes. He had the power to appoint a successor of his choice under the laws of Nemours."

She saw that her defiant words had incensed the Duke. She continued in a slightly more conciliatory tone. "I value your opinion, my lord, and understand that my disinheritance effects our future marriage plans. After all, when you chose me to be your bride, I was a wealthy heiress. As of now, I possess nothing but my dowry. Even though it is considerable, it cannot compare to the riches of Nemours. Therefore I understand it is your right to recant your marriage proposal. You are free to select a new bride, one who can bring you greater power and wealth."

The Duke's anger was diminished by her words, but his disappointment over the loss of Nemours, which he had hoped to appropriate, was partially mitigated by Polyxena's resplendent beauty. So obsessive was his desire for her that even in the face of this loss, she remained foremost in his mind. He shook his head.

"Cousin, you judge me too harshly if you believe my marriage proposal was based on financial gains. I desired you from the moment we met and because of this great affection and the respect I have come to have for you, I am compelled to wait patiently for our wedding day, when you will finally be mine."

Ludwig's erotic nature was intensified by his own passionate words. He encircled her waist and held her forcefully in his arms. "My beautiful lady. Now that I have proven my sincere affection, should I not be properly rewarded for my devotion? Let us end these cruel delays and fulfill our passion now."

His desire was further aroused by the sudden physical closeness to her. He grabbed her tighter and kissed her with unrestrained passion, ignoring her struggle to free herself from the brutal embrace. Finally, with an enormous effort, she twisted away from him.

"My lord," she declared with her usual daring. "Is this the respect you have for your future bride? Without regard for my sorrow? You propose to leave an indelible mark upon my honor. My lord, I request the courtesy of being left alone to mourn my father's death with dignity and respect. Any future meetings between us will take place only after you properly apologize to me."

She fearlessly looked into the Duke's eyes to emphasize her point. He was angered by the rebuff, but at the same time understood that he had exceeded the bounds of decent behavior.

Controlling his rage, he politely bowed and responded, "You have my apologies, my lady. But it is I who is offended by your open rejection of me. Your cold nature is evident, as if you do not desire the amazing pleasures and ecstasy of love. I say you are hiding behind your mourning. Thus I leave now as you request. Furthermore, because of my love for you, I defer to your wishes and will not oppose your father's will...*For now*." He glared at her for a moment, then turned and left the room without another word.

Polyxena was still shaken by his aggression and wiped her mouth to erase his wanton kiss. She thought about her last, more pleasurable embrace, and the image of Duccio's handsome face surfaced in her mind along with memories of the warmth and comfort she experienced in his arms. She recalled his confession of everlasting devotion and found herself filled with longing for him.

The Duke's tyranny continued to reign supreme in Lorengard-Lorraine. The oppressed people became desperate and began to rebel in isolated attacks on the Duke's forces. The rebellious were mostly young people, impatient and idealistic, and many sacrificed their lives in their desperate quest.

Ludwig's mercenaries were seldom overpowered by the citizen rebels, since the guards were heavily armed and had great advantage over those whose only weapons were pitchforks, wooden clubs and rocks. Nevertheless, the pitiful corpses they left behind tragically illustrated their determination to die rather than continue to live in bondage

Rebellion only stimulated his desire for revenge. The relationship between the Duke and Polyxena continued to deteriorate. Despite his reluctant apology for his sexual advances, he felt frustrated by the knowledge that Polyxena would not give in to his desires. The only way he could possess her would be though marriage. He despised himself for his obsessive desire for this unattainable woman, who both bewitched and intimidated him with her dignified courage.

Polyxena was relieved by his absence, but felt useless and imprisoned in the lavish marble palace. She had come to despise its grandeur. The suffering people and the growing violence over which she had no control depleted her resilience. She was overtaken by an ominous feeling of despair.

To finally crush the insurgency, Ludwig ordered his guards to break into homes suspected of harboring enemies of his regime. The resulting violence was oppressive and terrifying, and entire families were put to the sword.

Many young men who were suspected of being rebels were imprisoned, where they were tortured and forced to reveal names of so-called accomplices. The bloodbath Polyxena feared was becoming a reality. Terror spread throughout the land.

One morning, Polyxena's solitude was disrupted by a surprise visit from the Duke. Her anxiety began with his mere presence but escalated at the sight of his sinister smile. She knew it to be an emblem of evil tidings.

"Dear cousin," he began. "…I am here to share wonderful news! As you know the Dukedom is in turmoil because dissenters and rebels are provoking disturbances. We finally crushed the rebellion by the sword. Their loathsome carcasses now hang from our turrets, a symbol of uncompromising justice for all to see and fear! Blood has washed away the evil of dissension and we are victorious."

Polyxena used all of her self-control to maintain a calm face while he continued.

"We will have a celebration greater and more entertaining than the joust. A public execution of the leaders of the uprising. They will hang as traitors and their corpses will be drawn and quartered to instill terror in the populace and discourage future uprisings. The execution will occur in two weeks, which is the time needed to build the scaffold and viewing podium and send invitations across the land. And I am certain the spectacle will secure the Dukedom from future rebellions."

Polyxena swallowed her distress. "Dear cousin, you deserve commendations for your victorious endeavor against the dissenters. But I beg your indulgence, since I won't attend the executions, given that I find such spectacles painful to watch. Besides, the honor of victory is yours. It is appropriate that you revel alone in your triumph."

"Cousin," he angrily responded. "We must appear together at the executions and present a united front. You are the Duchess of Lorengard-Lorraine and you must not shy away from bloody spectacles necessary to administer justice. You must assert your position of power. A refusal to attend is unacceptable and I deny it."

Without waiting for a response, the Duke turned to leave the room. He stopped and turned toward Polyxena, slapping his forehead as if remembering something important. "By the way my lady, I did not mention that two knights of our acquaintance are among the condemned men who will face the gallows."

Polyxena's distress turned to panic and it was suddenly difficult for her to breathe.

Ludwig continued with venomous delight. "They are Duccio Degli Uberti and Philip of Rohann, whose lives you begged me to spare. They rewarded my generosity by becoming instrumental in the uprising to overthrow my regime. Death is too good for them. I will make them suffer and their agony will give me endless pleasure. In the hands of an experienced executioner, the hanging can be long and torturous. The rope will stretch their necks slowly, while they choke on their own blood, bringing them close to death. However, I will have them drawn and quartered while they're still alive and I will have my revenge."

Riding high on his dreams of retribution, the Duke left the traumatized Duchess in despair. She stood for a long moment, unable to absorb the hellish situation. However, with the thought of the horrors to be perpetrated against Duccio and Philip, her strength of resolve regained control. A look of icy determination hardened her face. A wise person seeing it, would know to take caution.

AT THE SIGN OF THE ELK

Along one of the narrow streets connecting with Normandy square in the heart of Lorengard-Lorraine, life appeared to go on uninterrupted by civic strife. The area was filled with markets overflowing with vegetables, fruits, and a variety of salted meats displayed on colorful carts. People of modest means who constantly crowded each other in the narrow space populated this noisy corner of the Dukedom. It was a typical market of the time, where shoppers ignored the pungent odor of the meats and fowls hanging prominently in the shop entrance as well as the putrid odor from abundant garbage scattered among stagnant puddles.

The most popular drinking and eating-place was a charming inn with a colorful carved elk above the door painted with the words: *SIGN of the ELK.*

Several steps down from the street level, a large public room stood tastefully decorated in rustic style. The high ceiling, adorned with dark wooden beams, made the room relaxed and inviting. A large wrought iron chandelier, brimming with candles, lit the room in a warm, comforting glow, and several long, narrow tables sat surrounded by stools to accommodate the clientele.

The guests were enticed by the strong, aromatic foods, including many salted hams, cheeses and preserved foods hanging from the ceiling. Assorted copper utensils hung on a large brick wall and reflected the warm candle light in their polished shine.

Monsieur Berthold Ballon was the Inn's genial host, a man in his late thirties with a jovial rounded face, piercing blue eyes, and a ready laugh. The good-natured man was short and stout, with a large belly that bounced when he walked.

He pranced around the room greeting guests with smiles and making certain their goblets stayed full. The free-flowing wine provoked gaiety and laughter, tempering the pain of life in the realm. Monsieur Berthold enjoyed the festive atmosphere of his inn and remained oblivious to noise from his intoxicated guests.

One day his vigilant eyes noticed a man sitting alone in a dark corner of the room, obscured by the shadows and shrouded by a flowing black mantle. Berthold felt uneasy about him, having noticed by the visitor's general appearance that he was an aristocrat. He admired the stranger's elegant, chamois-gloved hands. He recognized them as a luxury few could afford.

Berthold bowed and respectfully addressed the stranger, "You honor my establishment with your presence, my lord. May I be of service?"

The guest appeared startled by Berthold's voice and looked up at him. Berthold saw a red mask that concealed everything about the man's face but the brilliance of his eyes. He felt no particular surprise over the mask, since the aristocracy often traveled in disguise to protect their identity. This was especially true when they carried out illicit love affairs with lower class women.

"Monsieur Ballon," the visitor said with his voice somewhat muffled by the mask. "I am in need of your services, but it is not food or drink I require." The guest removed several gold coins from his pocket and gave them to Berthold, who was startled by the stranger's generosity. "Please introduce me to your friends who meet secretly in your establishment. I have something of great importance to tell them."

Berthold's face lost its color. Suddenly frightened and anxious, the gold coins felt as if they burned his hand. He dropped them onto the table. "My lord, I do not know what people you are talking about. There are no secret rooms in this establishment. Please take back your gold. I can't accept it for a service that I am unable to render."

He turned to leave the unsettling guest, but the stranger's commanding response stopped him.

"I am mystified, monsieur, that gold is not to your liking. Strange, my friend, because gold is so coveted that some people kill for it. But since you appear disinterested, I will convince you to assist me with metal of a different kind."

He smoothly pulled a shiny blade from his under cloak, which glistened in his hand. However, noticing the devastating effect his belligerent act had on the fearful host, who suddenly appeared ready to faint, he removed the dagger from sight and spoke in a gentler tone. "Be assured I have no evil intent. I did not mean to frighten you, but to assure you I have persuasive methods. My quest is vital and requires your help."

"Please my lord, do not tell me more," Berthold whispered. "Have mercy, your request could mean my death. What evil have I done that you should harass me so?"

"Monsieur my presence here only proves my friendship. For if I had evil intentions, the Duke's guards would already be at your door. Wasting time now only places us both in greater danger. We need to act and you must come with me while your guests are in this drunken stupor and will not notice your absence." Without waiting for a reply, the stranger picked up the gold coins and placed them back in the man's hand.

Berthold was aware he had little choice in the matter and that he could only hope the stranger was truly a friend. He led him swiftly to the far end of the room, where they passed through the door to the inn's wine cellar.

The men descended a long and winding stairwell to a room deep enough underground to protect the wine. The cellar was poorly lit, but had the pungent and inviting aroma of fermentation. The large room was cavernous with a rough, uneven floor and low ceiling. Many wine barrels were stacked atop each other against the walls, spouts pointing forward for easy access.

Berthold walked to the rear of the cellar and into an area swallowed by darkness. He felt for a lever hidden behind one of the barrels, then pulled it and caused the brick wall to rotate and reveal a large opening. Another door stood inside the mysterious entrance and Berthold tapped a special rhythmic knock. After a few anxious seconds, the door slowly opened with a sharp grating sound. A man appeared at the entrance, apprehensively looking around.

"Monsieur," he admonished the innkeeper, "I hope you have valid reason to interrupt our meeting. It is not prudent to come here when the inn is crowded. You could be followed, or worse."

"Forgive me," Berthold replied. "I was forced to come by this persuasive individual." He stepped aside to reveal the ominous stranger. At the unwelcome sight, the man at the door retreated into the room and defensively grabbed for his sword.

The hidden room was large enough to accommodate the many people secreted inside. They sat at a long wooden table that was lit by several candles, casting the room in a golden glow. The assembly consisted mostly of people from an older generation, dignified and aristocratic. At the moment, they all looked at the new arrivals with apprehension.

The stranger entered the room, bowed to the group, and addressed them—his voice still muffled by the mask, "My lords, please excuse my intrusion. Monsieur Berthold tried to dissuade me, but I forced him to bring me here to meet you and for very important reasons. He is a proven and faithful friend of your cause and he has my admiration and respect."

"Then who are you?" the man at the door challenged. "Your presence is unwelcome. We don't know who you are and we don't like your disregard for our privacy. We are friends privately gathered here to enjoy pleasant conversation and card games. Therefore, I request you leave at once. Our diversions are not your concern."

"My lords, please listen carefully," the stranger advised. "It is useless to deny the obvious. Serious reasons have induced you to gather in secrecy, not card games. I know many among you are noble subjects, faithful to the lamented Arsenio. Because you were loyal to him, you have been stripped of your possessions and now hover on the brink of poverty. I know you seek justice and that you want revenge against the cruel Duke of Saxe-Hanover."

The stranger approached one of the women at the table and bowed to her. "My lady Amelia, Countess De Vargas. Your nobility of spirit is known throughout the Dukedom. Kindly receive my compliments."

The Countess stood and spoke with both concern and curiosity, "Sir, whoever you are, if you truly have noble intentions, remove your mask. It is disrespectful to be addressed by a mysterious knight."

In reply, the stranger opened his mantle and showed a red cross clearly visible upon his chest. "I am a Knight Templar and I have come to reveal a crucial plan to you."

The Countess was not yet persuaded. "My lord, you may well be a Knight Templar on a noble quest, but you are still a mystery to us."

He chuckled. "Mysterious Templar…An interesting name. Perhaps you can address me in this fashion, since it is imperative to my mission that I remain anonymous. The Mysterious Templar begs your indulgence."

Angry mutters of displeasure erupted around the table. One man's impatient voice rose the sharpest, "We suggest you leave at once. Why does an honorable person need a mask? You could be the Duke's spy, sent here to harm us."

The Templar calmly responded, "My presence here best proves my friendship. If I had hostile intentions, there would be better methods available for causing harm. Here, I am one against many. If you wished to kill me, you could easily do so." With that, he placed his sword on the table and stood back, disarming himself in a gesture of friendship.

The Countess was reassured enough to respond in a conciliatory manner, "Very well, my lord. Since you wish to remain anonymous, we will acquiesce and let you explain your presence. I am sure my friends will grant you time to speak." Her tone did not open the question for debate.

The others remained silent.

Then the man at the door spoke in a tone of urgency. "My lord, whoever you are, sit down and let your reasons be known once and for all. Your presence here puts us in danger."

The Mysterious Templar ignored the invitation and remained standing while he began his story. The assembly quickly found themselves aghast at the plans he explained methodically to them. Finally, the least patient among them interrupted.

"Stop! If you are not the Duke's spy, sent to torment us, then you must be a fool. How can we accomplish the impossible things you describe? The costs involved are more than we have the ability to bear."

The Mysterious Templar pulled open his mantle to reveal a leather pouch, which he tossed onto the table. "Start with this."

It landed with a hard thump, breaking open the drawstring and releasing a multitude of gold coins that spread across the table, the glittering answer to every revolutionary's prayer. It represented a small fortune and the sight of it left the assembly speechless.

With that dramatic gesture, he grabbed his sword and turned to depart. Before he got to the door, the Countess De Vargas dared to ask, "Who are you, please, that you would entrust so much gold to us?"

"A friend," was the only answer the Mysterious Templar offered. A moment later, he disappeared among the shadows of the dark wine cellar and they heard his quiet footsteps recede while the gold coins continued to glitter in the candlelight.

CHAPTER NINE

THE EXECUTIONS

Preparations for the collective executions were complete. The Cathedral Square where Arsenio's funeral took place was now readied for a far more violent occasion.

The giant hanging gibbet included a sophisticated trap door mechanism created by an engineer, who was lavishly rewarded for the task. With the turn of a single lever, all of the condemned men would fall at once. The ropes were short enough so that the fall would not necessarily break the victim's neck. Some might die there, but others would survive. Then the most spectacular part of the executions would occur.

The condemned victims, dead or alive, would each have their feet and hands tied to four horses facing in four directions. When the steeds were spurred to a full gallop, the limbs would be torn from their bodies.

The Cardinal of Lorengard-Lorraine unsuccessfully attempted to protest the execution site because it faced the cathedral. He complained that it was as if the Duke, in his endless lust for blood and revenge, planned to challenge man and God alike.

Polyxena was anxious about the terrible day of the hanging. When the ungodly hour finally arrived, Ludwig came to her rooms to personally escort her and make certain she was by his side for the executions. The hatred she felt for him had become impossible to conceal and she purposely shunned eye contact with him.

She had allowed her handmaidens to dress her for the occasion without caring about the choice of gown or the styling of her hair. She felt as if the day was marked for her own execution.

"Dear cousin," he cried upon entering her rooms. "The joyous occasion of this day is increased by your loveliness. I have greatly missed it for many days."

"My lord, today marks a victory you have personally created, but I must admit I am repelled by the violent and bloody spectacle we are about to witness."

He stared at her for one blank moment, then quietly replied, "And I feel your distaste for justice is unworthy of a Duchess. It signals weakness, when you should rejoice with me and revel in the deserved end for these traitors."

Polyxena could not respond. With considerable effort, she smiled and placed her hand on his arm. Together, they left her rooms.

Up to that point in the day, the Cathedral square was trouble free. Armed guards stood ready to suppress any violent protests, mindful of the uprising at Arsenio's funeral. For this occasion, the Ducal podium was assembled directly across from the gallows for the finest view of the horrors of torture and the agony of death.

The podium was draped with crimson and gold to accent the two ostentatious thrones placed centrally on a dais. It accommodated the rulers of Lorengard-Lorraine plus the Ducal court, including Lady Flavia De Brezzé and the Baron Frederick Van Halt.

When the Duke and Duchess arrived in their coach, the crowd was already encircling the massive square behind metal barriers. The populace was silent and deeply sad. Anguish marked many of their faces. The more reckless among them looked with open loathing at the Ducal podium, but it was to no avail. The tyrant reveled in their hatred. It heightened his sense of invincibility.

When the wooden cart carrying the ten prisoners entered the square and approached the scaffold, a mournful silence fell over the citizenry like an oppressive shroud.

Polyxena watched the cart approach and felt that her heart was in her mouth. The rude wagon was an unworthy transport to carry so many vibrant youths to their cruel death.

When she spotted Duccio's tall and striking presence among the condemned men, it took all her willpower to conceal her distress. She could see the splendid knight searching for her face, defiant and proud. When he saw her, his eyes met hers while Polyxena's sense of helplessness cut her in two.

Philip was also in the cart with Duccio. He stood out among them with his striking light, blond hair, and as a knight, he faced his death with courage and dignity.

The Duke noticed Polyxena's distress, though instead of compassion he felt sadistic elation. He reveled in the sorrow and torment he was causing among the fools of his realm.

The tragic spectacle began when a herald in full dress regalia arrived on horseback, carrying a rolled parchment. He opened it and read it aloud in a voice that reverberated through the silent square.

In this day of our Lord, May 26, 1483,
As ordered by the rulers of Lorengard- Lorraine,
ten traitors who conspired against the Dukedom,
will be Hanged, Drawn and Quartered.
Their deaths will be an example to all those
who commit treason against the realm.
Since the conspirators are guilty of treason, a heinous crime,
they will be denied Christian burial and their corpses will hang
on the Dukedom walls as fare for the vultures.
Death to all traitors!

With those ominous words, a troubled murmur spread through the crowd. The condemned men were horrified by their impending profane deaths. But during those terrible moments Duccio seemed oblivious to everything except Polyxena, and he focused on her while the executioner prepared to force him from this world.

She could longer stand the thought of the horrors about to unfold and rose from her throne. She signaled her departure to the Duke and defiantly began to leave. Ludwig ignored his own breach of etiquette and forcefully grabbed her arm.

"Where are you going cousin?" he demanded. "Your place is by my side while justice is implemented. I deny your wish to depart."

Polyxena reached the limits of her tolerance. All the dignity and pride instilled by her patrician upbringing surfaced in her and she no longer cared about consequences. "I am the Duchess of Lorengard-Lorraine! A title I accepted as true and valid. Therefore, no one here is above me and can challenge my wish to retire." She freed her arm and left the podium, cautiously respected by all who overheard.

Although her defiance angered him, he was powerless to bend her will without making their discord public. However, his patience toward the daring and rebellious Polyxena had waned and the excitement of the chase had lost its luster. He began to seriously contemplate better, more efficient ways to make her bend to his wishes. He decided not to confront her, since that would take him away from the event at hand. Instead, he ordered the executions to proceed without delay.

But as if to further aggravate him, the bells of the Cathedral began to sound in a religious practice for honoring the dead. It was a clear gesture of defiance from the Cardinal, in showing such respect to condemned men. The bells seemed to signal the blessings of the church.

When the cart reached the gallows, the victims descended one by one, hands tied behind their backs. They were sad but remained dignified and their composure broke the hearts of the citizens even as it garnered their respect. Screams of despair erupted from relatives and friends of the condemned men.

Duccio felt himself beset with despair as soon as Polyxena disappeared. His only wish before dying had been to see the woman he loved with his last glance. It was as if she had also been taken from him in this terrible hour.

The condemned men were positioned in a straight line over the trap doors and the nooses were placed around their necks. The ominous drum rolls and cathedral bells continued and the many in the crowd bowed their heads in prayer.

Ludwig's eyes sparkled with perverse anticipation. He rose from his throne and stood for the best possible view, savoring their anguish. For one long moment he remained motionless and simply stared at the victims, rejoicing in their suffering. Then he abruptly signaled the hooded executioner to trigger the hangman's lever.

The executioner reached for the lever, but suddenly stopped. His arm fell motionless to his side and he collapsed with an arrow protruding from his chest. Before the crowd realized what had happened, arrows from unseen archers severed the ropes from the victims necks. A mysterious hand released the lever, dropping the condemned men through the opening and beneath the gallows.

Arrows continued to rain down on the guardsmen, killing many of them because they couldn't tell where the attack was coming from. Turmoil erupted in the square. The people were encouraged by the temerity of the attack, and many of them incited the insurgents to continue their deadly assault.

The Duke found himself faced with an unexpected uprising, and he was overwhelmed with ire and terror. He ordered his guards to suppress the revolt and return the prisoners to the gallows for execution. However, it was apparent that some mercenaries were fighting for the insurgents. Rebel marksmen armed with longbows had been placed in strategic areas, their weapons capable of piercing a knight's armor from more than 250 yards and a skilled bowman could release ten to twelve arrows per minute.

The constant barrage of arrows from all directions killed many guards, causing others to panic. The revolt began to favor the insurgents. Meanwhile, Duccio and Philip were safely under the gallows with the other condemned men. The surprise events seemed miraculous to them.

A conspirator under the scaffold speedily severed the ropes from their wrists and gave them swords. For a few seconds they stared at the weapons, wondering if they were dreaming.

Cold reality struck when they emerged from under the platform and saw the fierce battle in the square. They brandished their swords and charged the nearest mercenaries, swinging their weapons in raging fury and scattering mutilated bodies on the cobblestone.

"Friend!" Philip exulted. "What an unexpected joy to fight again by your side. If we die today, far better with sword in hand than death at the gallows."

Suddenly, at the far end of the square near to the cathedral, horses galloped into the area and forced open a large space in the crowd. The animals looked to have no riders, but were fully saddled. Their movements appeared to be guided, however, and after a few seconds, a man rose up on one of the horses from his hiding place on the side of the mount. He wore a black hood and mantle, his face shielded by a red mask. A large red cross emblazoned on his chest symbolized the Knights Templar. At the sight of the mysterious Knight, a voice rose from the crowd from one of the men who had already met the mysterious rider at the inn's concealed meeting room.

"It's the Mysterious Templar!" the stranger shouted. "Our champion. Long live the Mysterious Templar!"

The cryptic name spread throughout the square while frightened citizens welcomed the sight of a knight as their protector and a living reason to hope the day might be theirs.

"The Mysterious Templar..." the name was repeated by voices throughout the square.

In response, the Templar raised his sword and shouted, "Death to the tyrant!"

When an arrow from one of the hidden archers pierced the coat-of-arms over the podium, the Duke's bodyguards urged him to withdraw. The unstable situation put him in grave danger.

Ludwig was livid with ire, but knew they were right. He joined Flavia De Brezzé and the Baron Van Halt in making a swift exit from the square. By that point, the Cathedral square was a true battleground with corpses of the palace guards and injured guardsmen everywhere.

The Templar's plan of attack had intelligently utilized surprise in creating a successful assault and the insurgents had dealt a fatal blow to the Duke's superior forces.

The Mysterious Templar was the hero of the hour. He dispatched countless mercenaries from his place high in the saddle, securing the immediate surroundings and opening a path to the condemned prisoners.

Duccio, Philip, and the other condemned men were in the center of the square still engaged in a fierce and bloody fight against the mercenaries. The Templar signaled them to mount the waiting horses, and they jumped upon their steeds, shielded by the rebel archers.

The arrows from the hidden archers continued to devastate the Duke's mercenaries, who couldn't defend themselves against hidden archers. Many mercenaries ran for cover to escape the deadly arrows and charging horses. Taking advantage of the panic, the Mysterious Templar signaled the condemned men to follow him out of the cathedral square.

But it was at the peak moment of the daring escape when Philip saw an arrow flying toward Duccio. With no time to warn him, Philip quickly reacted by pulling the horse's reins so hard that the mount reared onto his hind legs, lifting Philip higher into the air and positioning him as a human shield. In an instant, the fatal arrow hit him instead. The heroic Philip gasped and fell to the ground, mortally wounded.

Duccio witnessed the sacrifice and immediately realized what his friend had done. He jumped from his horse to rush to his side. The Mysterious Templar also saw Philip's sacrifice and realized Duccio was also now in mortal peril at the side of his fallen friend. The knight signaled the remaining prisoners to continue in the path he had initiated for their escape. Then he rushed to grab two free riderless horses by the reins and brought them to the men.

"It's time for you to go," he shouted.

"Go my friend," Philip gasped to Duccio. "There is no time. Save yourself."

"Wait," Duccio cried. "I will help you to remount your horse and guide you to safety. If you cannot rise, then I will remain here with you. That arrow was meant for me, Philip. Why did you shield me with your body and sacrifice yourself for me?"

"Duccio," Philip whispered. "I have faced death countless times for anyone who paid me. It is an honor to die on my own volition for a true friend. I gladly shed my blood for you, my true brother, the only family I've ever known."

"You won't die," Duccio desperately cried out, trying to lift his friend's limp body. "I will get you out of here even if it is the last deed of my life."

Meanwhile the Mysterious Templar stood his ground in front of them and carved a whirling net into the air with the tip of his blade, brushing back several of the guards who were trying to ambush Philip and Duccio in their vulnerable position.

Despite his bravery and expertise, his position was precarious and little time was left to escape. "Go! While you can," he cried to them. "Make haste and follow me."

Philip tried desperately to get up and follow them, but his pain forced him to fall back, moaning in anguish. "I cannot make it. I know this wound is fatal. You will bring a cadaver to safety. Go, my brother. God is opening his arms to me, so get on your horse and run from this place. With my last breath I bless you for it."

Duccio shook his head. "If this is truly the end of your road, then I shall follow. But before I face final judgment, I will take many of these killers with me."

Philip struggled to pick himself up in spite of his pain, but blood began to flow from his mouth. The shadow of death fell over him.

"Why do you defy me, friend? Did I forfeit my life for no purpose? Save yourself and live. Only your survival can justify my death." With those final words, Philip fell back, now close to death.

The Mysterious Templar continued to fight with valor, but he was heavily outnumbered by the guards. They were about to overpower him when some of the insurgents came to his aid and gave the Templar and Duccio a few more minutes to escape.

Duccio could no longer deny his friend's final wish for him to abandon the battle ground. He knelt by Philip's side and kissed him with brotherly love. "Farwell my friend," he whispered. "My true brother. May the Lord grant you the joy denied you in this life."

When Philip realized Duccio was leaving, a moment of joyful relief shone in his eyes. He resigned himself to his destiny with a final sigh and gave up his soul.

"Heavenly Father," Duccio prayed. "Open your arms and welcome Philip of Rohann into your kingdom...I go!"

Duccio rose from his friend's side, sword in hand, driven by pain and despair. He swiftly killed two mercenaries still in his path and finally mounted his horse along with the Templar to escape the cathedral square.

The square was a gruesome theatre of death. Ten rebels met their end on that tragic day, but more than a hundred of the Duke's men were slain. The square was drenched in their blood.

The Duke was left to pace the castle floor, seething with rage and terrified by the day's revolt. He silently vowed to make his henchmen suffer terrible reprisals for failing to squelch the revolt and leaving him to witness the crushing defeat of his men and be forced to run for his life.

He was especially distressed by the unexpected courage and resilience of the people, whom he had regarded as demoralized and helpless. The day had shown him that in reality they were dangerous adversaries, more than capable of overthrowing his powerful regime.

THE LOVERS

Following the uprising in the cathedral square, Polyxena remained secluded in her rooms. She had no further contact with the Duke, who demonstrated his contempt for her departure from the executions by completely ignoring her. The arrangement pleased her, leaving her with more freedom to move about on her own.

The Duke was preoccupied with concerns for his own security and barricaded himself in the palace. The sudden appearance of this man whom the people called 'The Mysterious Templar' had put him in constant fear for his life. He couldn't understand how the uprising occurred, since such a display of force and arms was so costly to compile. He knew of no one among his people who possessed such riches, since he had already confiscated the valuables of the affluent citizens of Lorengard-Lorraine. He had already ceased being concerned with Polyxena's loyalty, since he deemed her powerless after her disinheritance.

Polyxena favored her time alone, preoccupied with the people's wellbeing and distressed by her own position as a powerless ruler. She found no relief until the day Davina entered her rooms, excited and joyful.

"My lady, I have received wonderful news from our usual source. It's a verbal message, for reasons of safety."

"Tell me, then. Don't keep me in suspense."

"The purpose of the message is to ease your mind and assure you that Duccio Degli Uberti is safe. The noble knight sends you his personal greeting and his continued fealty and pledge to serve you."

Polyxena did not respond, but Davina could see she was joyously relieved by the news.

"My lady, I have witnessed the great sadness you have endured since the fateful day of the executions," she said. "I know your sorrow is over the death of Philip of Rohann and your overwhelming concern for the safety of Duccio Uberti. This leads me to believe the time has come to end your loneliness and allow a reunion with him. We could leave the palace in the usual hidden way, since we are being openly ignored by the Duke and his guards. I believe no one will miss our presence."

"Do you think it would be wise to take such a step? I fear my presence could endanger the valiant knight."

"Wise? Certainly not my lady, but necessary, since I know you have spent many lonely hours. After so much sorrow you deserve to realize your hidden desires. Thanks to the secret passage, I believe we can go in relative safety."

Polyxena was filled with joy and warmly embraced the maiden. "Then yes. Let's go tonight. I cannot deny my eagerness to be with Duccio again, who is always on my mind. However, danger lurks everywhere in this palace. It would be prudent to wear masculine clothes to shield our identity. They will also allow us to move more freely if we need to defend ourselves against our enemies."

With haste, the young women changed their clothes in preparation for their departure. They remained cautious over the presence of prying eyes, knowing themselves to be in an arena filled with schemes and intrigues.

In a different part of Lorengard-Lorraine, far away from the opulent Ducal palace, Duccio was safe in a comfortable room on the upper floor of a modest dwelling. Although it was the middle of the night, he was fully dressed, as if he had no desire to sleep.

He sat on the side of the bed in meditation, but from time to time rose to pace the room or to the open window and breathe the fresh air to calm his anxieties. He projected the aura of a man who had matured in just a few days, evolving from an emotionally charged young man into a somber and reflective adult.

When he heard soft sounds of someone walking in the hallway outside, he reached for his sword and threw open the entry door and saw a retreating figure barely visible in the shadows. But the mysterious guest quickly lowered the hood of her cape to reveal Lady Davina of Devonshire.

Duccio immediately lowered his weapon and bowed. "Lady Davina. I am honored by your presence. Please forgive my hostile reception, but your visit was so unexpected, it surprised me. Please enter my humble room. You are most welcome."

She responded with a smile to his cordial greeting and curtsied, but she did not enter.

"What news do you have of our lady? Is she well? Are you here to deliver evil tidings? Please answer and relieve my concern."

Davina smiled and stepped aside, allowing Polyxena to appear from the shadows and stride into the room. She quickly removed her hood and allowed her lustrous hair to fall over her shoulders.

The sight of her in the torch light stunned Duccio. He regained his composure and knelt to kiss her hand. With his head bowed, he remained respectfully silent and waited for her to address him.

Polyxena was moved by Duccio's gesture of devotion and was overcome by strong emotional feelings. However, she spoke in her usual calm and dignified manner in a voice filled with kindness.

"Sir Knight," she said. "Only a few hours ago, after much concern, I received news that you were safe. Your welfare has been constantly on my mind since the recent uprising. I value you as my most loyal and devoted ally and as a friend to the people of Lorengard-Lorraine. I wish to convey my appreciation and affection for your gallant efforts."

"My lady," Duccio responded. "…it is a great day that allows me to be in your presence again. In this moment I am the happiest of men."

But Duccio's passionate feelings were restrained by the oppressive etiquette placing a barrier between himself and the beautiful Duchess he loved. Lady Davina's presence added to his uneasiness, but the astute young woman displayed discretion and left the room to give them privacy.

Finally alone with Polyxena, the passion he tried so hard to suppress was plain upon his face. Polyxena felt herself overwhelmed by the sight. She was suddenly inundated by the warmth and pleasure of her emotions for him. She remained quiet, as if confused and unsure of herself in this novel situation, leaving it to Duccio to break the silence.

"My lady. I am moved by your concern and the unexpected joy of your visit. Comfort has been in short supply here, and as I'm sure you can see, the blessing of sleep has been denied me since the death of my dear friend, Philip."

"I know about his tragic death and I grieve for the loss of such a valiant knight. Allow me to express my sincere condolences. I know you loved him as a brother."

"Your compassionate words are a calming tonic. After the pain of Philip's passing, my greatest torment is knowing he died to save my life."

"I am aware of his heroism, and I can assure you it is also well known among the people. They respect his memory, and may the good Lord reward his gallantry."

Duccio remained silent for a long moment, then sadly continued, "What torments me is the image of him lying abandoned in that tragic square. With his last breath, he urged me to leave him and save myself. But I have been in the dark about what happened to his remains. Knowing the Duke's cruelty, it is likely that he is hanging on the castle walls and is desecrated by the vultures." With those devastating words, he sobbed and covered his face.

Polyxena placed her hand on his shoulder and soothingly addressed him. "Do not torment yourself with that image, Sir Knight. I ordered your friend's body to be removed from that tragic square. Noble and courageous citizens helped me do so. He sleeps in a Christian tomb unknown by the Duke and safe from revenge and desecration."

Overcome with relief, Duccio gratefully kissed Polyxena's hand. "How can I thank you for your kindness toward my friend? It gives me great comfort to know he is resting in peace…But why did Philip sacrifice his life?" he asked. "Was it merely so I could live? My existence is burdensome and living is becoming more difficult each passing day. My desolate existence offers only violence and death!"

Polyxena approached Duccio, deeply concerned and moved by his despondency. But she thought it inadvisable to display too much compassion, fearing it would further humiliate the proud knight.

After his brief display of depression, Duccio regained his dignity and continued to look at Polyxena with a mixture of love and deference.

Finally, she addressed him, "Why are you so silent, Duccio? Have you nothing further to say to me? Strange. I recall the intimate thoughts you shared with me before. Then your passion for life and your chivalrous nature held no unworthy thoughts about imminent death."

Her challenging words hit the mark. Duccio was shocked and disturbed by them. "My lady, you address me in this manner? Why do you remind me of issues I have tried desperately to forget? I regret my inappropriate behavior toward you and my confession of love. I realize it shocked and affronted you."

"Well my lord. Have your feelings toward me changed? Has the passing of time and your grief for your friend mitigated your love for me?"

"My lady, since you asked, I am compelled against my wishes to speak openly. Yes, my feelings have changed. The hopelessness I endured in your presence has become despair because I am denied the privilege and joy of being near you. During the tragic day of the executions, my mind was oblivious to my incumbent death, because you were there and your lovely presence overshadowed everything, including the ominous gallows. Therefore, my lady, I have nothing else to say except this is the measure of my love for you."

After his passionate confession, Duccio deferentially lowered his eyes, feeling diminished compared to the woman he loved, the Duchess he had pledged to serve and protect.

His words filled Polyxena with a mix of trepidation and joy. She was aware of their difficult social position and concerned that his poverty diminished his esteem for himself, even though he was a noble knight. To dispel the uneasy moment, she moved toward the window and pointed outside.

"Look, Duccio, outside this window lays the world filled with injustice and unfairness. In this limited space, humans toil, enslaved, and held captive by their own inequities and the Duke's unjust laws. But I propose you and I leave this sadness outside and close the shutters on this window to remove it from sight. Now we are finally alone in our own world, removed from toil and sorrow. And for the present moment, we are two perfectly equal creatures of God who are in love with each other."

At the instant Polyxena pronounced her words of love, she blushed violently, but the effect on Duccio was that of a lightning bolt. Overwhelmed by the power of her revelation, he fought to regain his composure and joyously addressed her.

"You love me, my lady? This is a miracle too beautiful to be real! I am afraid of dreaming. Please repeat those blessed words and let them fill me with jubilation."

"Duccio, on that terrible day of the executions, my heart was broken and I felt devastated when you walked toward your death. It was as if I was witnessing the end of my own life. I know now that I loved you from the beginning, but I was unaccustomed to the powerful emotions you stirred in me. I love you as I have never loved before."

Duccio stared at the woman he so desperately desired and whom he had considered unattainable. It was difficult to grasp that his wish had suddenly come true. He eagerly approached her with anticipation. She had a bright, welcoming smile upon her face when he took her in his strong and virile arms. He kissed her lips with smoldering passion, expressing his entire ardor for her at last.

Polyxena reveled in Duccio's warm embrace, feeling complete and happy for the first time in her life.

"My lady," Duccio whispered.

Polyxena quickly placed a finger upon his lips, shaking her head in a sign of mild reprimand. "Not 'my lady.' I am merely Polyxena to the one I love."

Duccio smiled and caressed her shiny, flowing hair. "Polyxena...My Polyxena. A name I uttered a thousand times as an unattainable dream. Today through some sort of magic you are in my arms, and now all I want is to hold you close and keep you safe from danger."

Suddenly he lowered his voice, "Forgive me, but I cannot dismiss the awful truth that you are promised in marriage to the evil Duke, a man who has total power and control of your life."

She responded by taking Duccio's hand and guiding him to a small makeshift altar in a corner of the room. She bowed with devotion before a crudely sculpted wooden cross, genuflected on a kneeling bench, then signaled Duccio to join her.

"Heavenly Father," she prayed aloud. "Look with kindness upon your servants, whose aspirations are placed in your loving hands. Bestow mercy upon us and bless the union of our souls."

She turned toward Duccio with a loving smile. "I, Polyxena of Nemours, take you, Duccio Degli Uberti to be my husband. With God's blessing, I pledge my fidelity and love, and I promise to honor you above all others, as long as we both shall live."

Duccio's eyes were filled with love and gratitude while he responded, "And I, Duccio Degli Uberti, here in the sight of God, take you, Polyxena of Nemours, to be my beloved wife. I pledge to you my undying love and devotion, as long as I shall live."

Polyxena removed a magnificent gold ring from her finger depicting the coat-of-arms of Nemours, with a large sparkling emerald in the middle. She placed the gem in Duccio's palm.

"Take this ring, my husband. Hold it close to your heart but keep it out of sight so it does not draw undue attention and bring you harm. It may be true that our pledge is known only to God for the time being, but the ring is a symbol of my undying devotion to you."

The young couple joyfully embraced and held onto each other with fervor and love. Duccio was still overcome by the rapture of the moment, but was the first to speak. "Polyxena, my bride. There is no sweeter sound in the world to me than these wonderful words. If I should die tomorrow, I shall be content, because I have realized my true aim in life. With your love, my beautiful lady, you have given my life purpose, and I thank God for having bestowed upon me the greatest of gifts."

The happy couple then forgot everything but their overwhelming desire for one another and passionately embraced.

†††

CHAPTER TEN

THE RETURN of the MYSTERIOUS TEMPLAR

Rotund and genial innkeeper Berthold Ballon stood before a large mirror in the small apartment he occupied above the 'Sign of the Elk' and admired his reflection. His fleshy frame was clad in opulent garments woven with the finest of silks and precious brocades, included a formfitting jacket and vest tailored to his corpulent form. He wore calf-length matching trousers to better display his white silk tights and velvet shoes that were fancifully decorated with small bows. A silk cloak and elegant hat with an ostrich feather completed the ensemble and awaited him on a nearby chair.

He turned in all directions to view his reflection, satisfied and proud of how he looked. He expressed himself with pride. "The generous gift from the Mysterious Templar was put to good use. I finally have a wardrobe worthy of my genteel form and gracious self. At last, one of my life's desires has been realized."

Then he abruptly felt his enthusiasm tempered by an unpleasant thought. It rose from his mind's recesses and deflated his zeal in an instant. "But how will this elegant wardrobe fit in with my modest station in life? In reality, I will not have much use for all this lavishness because of the questions it will bring…Oh well. Questions or not, I can picture how envious they will feel upon seeing me in such elegance. Why, I could be mistaken for a Count, or perhaps even a Duke."

He stopped his monologue, suddenly alarmed. "What if I attract thieves and assassins? Because of these splendid garments, they may confuse my humble status for one of wealth. They might even cut my throat to rob me." He shuddered at the thought.

"Well, I will simply have to conceal my attire under a common wrap. It will be visible only to myself and I will secretly enjoy the sensation of being a nobleman in these rare and expensive fabrics."

At that moment, he heard footsteps in the corridor hastily approaching his room. Under the doorway arch, he saw the commanding figure of the Mysterious Templar clad in his familiar black mantle and crimson mask.

"The Templar," Berthold whispered. He quickly regained his composure and approached the distinguished guest, bowing in deference to him. "Welcome, Sir. Welcome to my humble home, my powerful lord. You honor me with your presence." With that, Berthold respectfully stepped to the side of the door and motioned for the Templar to enter.

The Templar walked in and spoke softly, "Thank you for your warm welcome. Your home is a place where goodwill dwells, and in the name of friendship, I need to ask you once more for a special favor."

The host bowed again and directed the Templar to a chair. "Please be comfortable, my lord. I am eager to help if I can. You may count on my full cooperation." He could almost feel his next set of new clothing already on his frame.

"Very well," the Templar answered in his muffled voice. "Tell me, how do you purchase and obtain the wine for your tavern? Is it by delivery or do you personally travel to get it?"

"Most times, I send an assistant to the surrounding vineyards to make the necessary purchases. If the beverage is special vintage or imported from afar, I go personally to ascertain its quality and taste. I am proud to say, I serve the best wines from the Rhine regions, and some come from faraway Spain."

"How do you transport the beverage to your tavern?"

"I use an old cart filled with wine barrels and pulled by my dependable Normandy horses."

"By what avenue do you exit the Dukedom?"

"Well, I usually exit by the Valderani door located in the old section of Lorengard-Lorraine near Piazza Balan."

"Yes…yes," the Templar answered, deep in thought. "I am familiar with the area. Begging your indulgence, I have one last question. Are you familiar with the guards posted at that particular exit?"

"Actually, I seldom travel outside the Dukedom. However, during those infrequent occasions, I often meet guards who are loyal and frequent guests at my inn."

"Excellent. You have given me the information I needed, my dear Berthold. Now one final favor, I must request your assistance and company on a special journey outside the Dukedom. This outing, barring unforeseen incidents, should be completed in a day."

Berthold was suddenly alarmed. "A journey my lord? Will there be danger and threats to our lives?"

"I cannot deny the danger," the Templar curtly responded. "There is much peril involved. To remain safe from it we will have to rely on a fortuitous mix of good fortune and trickery."

"My God!" Berthold replied, openly terrified. "Why do you require my help? For such a dangerous journey you should be surrounded by men of arms who can protect you. The only lethal weapon I am familiar with is my frying pan, which will bring you little assistance if you are attacked."

"You are wrong, my dear Berthold. With a large group of mercenaries, we would be an obvious target for the Duke's guards and thus in far greater danger. No, my plan is more prudent. However, I understand your resistance to participating in such a dangerous endeavor. Of course, the choice is yours. You are free to refuse, if that is your decision."

Berthold's fear was tempered by the great respect he had for the Mysterious Templar and he felt the pride of having such a gallant fighter ask for his help. "My lord, will this undertaking benefit the people of Lorengard-Lorraine?"

"Anything that challenges the power of the Duke, will be good for the people."

In response, Berthold mustered his courage. "I am with you, my lord. I will do it for the good of the people in our fight for freedom." And, he thought without saying so, perhaps a few more additions to his expanding wardrobe. But Berthold was terrified by the grave dangers he would face. He was aware that his display of courage before the Mysterious Templar was bolstered by his respect and fascination for the mysterious knight.

"We leave early tomorrow," the Templar responded. He placed his chamois-gloved hand on the host's shoulder. "I thank you, my friend, for the people. And with the help of God, I know we will bring our mission to a successful conclusion. Let us meet tomorrow at seven o'clock in the morning at Piazza Balan. I will wait for you in front of the church of Saint Gregory. Be punctual and bring the wine cart. Remember also to secure legal passes so we can exit the Dukedom. Farwell my friend. Till the morrow."

The Templar made a hasty exit from the room and disappeared like an apparition into the darkened corridor.

Berthold remained silent, temporarily paralyzed with fear. Finally, he stood and walked to the mirror, once more admiring his rich attire. He mumbled to himself, "This is a most inopportune time to die. I guess it is fated I should not easily wear such sumptuous garments or enjoy the illusion of being a fine gentleman without such travails."

Suddenly fearful, he clinched his fists. "Why was I so reckless to join in a task that will probably end in disaster? All to impress that valiant knight with courage I do not possess...to hide my cowardice from him. But I am sure that the recompense for my foolish boasting will be the loss of my life." With a deep sigh, he said, "If this is my destiny and death is imminent, I will at least dress properly for the final meeting with my maker. Tomorrow, when I engage in what may well be the final acts of my life...I will wear these exquisite garments and place my life in the hands of God." He crossed himself and turned back to the mirror.

The following morning at the determined hour, Berthold was on his way to the meeting place, trembling with dread. He recited endless prayers to relieve his fear and anxiety, but still went forth as expected. When he reached Piazza Balan and the ancient church of Saint Gregory, it was early and few people were walking about. Dawn was approaching and early sunlight bathed the area in a soft pink glow that gave Berthold some measure of solace in spite of his dread.

The majestic portals of the church loomed before him, but he did not see any sign of the Mysterious Templar and felt slightly alarmed by his absence. He cautiously looked around without bringing attention to himself until he was startled by a familiar muffled voice.

"I am here, monsieur Berthold. Please come closer."

The host turned his head toward the sound and noticed a beggar sleeping on the steps of the church, wearing only a torn mantle and hooded cape. But as Berthold approached, the beggar pulled back the hood just enough to reveal his crimson mask, then slid it forward once more.

"My lord, I did not recognize you dressed like this." Berthold said, startled.

The Templar slowly rose. He stood with hunched shoulders and when he took a few steps, he limped like a crippled man. He approached Berthold's wine cart, and after making certain he was not seen, mounted with catlike agility and hid among the empty wine barrels. He crouched with his hooded head resting on his knees, feigning sleep again for anyone who might observe them. "Come friend. Let us be on our way."

Berthold obeyed the order in spite of the fear assailing him. With no respite from his agony, he went forth reciting prayers and hoping a merciful God would help him in his hour of need.

When they arrived at the Valderani doorway, they were stopped by a guard. He approached with an intimidating stride that further contributed to Berthold's helpless panic. "Show me your merchant permit and your pass."

Berthold deferentially handed the guard two rolled pieces of parchment and said in a tight voice, "I am on my way to the Vineyard of Ruann-Sensere to retrieve some wines for my inn."

The guard nodded at Berthold's words while he investigated the cart. He struck the barrels with his hand to verify they were empty. At that point, he noticed the immobile form of the beggar sleeping in the back.

"Who is this person?"

"My assistant, Ramon Gerard. His pass and personal papers here are in order, as you can see."

"Why is he sleeping? He looks like a lazy excuse for a helper. Come on, young man, get up! Let me have a better look at you."

"My lord," Berthold quickly said, praying to God and all the Saints. "…please let him sleep. He had a difficult night and is trying to recoup. He is young and foolish, as you can understand."

He winked at the guard with feigned joviality and continued, "Women and wine are an exhausting combination even for the young. Although, most of the time, he is a valuable worker at my inn, 'The Sign of the Elk.' Have you heard of it?"

At the inn's name, the mercenaries' demeanor changed and he smiled, speaking to Berthold with a friendlier voice, "You sir, are the proprietor of that tavern?"

"Yes, my lord, Berthold Ballon at your service."

The guard patted the fleshy host on the shoulder, beaming with a sudden display of friendliness. "It is a pleasure to meet you, my lord. You offer the best refreshments at your inn. A few days ago, I tasted a delicious wine there, far superior to the swill served at other taverns in Lorengard-Lorraine. It was worthy of the Duke's table."

"I thank you my lord," Berthold exclaimed. "Without fear of appearing immodest, I take pride in serving my guests the best wine I can buy. This is why I am taking this trip, to acquire an unusual Spanish wine of such rare quality and vintage as to rival gold."

"Excellent, my lord," the guard responded with his mouth watering at the thought. "Go to your destination and return as quickly as possible. I am eager to taste that delicious nectar."

"I promise, my lord," Berthold answered. "When I return this very evening, you will drink the first glass of this special wine to my heath."

"Go then," the guard said, hitting one of the horses to spur it on. "I'll be on guard tonight, and you will find me eagerly waiting your return."

Berthold gladly obeyed and incited his Normandy horses to move faster. His heart beat with such violence it made him breathless, but he was relieved and looked gratefully upward in thanks.

The wine cart bounced over the rough terrain, and soon was far away from the door of Valderani. Once they were safely away, the Templar rose from his crouching position. "Well done, my friend. You have eluded a grave danger. The people of Lorengard-Lorraine will be forever in your debt. We are close to our destination, Berthold. Slow down the horses. Do you see that magnificent oak tree? Go toward it. Hidden behind it, there is a narrow path through the trees. Take it without concern. It is wider then it appears and can comfortably accommodate the cart. Once we are safely hidden by the trees, find a suitable location to secure the conveyance and the horses."

Berthold followed the knight's instructions and entered the hidden road. But he was startled by the ominous sound of horses. Fearing enemies, he was filled with panic.

The Templar quickly reassured him, "Have no fear my friend, this place is safe. Stop here and fasten the horses to the surrounding trees. I shall take care of the rest."

Berthold obeyed. He tied his horses securely, and then placed a bucket of water on the ground next to them and scattered a small bundle of hay. Finally satisfied, he began to unwind, waiting for the Templar who disappeared into the trees.

The mysterious knight returned followed by two magnificent black stallions, fully saddled and exuding vitality. The Templar mounted one of the steeds and called to Berthold, "Come friend, time is of the essence. We must leave this place at once."

"My lord, you must be jesting," Berthold exclaimed. "How can I ride this restless beast, who breathes fire from his nostrils? Never! I shall fall like a rock and break every bone in my body."

The Templar laughed. "Do not worry, Berthold. Your horse is docile to every command. Besides, a brave man like yourself who faced the Duke's guard with temerity will not tremble at the sight of a simple horse, will you?"

The Templar's obvious flattery nevertheless hit the mark and calmed Berthold. He was an easy target for praise from someone he so deeply admired. With all the enthusiasm of a man climbing the gallows, he mounted the steed and oppressed it with his sizeable weight. The unfortunate horse emitted a sharp grunt of protest.

"Galia, Amir," the Templar cried, spurring both horses into action.

The splendid animals responded immediately to his command, loping away toward an open valley covered with a deep green carpet. Once in the open spaces, the stallions launched into a full gallop in exhilaration. Berthold was terrified by the horse's unaccustomed speed and held on for dear life, but within a few more moments, he began to relax when he saw how well the horse responded to his commands.

Once he was able to abandon his fear, Berthold focused on the destination and the reason for the mission. He rode forward to flank the Templar. "My lord, if you please, I am eager to learn where we are going and why."

"We are approaching a place near Lorengard-Lorraine," the Templar replied. "...that is known only to me. You will be the first besides myself to know its location and observe the secrets held within."

"Thank you my lord," Berthold answered. He felt moved by being included in the Templar's secret, but would not have minded knowing exactly what he meant about hidden places and special secrets.

"You honor me," he continued. "I, ah, hope to be worthy of your faith, my valiant Knight."

"We are going to a place that holds the key for the survival of the Dukedom. Our quest is to secure a small part of the treasure concealed there. I cannot disclose more about the source of the bounty, even to you. But I will tell you that it is part of a far greater treasure whose location is known to me."

The thought of a fabulous treasure fascinated Berthold, but he forced himself to remain silent while the Templar explained.

"Your wine barrels are the perfect hiding place to transport our precious cargo. Accordingly, I have secured the finest wines available, those whose worth is widely known. In your cart, they will be a perfect subterfuge to reopen the doors of Lorengard-Lorraine."

A free shipment of fine wine. Berthold immediately saw the reasoning in this explanation and he felt his attitude shift to a more pleasant note. He noticed that he had actually begun to enjoy the invigorating spring air and the beautiful fields, brimming with flowers.

Soon, they reached the edge of the valley and entered a thick wooded area filled with majestic trees and foliage. They followed a narrow snakelike path through the greenery. The Templar was familiar with the maze-like conditions and advanced along the winding path without difficulty.

However, a treacherously hidden rope pulled by mysterious hands suddenly snapped upward to obstruct their pathway. The horses spooked at the movement and bucked in fear, causing the unfortunate Berthold to be thrown to the ground just as he had predicted. He only escaped injury thanks to his natural padding.

The four men who conceived the trap emerged from the bushes brandishing swords. Berthold was so startled by them he raised his eyes in a plea for Divine help.

But the Templar had remained on his horse and had a considerable advantage over the attackers because of it. He charged them, sword in hand, displaying a masterful use of arms. Without mercy, his trusty stallion trampled one of the villains, mangling him at the same time that the Templar's sword skewered a second. He immediately engaged the third man, who now understood his mistake and fought furiously to survive against the Templar's onslaught.

The fourth remaining hostile so feared for his life that he canceled his plan to challenge the knight. He eyed Berthold instead, sitting on the ground paralyzed with fear. The fourth assailant approached him with a sharp dagger in his hand.

Berthold leaped to his feet with unexpected agility and sprinted like a gazelle into the thick foliage and surrounding trees with his assailant close behind.

Unfortunately, for the beleaguered Berthold, the vegetation was too dense to pass through with the speed he needed. Unable to advance and driven by terror, he climbed a tree and clawed his way up into the highest branches.

But the attacker arrived at the tree trunk and leaped high enough for his dagger to puncture the bottom of Berthold's pants. Berthold grabbed for the branches above him, but they could not support his weight. He fell with a terrified scream.

Miraculously, his foolish assailant was directly below him and broke Berthold's fall with his own body. Berthold flattened him like a pancake.

It took him a few moments to clear his head after the impact, but then he realized that not only was he unharmed by the fall, but he was no longer in danger. His nemesis appeared to be dead beneath him, his neck broken by the impact. The miraculous turn of events filled him with pride, for clearly, his prayer had been answered and his superior spiritual standing confirmed. He remained seated on the carcass like a hunter with a trophy.

The Templar soon joined him, having dispatched his own enemy, and was amused and relieved to see Berthold sitting on the pitiful remains of his opponent and wiping sweat from his brow.

"Look my lord, I also conquered my vile adversary," he announced. "And without weapons."

The Templar laughed out loud. "Well done Berthold," he cried. "A good warrior uses any resource at his disposal."

"My lord," asked Berthold. "Do you believe this trap was ordered by the Duke?"

"I doubt it my friend. He knew nothing of my plan and you were the only other person involved. Besides, our assailants were nothing more than common thieves...unskilled in swordplay and lacking intelligence, judging by your adversary's condition. No, Berthold, the Duke surrounds himself with ruthless mercenaries...the best money can buy. If they cross our path, they will be fierce enemies."

Berthold stood up from the crushed body of his victim and brushed the dust from his clothes, examining himself for injuries. A moment later, he cried out in alarm.

"What is wrong my friend?" the Templar asked. "Were you hurt in the fall?"

"No, my lord. No. Please look at my beautiful, elegant garment. Cut to shreds. It cannot be mended. It was the only one of its kind and is totally destroyed."

The Templar was surprised by the explanation. "It seems imprudent to wear such valuable attire on this difficult journey."

"I must confess," Berthold replied. "I knew this journey could be my last. If so, I wished to be properly dressed for the Hereafter."

The Templar kindly placed his hand on Berthold's shoulder and spoke with renewed respect, "Do not fear my friend. I will personally provide you with one of the most elegant wardrobes available. With my help, you will become the prime exponent of style in the Dukedom. Now we must be on our way. Time is of the essence."

Beaming with anticipation, Berthold dried his eyes and followed the Templar into the lush greenery, where they quickly disappeared.

THE ECSTASY of LOVE

After the marriage celebration, Duccio and Polyxena enjoyed blissful months of intense passion and joy. Hidden from the world, they lived in a modest room nestled in

Lorengard-Lorraine at a location known only by loyal and trustworthy friends.

They created a special place for themselves, far removed from the toils and sufferings of life in a utopian existence. Still, they remained aware of the need to be prudent, knowing that if they were discovered, there would certainly be tragic consequences.

On one of their happy days together, they lay in bed holding each other in a tender embrace. Polyxena rested her head on Duccio's chest while he caressed her and savored their blissful state.

"Polyxena, my happiness is overflowing and is more than is due any man in a lifetime. I dare not ask for anything else, because it would be ungrateful to the power that endowed me with this perfect love."

"Duccio, I feel truly alive for the first time. At last, I know that the darkness of human existence can nonetheless be filled with unexpected joy. The dark cloud that seemed to hover over me throughout my life has finally lifted. All this is possible because of your love for me and I love you as I never have before."

"Polyxena, for you I live and for you I am ready to die. If such an event should ever come to pass, know that I will always be grateful for the blessings I have received in the treasure of your love."

At those words Polyxena felt herself suddenly beset by a sense of impending doom. She held him tightly, hoping to obliterate the sudden fear that dominated her.

Duccio embraced her. "What is it? Why are you trembling? You are safe in my arms and have nothing to fear."

"Duccio," Polyxena answered in her sudden anguish. "Your words made me suddenly terrified of losing this blissful state, that seems too wonderful to last. For an instant, I felt the cold hand of death in my heart and I am frightened by the thought of being separated from you. If any calamity should befall you, my heart will cease beating from sorrow, because without you, I long only for death."

"Please, Polyxena," Duccio firmly responded. "...don't speak with such hopelessness. Your words hurt me like a dagger. I beg you never to contemplate suicide. If I die prematurely and you ended your life in response, I would become the most ill-fated person that ever crossed your path, and I am certain that, even in my grave, I would feel the agony of having caused your death. I love you too much to harbor any possessiveness toward you. I only wish to bring you joy and share with you whatever time we have in this world. Don't forget, I am a man of arms. Death's shadow follows me every day of my life. But I will never give in to the fear of it, because it is only knightly chivalry that defines me and makes me worthy of your love."

The handsome knight stood proudly before Polyxena, with his heightened emotions stirring the rapid beating of his heart. The dignified expression on his face made him appear more mature then his young years, and the effect only heightened his appeal in her eyes.

Duccio's gallantry, noble enough to make her feel proud and fortunate to be loved by him, aroused her passion. "Thank you, my husband," she said. "Your courageous words remind me once more how well I placed my feelings. I feel humbled by your wisdom and your kindness. You make me want so much more of the beauty that life can offer. The joy I experience in your arms is so sublime I wish it could last forever. It helps me set aside the cruel realities in my mind and the awesome responsibility I face every day."

Duccio smiled and approached her, beset by passion. She playfully eluded him and with a bewitching smile upon her face, slowly removed her robe, letting the garment fall softly to the floor and uncovering her perfect form to the man she loved.

The sight of her voluptuous body once again aroused Duccio. In that glorious, sensual moment, she appeared more beautiful and desirable in his eyes than ever before.

She opened her arms toward him, beckoning a tempting invitation and filling his mind with pleasure. He responded eagerly by embracing her and passionately caressing her silky skin. He kissed her lips with such desire he took her breath away. Polyxena melted in his arms and in the sensual embrace they reached the height and ecstasy of love.

In the weeks following that eventful day, Lorengard-Lorraine was beset with continued acts of rebellion. Revolts against the Duke's cruel authority became bolder and more audacious, following the mysterious appearance of the man known only as the Mysterious Templar.

Polyxena was gratified by the Duke's fear-inspired absence and delighted in her resulting ability to move about the palace and Dukedom without his interference. She lived for the special times in Duccio's arms.

However, despite her newfound freedom, she still felt herself beset by the ominous feeling that she was being watched by someone evil. The sensation caused her to fear deadly peril to Duccio, so much so that she began to prudently abstain from visiting him in their secret love nest, in spite of the anguish brought by the imposed separations. She allowed agonizing days to elapse until she could no longer bear the loneliness.

One night, accompanied by the faithful Davina and shielded by darkness, she walked through long corridors and eluded the many guards throughout the palace until she reached the palace chapel. An imposing marble altar and beautiful mosaics crowned the exquisite sanctuary. There Polyxena and Davina entered and devoutly crossed themselves, thankful that the chapel was empty at that late hour.

Polyxena walked to a large marble basin of holy water perched upon an elaborately decorated column located in a far corner of the chapel. It was barely visible to the eye, shrouded by darkness. She looked around to guarantee the absence of unwanted company, then placed her hand under the basin and searched for something hidden. A moment later, the marble vessel rotated to the side and uncovered a large opening in the chapel's floor.

Polyxena and Davina entered the open space without hesitation and hastily descended the stairs. Slowly, the marble basin rotated back to its original place and closed the concealed opening. But the secrecy she hoped for was flawed in that moment. A shadowy form appeared in the recesses of the chapel and eyes flashed in the dark.

Unaware of the intruder above them, Polyxena and Davina continued their descent into a comfortable area illuminated by many torches already lit in anticipation of their arrival. The secret passageway connected to the palace stables and had been created decades earlier to offer an emergency exit to the nobles of Lorengard-Lorraine if they needed to reach their mounts in secrecy.

She learned of the passageway in a special message sent by a nameless friend and believed that the helpful stranger was the Countess De Vargas, a woman renowned for her bravery and loyalty. She was close to Arsenio's' family and familiar with the palace and its surroundings. When they arrived at the stable, Polyxena and Davina discovered two saddled horses waiting for them. The animals were always ready when needed, thanks to the help from a mysterious and loyal friend.

Late in the evening, Duccio paced alone in his room, unable to sleep. The latest separation from Polyxena and his constant concern for her welfare filled him with anxiety. When he finally heard her soft footsteps in the corridor, he eagerly ran to her and lifted her sinuous body in his arms, passionately embracing her.

Polyxena melted once again into the warmth of his arms and felt the sensual, comforting sensations fill her with delight.

"Polyxena," Duccio exclaimed. "My wife, my love, you are finally here." He held her as if she might disappear. "I was frantic with concern. I thought something terrible happened to you. Why didn't you send a message? A word to alleviate my anxiety?"

Polyxena responded tenderly, "I am sorry to have caused you anguish, Duccio. But I felt it would have been imprudent to contact you because of a feeling of doom that has been plaguing me. At times I have thought I was being watched and followed by someone evil and I feared coming because it might cause you harm. I also suffer terribly during our separations and constantly long to be in your arms again."

Her words aroused Duccio's desire and he kissed her with ardor. She responded with abandonment, forgetting in the pleasurable moment that they were in the corridor and not safely alone in his room.

They laughed happily, amused by their recklessness, and for a few moments forgot all their grievances. They were simply two young people in love, delighted to be in each other's arms. Duccio finally lifted her, carried her into the privacy of his room, and closed the door behind them.

The hours they spent together flew by and when the bland light of morning cruelly appeared, she quickly got out of bed, fearing a late departure.

"Polyxena please don't go just yet," Duccio implored her. "When you go, the beauty of my life leaves with you."

"No Duccio, it wouldn't be safe. It is necessary for me to leave even if my heart breaks every time we part. I love you so much and each day I love you more intensely than before."

Duccio teased her by feigning displeasure. "If you love me more now, I guess you did not love me enough before. At least, not as much as I loved you."

"Come my love." Polyxena laughed. "Before, I loved a handsome knight, who with his striking presence and valor, attracted many maidens in the Dukedom, including me. I have since learned you are a man with incomparable nobility and kindness and your great ability to love has made me feel complete."

Polyxena tenderly kissed him to diminish his sorrow at her departure. Then she made herself rise from the bed and quickly dressed, fearing the danger of further delay.

Duccio sat disheartened, reluctantly compliant to the need for caution in their dangerous situation. With his generosity and loving heart, he wisely decided not to cause Polyxena more sorrow by speaking gloomy words.

"We will be together soon my love," he exclaimed. "And the sun will shine again for me in your presence. Forgive my weakness and selfishness. I am truly happy and blessed to have had you in my arms, and I will not ask for more. You told me once, Polyxena, that in this room we are equal before God as husband and wife. However, outside, in the real world, you are the Duchess of Lorengard-Lorraine, a title the noble Duke Arsenio wished you to have to protect his people. Despite the restrictions upon you, the title still retains great value, and you can do much more to help the citizens of the Dukedom than I could. We are only two people, and they are so many. They are desperately in need. Therefore, you must protect your safety. Not only for my sake, but more importantly for the good of Lorengard-Lorraine."

Duccio's unselfish words moved Polyxena, but they somehow added to her anxiety and to that strange, impending sense of doom that haunted her. They held each other in a final embrace and kissed.

"See you soon, my beloved wife," he finally said as she walked to the corridor. When the feeling of dread overwhelmed her once more, she stopped, impulsively embracing him again.

"Kiss me, my love, one last time before I leave you."

Duccio, surprised by her anxiety, kissed her tenderly and caressed her beautiful face. He tried to diminish her concern with soothing words. "Do not worry, my Polyxena," he said. "No matter what the future holds, we should be grateful for the happiness we shared. We are fortunate people who have been blessed with the majesty and perfection of love."

They kissed each other for a long and passionate moment. Then she gently released his hand and swiftly walked away.

Duccio stood watching until she disappeared into the darkened corridor. When he reentered his room, he closed the door and fell upon the bed. The intensity of his emotion burned inside him, and he took a deep breath to regain control of his emotions. Her distress had deeply affected him and made the pain of separation worse than before.

The sound of steps outside the door roused him, and joyfully he leaped out of bed. "Polyxena," he cried with relief and ran to the door expecting to see her. Instead, he opened it to find five mercenaries armed to the hilt. They shoved their way into the room in a manner that revealed their deadly intent.

Duccio quickly recovered from his surprise. With skilled self-control, he retreated into his room and snatched up his sword, then spun to the men and swung the blade toward them, forcing them to back away.

"So my lords, you are here to commit murder," he spat. "I am singularly honored. Five against one. Whoever sent you knows my worth."

Duccio grabbed a nearby stool with his free hand and threw it against the assassins, taking advantage of their momentary distraction to plunge his sword into the chest of the nearest one, who cried out and collapsed, mortally wounded.

His expertise in swordplay kept his foes at bay while he retrieved the fallen assassin's sword and armed both his hands to ward off the group's attack. The assassins pressed forward, thrusting their blades and parrying his thrusts, but even at four to one they struggled to dominate the fight and were filled with frustration at Duccio's fighting skill.

He continued to inflict painful, strategically placed wounds in their thighs and chests to weaken their attack and make them more vulnerable. Their apprehension grew high against the unexpected skill of their victim, made worse by the fact that Duccio taunted and challenged them as if he knew no fear in battle.

"I see the fight is becoming unequal, my poor lords," he cried. "Now there are only four against one. Oh, I am mistaken… I meant to say three." With a quick motion of his right hand, he buried his sword into the throat of the fourth mercenary, who fell fatally wounded, choking on his own blood.

The fighting intensified, with the assassins now reduced to three and two already wounded. Their injuries restricted their movements, leaving Duccio to eye the window as a possible avenue of escape. He could make it through the opening, but he also knew it was too high for a safe landing. His only potential escape was through the doorway that remained blocked by three determined assassins.

In his eagerness to escape their death trap, he got too close to the door, allowing one of the killers to deliver a wound on his left arm.

The attacker triumphantly cried, "You are wounded, sir knight."

The other two laughed in relief and contempt for their victim.

"And you my lord…are dead," Duccio replied. With that ominous warning, he hurled his sword like a javelin and impaled the boastful killer, who fell lifeless to the floor.

Despite his wound, he continued to fight with ferocity and held his sword in both hands to raise it for a powerful strike. In a single stroke, he severed the head of another assassin. The body remained standing for a brief chilling moment, then collapsed. Blood splattered everywhere, staining him and the last assassin, who by this point was pale and clearly terrified.

Duccio ferociously went after the last attacker and fought his way to the door. The man openly trembled after witnessing the knight's phenomenal skills and seeing the violent deaths of his comrades. By now he clearly realized he was dueling a superior opponent.

Duccio observed the man's state of fear and taunted him with utter disdain, "It's obvious my lord, that assassins like yourself give death well but receive it poorly! For once in your despicable life, show some courage and die like a man."

While fighting, Duccio had managed to remove the last obstacle from the doorway. He kept the last assassin on the defensive while he turned his back to the door to retreat out into the corridor while still fighting off the last attacker. With a few more well-placed strikes, his sword found its mark in the chest of his opponent. The last of five assassins collapsed at the feet of the victorious knight with a bloodcurdling scream.

But at that moment, a strange look of stunned surprise flashed across Duccio's face. He dropped his sword and desperately grabbed his chest where the tip of a sharp blade surfaced, thrust through his back by the hand of a coward. With desperate strength, he turned around to face a sixth assassin who had lain in wait for him. Duccio saw Baron Van Halt, wearing a repugnant look of triumph.

"Miserable assassin," Duccio hissed. But his strength abandoned him and he fell backwards to the floor, thrusting the tragic sword further through his body. A scream of pain erupted in his throat and with death already looming upon him, he grabbed the gold chain that held the precious emerald ring given to him by Polyxena. He lovingly kissed it and with his last breath, Polyxena's image appeared before his eyes, miraculously removing all of his agony and any trace of fear. By the time he exhaled his final breath, he was at peace and ready to give up his soul.

The Baron stepped into the room and approached Duccio's body, taking a coward's delight at the success of his crime. He disdainfully looked upon the corpses of the incompetent assassins, so easily overpowered by Duccio's amazing ability and prowess.

He quickly retrieved the ring and its gold chain from Duccio's hands and gazed with joy at the emerald stone. The sight of the Nemours emblem on the jewel made him laugh out loud.

"Well! The coat-of-arms of the house of Nemours. Our beloved Duchess was truly generous to bestow such a splendid gift on a humble servant." With a satanic smile, the Baron left the room carrying the jewel, leaving Duccio shrouded in a pool of blood.

†††

CHAPTER ELEVEN

THE SAD SUMMER HEAT

It was in the early hours of the tragic day of Duccio's murder that Polyxena received an unexpected visit from the Duke. He entered her rooms with a haughty disregard for interrupting her without advance notice.

Polyxena was careful to welcome him and to keep herself composed in his presence, but she felt a terrible dread.

Ludwig, however, was jubilant. He savored her helplessness and gleefully rejoiced at her obvious efforts to control her fears. He felt elated by the devastating blow he was about to inflict.

"I'm certain you will forgive my unexpected visit at this hour when you hear my news. It is important enough to compensate for my indelicacy, because I am here to let you know that only a few hours ago, a sworn enemy of Lorengard-Lorraine has been brought to justice," he slowly and deliberately paced the next words.

"His body rests in a pool of his own blood in the very place where he tried to elude our revenge. Since I know how devoted you are to our cause to eradicate enemies of our government, and how loyal and faithful you are to me in your promise to become my bride, I am here to reward your loyalty by sharing this great triumph with you. Now that I have fulfilled my duty, I bid you a good morning and, with your permission, I will retire."

With those sardonic words, he slowly walked toward the exit.

"Cousin," Polyxena cried, overwhelmed with dread. "What is the name of this enemy?"

The Duke stopped and turned with a sneer. Staring coldly at Polyxena, he quietly replied, "Oh, the name is of no importance, belonging to a vile traitor whose life you once begged me to spare…and who, without gratitude, conspired and plotted against me. But the name, the name. What was it? Oh yes…Duccio Degli Uberti."

Polyxena's scream of shock reverberated through the room until all her breath left her and she collapsed unconscious upon the floor.

"Wretched woman," he exclaimed, burning with jealousy. Without another word, he stormed away and abandoned Polyxena in her grief. He was unable to comprehend why the beautiful woman scorned his amorous advances, favoring someone who was a mere bodyguard, a servant.

Davina had stood in the background and witnessed the terrible scene. Now she rushed to aid her lady. She carefully lifted her head and tapped her cheeks to revive her. Polyxena opened her eyes and looked about in confusion, disoriented and nearly in a trance from the terrible shock. Her pain was unbearable.

"Duccio," she moaned. "I killed you with my love. I am responsible for your death." Gasping for air, she sat on a nearby bench and struggled to catch her breath.

Davina searched for words to somehow ease Polyxena's despair, "Please, lady. Why utter such terrible and unfair words about your love? The noble knight would have been long dead if you had not intervened to the Duke on his behalf. You gave him your love, and he experienced great joy. Wherever he is now, he blesses you for it. I know that the candle of his life burned out too soon, but it burned so brightly! Please hear me my lady. I would gladly forfeit my life to experience a sublime love such as that, even for a little while."

She embraced Polyxena with affection, and her kind eloquence gave Polyxena a measure of respite.

She regained some control and reclaimed enough dignity to fondly address her faithful friend. "Thank you my dear friend. I appreciate your compassion. It gives me solace in this tragic hour. But I must also request one more great favor from you. Please leave me alone with my sorrow. I promise to call you if I should need your help."

Davina was frightened by the sound of those words and shook her head in vehement denial. "No, my lady, please let me stay. This is not a time for you to be left alone."

Polyxena understood her meaning. "Have no fear, Davina, I will not harm myself...I promise you and I swear upon Duccio's sacred blood. As the Duchess of Lorengard-Lorraine, my people are in need of me and I will not abandon them. Besides, there is much I have to avenge."

At the reassuring sound of Polyxena's words, Davina respectfully bowed and left the room. Polyxena sat without moving for a long time, immersed in thought. Eventually she took a deep breath, squared her shoulders, and grabbed a black hooded mantle from a large wooden chest. She placed it around her shoulders and hurried from the room.

Duccio's untimely death quickly became common knowledge throughout the Dukedom. The noble knight was renowned for his valor and widely respected for his staunch loyalty to the late Duke Arsenio. In his death it became apparent that he was beloved by the people.

His handsome appearance and his fearlessness in combat had made him favorite among the maidens in Lorengard-Lorraine. In their passionate zeal, they had pined in vain with romantic dreams of him. Now that the object of their infatuation was gone, torrents of tears flowed from many of them.

His body itself attested to his incredible valor at the moment it was found, surrounded by the bloody corpses of his assassins. The sword still in his back also proved the cowardliness of his executioner. A story circulated that Duccio wore a peaceful look upon his handsome face, even in death, as if some force had calmed him in during his final agony. Minstrels created songs honoring the legendary knight's life and death.

The most popular version recounted a mysterious young woman shrouded in black who embraced and kissed his lifeless body. It was said that with considerable strength, she then stood and removed the sword from his body, kissing the blade just as she had kissed his lips, while swearing to avenge his cruel murder.

What the minstrels did not know and could not write was that along with a loyal female friend, the woman in the black shroud took possession of his body and honored him with a secret Christian burial where his mortal remains could not be dishonored.

Summer was unusually hot that year. The relentless sun scorched the earth, drying streams and rivers. A widespread drought soon accompanied the heat, while clear skies reigned and rain was nowhere seen. Eventually the drought reached critical proportions and the many fountains of Lorengard-Lorraine, which usually overflowed with crystal clear water, spewed nothing but runny mud the color of rust.

It became necessary to dispense water by strict rationing. If anyone appropriated more than their share, they were subjected to the penalty of death. Endless lines of distressed citizens formed seeking the limited rations. The drought was yet another added woe for the besieged people, who were overwhelmed by the endless torments dealt by a cruel destiny.

One burning afternoon, one of the townsmen whose face appeared unusually gaunt and flushed had unsteadily approached the fountain. He used the last of his strength to stagger to the destination, then collapsed there when he arrived.

Several people approached to give him aid, and one showed the generosity of filling his own cup with water and pouring it over the man's face to revive him in the blinding heat. But a moment later the eyes of that good Samaritan filled with horror as he recoiled backward and screamed.

"God help us, he has the plague! God help me, I touched him. The plague!"

Cries of alarm immediately echoed from voices in all directions, for the Black Death was known to be more deadly than war.

Several guards were attracted by the disturbance and rushed to the fountain. Hearing the crowd's panicked cries, they carefully approached the sick man and quickly verified that he was truly a plague victim. They exchanged a few private words, then sent the youngest one galloping away on a mission. Within a few moments he rode back to the scene carrying torches.

The guards surrounded the sick man, without hesitating at all, poured lamp oil over him, and set his clothes on fire. The intense heat brought him back to consciousness, but he only screamed once before the heat-sealed his lungs, but he tried to stagger to the fountain. He came within a few steps of the muddy water before he was quickly engulfed by the flames and fell helplessly to the ground. His body kept fighting the flames but the most awful aspect was that he could no longer make a sound and the battle went on in silence.

The community had no time to absorb the effect of that terrible silent death play. Within a few hours, it became apparent that the inhumane execution didn't stop the pestilence. New bubonic plague cases spread like wild fire throughout the Dukedom.

It arrived with all the usual horrors of random death and final agonies, but it also included a particularly devastating side effect in that it forced a temporary halt to the rebellion that had begun to give the people a ray of hope against the Duke's cruelty.

While the Duke was relieved by the temporary truce, he was far more concerned over the ghastly pestilence. He ordered the Ducal palace closed and inaccessible to anyone from the outside, under the penalty of death. The palace's lavish provisions of food, wines, and water remained available to the privileged few, so that a festive spirit of denial was allowed to prevail uninterrupted at court.

Secure in their lofty powerful positions, the aristocrats felt immune from the plague in their luxurious, inaccessible world. But the devastation continued to mercilessly sow death among the unfortunate citizens.

Polyxena remained in mourning over Duccio's death and locked herself in her private rooms, leaving only to fulfill necessary duties as Duchess. The few who saw her looked upon a face that was pale and nearly lifeless, as if her soul had already joined Duccio in death but her body moved under the power of an iron will. Her only solace was solitude, while the Duke failed to grasp how she could prefer a mercenary of no social standing over a powerful ruler like himself.

Flavia discovered to her pleased surprise that her fortunes rose again thanks to Polyxena's fall from grace. She was overjoyed to be back in the Duke's favor. Now she was seated at the Duke's right side during banquets and social events, receiving his undivided attention. His newfound devotion made her dream again of the elusive Duchess crown. At last, it appeared to be within her grasp.

As if to dispel disease with gaiety, orgiastic feasts became the order of the day. Debauchery reigned supreme in the palace now that the Duke had replaced the virtuous Polyxena with Flavia, and her availability, who dutifully tended to his lust with unquenchable thirst for sensual pleasure and a sustained desire to satisfy the Duke's passion. She did not engage in lovemaking so much as she labored in the nude to achieve her dreams of glory.

For weeks, their sexual encounters were frequent and uninhibited, fueled by insatiable lust and the unrestrained drinking of spiced wine. They aspired to pleasure while remaining oblivious to the suffering of the plague victims and to the gruesome sight of bodies piled on funerary carts for transport outside the city walls to be burned.

Weeks elapsed under a relentless sun that scorched the earth to a dull brown. The Black Death rained down upon the people, but the sky surrendered nothing.

One hot August night, the Duke and Flavia retired to his apartment at an early hour following another ritualistic feast. They were both giddy from wine consumption and in the intense heat, their lustful desires intensified.

In their rooms, the Duke collapsed onto the bed and gazed with drunken lust at Flavia, who was equally eager to remove her clothes under combination of heat and wine-fueled desire. He stared at the voluptuous, exciting, and sensual creature while she responded to his sexual overture by removing her veil with a single stroke and displaying her magnificent body.

It shocked and baffled her to see the Duke's wanton look change in an instant to one of horror. He screamed like a man possessed and pointed to her naked chest.

Overwhelmed with fear Flavia lowered her eyes and staggered backward at the sight before her, then joined the Duke in his scream. Several of the black buboes known as the 'messengers of the plague' blemished her perfectly white skin. Instantly hysterical, she imprudently accosted the Duke in search of comfort, but his revulsion and fear compelled him to stagger back from her.

"You have the plague," he screamed. "You are unclean! Come near me and I'll kill you like a dog."

Flavia collapsed to her knees, begging for a show of mercy he had no strength to give. The Duke was overwhelmed with terror and continued to scream at her, "You have the plague. Guards, come to me. *Guards*!"

Two mercenaries flew into the room, swords ready. They were stunned to see the Duke so agitated, but instantly understood his concern when he pointed to Flavia and cried out, "She is infected with the plague. Get her out. Get her out!"

"Have mercy," Flavia pleaded, overwhelmed with terror.

But the Duke's fear surpassed all concern for her and he continued to shout, "Remove her from the palace. Hear me you fools. Take her away!"

The guards hesitated, fearing the plague even more than the cruel Duke. This fueled his fury and he screamed louder, his voice reverberating down the corridor and sending a wave of anxiety sweeping through the palace.

Polyxena and the Baron Van Halt responded to the Duke's cries. When they arrived at his apartment, they were shocked to see him disheveled and terrified, lacking a leader's dignity in a crisis. When they approached him to inquire about the distress, he pointed to Flavia with contempt and revulsion.

"She is infected with the plague. She must be removed from the palace at once, before the Black Death destroys us all!"

Flavia was so terrified by the Duke's words that she was about to faint when Polyxena compassionately clutched her to prevent the wretched girl from falling.

The Duke, shocked by Polyxena's recklessness, shouted angrily. "What are you doing foolish woman? Haven't you heard me? She has the plague."

Polyxena remained detached and continued to hold Flavia until she could carefully place her on a nearby chair and cover her naked body with a blanket. "I have been exposed to the plague before," she told the Duke. "…and I seem to be immune."

The Baron concurred. "I also do not fear the plague, my lord, knowing I am immune."

"Very well, you can all stay here if you wish," the Duke fairly growled at them. "However I will move my residence into the east wing of the palace with my guards and servants. I intend to remain there in complete seclusion until the plague subsides. You all can remain here, but do not trespass into my new domain…under penalty of death."

He turned to the Baron Van Halt. "You, my lord, will be in charge here until the crisis ends, commanding the Dukedom in my name."

The Baron bowed and stepped aside to allow him clear passage from his rooms. Without further discourse, the Duke Ludwig quickly left his apartment, followed by his guards, leaving Polyxena and the Baron alone with Flavia.

Polyxena brought a cup of wine to Flavia's lips, then urgently addressed the Baron, "My lord, to help lady Flavia, I need fresh water to prevent her from developing fever and keep her body as cool as possible. For added safety, I suggest we burn her clothes and bed coverings, replacing them at once with fresh linens."

"As you wish, your grace," the Baron responded.

Flavia spoke in a voice choked with fear, "My lady, is it possible to survive the plague? Is there any hope for me?"

"Do not fear my lady," Polyxena answered benevolently. "Many survive the plague, if they are well cared for. I pray you will be one of them."

Inspired by his sadistic nature the Baron preferred a more cruel response. "Have you ever seen the plague's visual results on the bodies of the survivors? It leaves you horribly scarred and disgusting to the eye. I imagine it will be so distressing to see your delicate complexion destroyed."

Flavia was terrified by the venomous words and screamed incessantly until she fainted, overwhelmed by despair. Polyxena gave the Baron a murderous glare that silenced his tongue and quickly drove him from the room.

For the next several days, Polyxena remained at Flavia's side to care for her. During the ordeal, she managed to close her eyes from time to time, attempting to renew her depleted strength. Her compassionate nature prompted her to care for Flavia and served to suppress her feelings of devastating pain and loss over Duccio.

Flavia soon developed a high fever in spite of the constant care afforded her and rapidly began to lose her battle with the plague. Within days, blood began to run from her nose and mouth, the Plague's ominous sign of imminent death. Polyxena found the metamorphosis of Flavia's once-beautiful face a terrifying sight to behold.

Still she fought to control Flavia's terrible fever by constantly applying and changing cold compresses, blotting her face and chapped lips with cool water.

Flavia looked up at Polyxena with boundless gratitude, her once haughty demeanor replaced by respect and admiration. She said with great effort, "How strange to think that you, my lady, are the only one who cares for me and has compassion for my suffering. I deeply regret hurting you. I was jealous and threatened by your gracious presence and the Duke's obvious attraction to you. You must know I was instrumental in Arsenio's downfall…and despite the fact that he loved and trusted me, I betrayed him."

Flavia sighed desperately. Her voice was drowning in blood and she fought for every breath. Polyxena lifted her to ease her breathing and placed drops of water in her mouth while she gently urged her to conserve her strength. But Flavia resolutely continued her deathbed confession, as if hoping to atone for her sins before facing eternity.

"Forgive me my lady, if you can. For I was also responsible for Duccio Degli Uberti's death."

At first Polyxena could not believe the devastating words and told herself Flavia was delirious. The ravaged young woman continued, "I had no ill will toward him, but I was spurred by my overwhelming desire to hurt you. I noticed you were unusually joyful, and as a woman, I assumed that you were in love. Since I knew the Duke couldn't be the object of such affection, I followed you, trying to expose your betrayal to him and bring about his merciless revenge.

"On that day, I found the hidden passage used by you and your handmaiden to exit the palace. I followed and saw your meeting with the noble knight and recognized the love you had for each other. I returned and informed the Duke at once, aware that he would seek retribution and would fulfill my desire to destroy you."

Flavia stopped for a few seconds, unable to breathe, but with incredible resoluteness and a desperate desire, she continued to confess her sins in the hope of saving her soul, "Oh my lady. How can there be any hope for someone like me? Can you find it in your heart to forgive me, after all the suffering and evil I caused? I want you to know how sorry I am and how much I despise myself."

Polyxena could no longer hold her compassion. "You ask too much of me. I am in mourning and I cannot forgive the terrible pain and sorrow you caused. But I do not curse you. You must place yourself in the hands of God and trust that he will forgive you."

"How can I hope for mercy?" Flavia pleaded. "I sinned too much. There is no forgiveness for one like me. I am sure Arsenio and Duccio are also cursing me from the grave."

"Let them rest in peace," Polyxena told her. "They sleep serenely in oblivion. They no longer experience the agony and anxieties of the living."

But Flavia was too tormented and fearful to be silent. "They are all dead," she cried out. "Forgive me, Arsenio, have mercy. No…No!"

She suddenly sat and bolted upright on the bed with a wild look and grabbed Polyxena's hand with desperate strength. "No! Arsenio is not dead, he lives, I tell you, he lives. He is not dead."

Polyxena was moved by Flavia's hysteria and tried to comfort her by refreshing the cold linens on her face. "You must calm down now. It serves no purpose to torment yourself."

But Flavia remained wild-eyed and screamed once again, grabbing Polyxena's hands tight enough to cause pain. "Arsenio lives, my lady!. I tell you he is alive. He lives!"

"I believe you, lady Flavia. Please, you must calm down."

"You think that I am delirious," Flavia countered. "But no, my lady. For the first time in my miserable life, I see clearly. And I am so ashamed."

Polyxena was struck by how rational Flavia sounded even though her words were not believable. "How can it be that Duke Arsenio is alive?"

Flavia seemed to realize she finally had Polyxena's attention and with relief she continued. "Arsenio did not die that fatal day. He was only rendered unconscious and taken away, to let everyone believe he was dead."

"But why, Flavia? And whose shrouded body was laid in repose at the funeral?"

"My lady, it was Luca Morosini. Arsenio's head guard. He was killed the same day Arsenio was sequestered."

Polyxena was stunned by this. It was unbelievable, but still not something she could ignore. Her forehead beaded with cold sweat. "Why did the Duke spare Arsenio's life? Knowing how cruel he is, I find it hard to believe."

"Superstition, my lady. The Duke is terribly superstitious! He once told me that a mystic, his grandmother I think, foretold his future in which he would be rich and powerful. The only threat to the fulfillment of his victorious path was the deliberate killing of any family member because a curse would be upon his head.

"Perhaps he did not believed the story, but at the same time, he was afraid to tempt fate. And so in order to destroy the cousin who stood in the way of his path to power, he decided to make him disappear. Not to kill him, but only to let everyone believe he was dead. It worked well for him."

Polyxena recalled often hearing the Duke speak of his tendency to believe in superstitions. With that, Polyxena accepted the possibility that Flavia was speaking the truth. Along with everyone else, she had also never been permitted to see Duke Arsenio's body. It was therefore at least possible he was still alive. Suddenly, Polyxena felt genuine hope for the first time in weeks.

The enormous effort required for Flavia's confession depleted her before she could reveal more and she fell back onto the bed unconscious. Polyxena desperately tried to revive her by putting cold water upon her face. "My lady please. Where is Arsenio? Please!"

Flavia's eyes fluttered for a moment. Though dying, she made a tremendous effort to respond, "They never told me... Maybe far away, or nearby in some secret place..." She desperately grabbed Polyxena's hand and whispered, "Find him, my lady. If he lives...and beg him to forgive me. Oh, forgive me, Arsenio."

She gasped and her body jerked like someone falling into a precipice. Then, little by little, she released the hold and her hand fell motionless upon the sheets.

CHAPTER TWELVE

THE SEARCH

The weeks that elapsed after Flavia's death were filled with anxiety and sadness for Polyxena. Rather than providing consolation, Polyxena's sense of helplessness was only increased by the claim of Arsenio's continued survival. She desperately wanted to believe he still lived but had no way to acquire more information's.

Who could she ask? The dreadful situation preyed upon her. She knew she had to somehow find the Duke of

Lorengard-Lorraine, if he lived and help restore him to his rightful power. The people needed him. She also felt certain that if anyone suspected she knew Arsenio was alive—his life would be forfeited by his captors.

She made several trips to the Palace dungeons under the pretext of inspecting the area for new cases of plague. She knew the effort was likely to prove futile, since it was highly unlikely Arsenio would be held in such an obvious and accessible place, but she needed to begin somewhere.

The Duke of Saxe-Hanover segregated himself in a prison of his own making. His fear of the plague made it impossible for Polyxena to get clues from him to find Arsenio. She knew the only person who could have knowledge of Arsenio's whereabouts was the Baron Van Halt, the Duke's most trusted ally. If Arsenio truly lived, The Baron was sure to be someone who knew his whereabouts.

For many days, Polyxena secretly dedicated her attention to the Baron. She followed him everywhere, with discretion, hoping his actions would shine a light on the unsettling mystery. However, as time passed she discovered no clues as to Arsenio's location.

She no less determined to solve the mystery because of it, especially when it concerned a matter of the Dukedom's stability and survival. She continued her relentless surveillance of the Baron in spite of the fact that it continued to appear futile.

She became familiar with the smallest details of the Baron's routine, the way he inspected the palace guards each day, his daily reports on the plague in Lorengard-Lorraine, and the duties he assigned to the mercenaries throughout the Dukedom. He was extremely busy in his newly acquired position and his daily routine always ended in his private chambers, down at the end of a long corridor in the palace's west wing.

She noticed, however, that these daily visits were performed alone and that he usually remained in his room for only an hour. The area was deserted and unguarded, shrouding his activity in secrecy.

No other option was left to Polyxena but to investigate the Baron's chambers. After taking care to be certain she was alone and away from prying eyes, she entered the long corridor and hid in the furthest end behind a decorative armor.

Fortunately for her, the Baron was fastidiously punctual in all his endeavors and arrived at his usual time. As soon as he reached the door to his private chamber, he released several keys from a metal belt ring. Polyxena could see that he selected one, golden in color and small in size and unlocked the door with it. She got a glimpse of the Baron's room as he entered before he closed the door behind him. She heard a clicking sound as he relocked the door.

Silence returned to the corridor. After waiting a few minutes, Polyxena felt secure enough to come out from hiding and carefully approached the door. She pressed her ear against it, but didn't hear anything inside. With her heart beating wildly, she bent to look through the keyhole, but the key was still in the lock and blocked the view.

She withdrew to her hiding place in frustration, waiting for the Baron to come out. Again, he was punctual in leaving, quickly locking the door and returning the golden key to his belt. Then he turned and disappeared into the long corridor with a determined stride.

Polyxena let a few moments pass before she emerged from hiding. Once again at the mysterious door, she looked through the unobstructed keyhole. This time she could see an elegantly sculpted desk against the far wall, stacked with manuscripts piled in disarray. Nothing appeared unusual or suspicious. She tested the door's handle but as she suspected it was securely locked.

She had to take possession of the key. There was little enough hope of finding clues of Arsenio's existence in the Baron's chamber, but it was necessary to follow even improbable leads to find a way to confirm whether he lived or not, and if so, restore the Prince to his people.

The next day, lady Davina brought Baron Van Halt an invitation from the Duchess of Lorengard-Lorraine to be a guest in her private rooms. The special favor from the beautiful lady was eagerly accepted. He arrived punctually, dressed all in black to enhance his flaming red hair while also camouflaging his prominent belly. A handmaiden escorted him to the antechamber, where he was quickly joined by Polyxena.

The amazing beauty of the enigmatic Duchess had the same seductive power over the Baron as it did with so many men. He made a gallant show of kissing her hand.

"Welcome Baron," she greeted him. "It was gracious of you to respond to my invitation." She withdrew her hand, which he appeared determined to take home with him, then sat on a divan and gestured to a nearby chair for the Baron.

"Your grace," he said with a smile of pleasure. "You honor me with your cordial invitation. How may I be of service to you?"

"Be of service? Of course not." She smiled. "I desire the company of a friendly person. Since the untimely death of lady Flavia and the Duke's self-imposed seclusion, sadness and boredom reign in the palace. I thought it would be pleasant to engage in an enjoyable conversation with a genial person like yourself."

Polyxena disarmed him with another convincing smile. The Baron was not inclined to ask why she should appear so convivial despite the tragic turbulence in her recent life. Her friendly reception not only flattered him, it gave him a lusty form of hope.

"My lady, you can always count on me. If I can serve you, it would be my pleasure to oblige."

"Please, my lord," Polyxena seductively answered. "It is not service from you I require, but as I said, simply to be in the company of someone of my own choosing…A person I admire."

She gazed enticingly at the Baron with her magnificent green eyes and her seductive manner filled him with desire. She took note of the Baron's receptiveness and clapped her hands, summoning Davina to bring in a gold carafe filled with wine and two splendid gold goblets.

"Kindly join me in a toast with this full-bodied wine from the golden vineyards of Nemours," she said, and motioned for Davina to fill the Baron's cup.

With that, pleasant fantasies left him and his face darkened in suspicion. He eyed the filled goblet but made no move to drink. Polyxena teased his sense of manhood by lifting his goblet and drinking deeply from it. Then she offered it again to him with a flirtatious smile.

"If you please my lord." She smiled. "I am sure the Duke would approve of our friendly encounter. Besides, he is not here to share this intimate moment. As you see, we are quite alone."

Her seductive manner hit the mark. Without further hesitation, the Baron grabbed the goblet and put his lips in the same area where she had placed hers.

For the next few minutes, Polyxena continued to hide her disgust and managed to convince him of her pleasure at his company, while Davina made certain that the Baron's golden goblet was never empty. He was a heavy drinker who gave himself over to the wine with gusto. Little by little, he began to lose his dignity.

Polyxena signaled Davina with her eyes to leave her alone with the Baron. A few minutes later when he realized they were now completely alone together, he felt himself overcome with desire. Her obvious receptiveness aroused him, especially when she removed the goblet from his hand and purposely brushed her fingers against his burning lips. She saw the Baron losing his self-control while he looked at her with open hunger.

Polyxena lifted the carafe and again filled the Baron's cup while gazing into his eyes. He felt himself hypnotized by her stare and distracted by her beauty, so much so that he did not notice when she opened the top of a special ring on her right hand and let a smooth white powder fall into his cup. It disappeared into the wine.

The Baron gladly accepted when she seductively handed him the goblet, showing him a smile filled with pleasurable promises. He seized the cup and drank without hesitation.

"My lady, you are too beautiful," he said, gazing into her stunning eyes. He tried to focus on their color but realized he was having a hard time getting his vision to clear. A strange feeling overwhelmed his body.

He began sweating profusely, warmed by a sudden unnatural sense of heat in his limbs. He loosened his collar to ease his breathing and cool himself.

"I will open the window," Polyxena soothed, as if all he needed was a fresh breeze.

He nodded but nevertheless gradually closed his eyes and allowed his head to drop forward onto his chest. In another minute, he was unconscious. When he began a deep snore, Polyxena softly called Davina to rejoin them.

"Please make haste, we must move quickly. The sleeping potion will wear off soon and he will awaken." Polyxena gently removed the man's belt and took the heavy key chain, then quickly sorted through the keys. With a sigh of relief, she recognized the small golden key the Baron had used to enter.

She removed it from its chain and approached Davina, who stood ready with two pieces of fresh clay.

Polyxena quickly placed the key in the clay and squeezed the two pieces together, obtaining a perfect impression. With special care, they cleaned the precious key, removing all residues of clay, then swiftly replaced it back on the belt of the sleeping Baron.

"Davina, I need this key as soon as possible," Polyxena exclaimed. "You know what to do, but please be cautious and stay safe."

The faithful handmaiden quickly left the room while Polyxena sat on the divan, holding the golden goblet in an imitation of someone merely relaxing and sipping wine. Within several minutes, the Baron began to waken. She was uncertain of his reaction to her sleeping potion and hoped he would attribute his grogginess to the alcohol.

Finally, he slowly awakened. His first impulse when he opened his eyes was one of suspicion. He jumped unsteadily to his feet, sword in hand, ready to defend himself. After a moment, he wiped his eyes and assessed the situation, noticing that there was no apparent threat.

He looked over at Polyxena, comfortably sitting before him and feigning surprise at his alarm. Suddenly embarrassed by his paranoid behavior, he bowed before the Duchess. "Pardon me, my lady. It is unusual for me to be so completely overcome by wine. I am embarrassed by my indelicacy and beg your forgiveness."

"Please my lord, do not concern yourself," Polyxena lightly responded. "You must be tired from all the heavy responsibilities placed upon your shoulders. Besides, the wines of Nemours are notoriously strong and go quickly to your head. My advice is for you to retire early and get some needed rest to refresh you and make you feel vigorous again." She stood and lifted her goblet to him. "Until our next meeting, my lord, which I hope shall be soon."

The Baron felt himself truly flattered by the Duchess's accommodating attitude and passionately kissed the hand she extended. He left Polyxena's apartment with the triumphant stride of a man who has made a conquest.

The next evening, more than an hour before the Baron's scheduled visit, Polyxena entered the west wing of the palace. It was devoid of guards at that late hour, so she quickly traversed the long corridors while her heart beat hard against her chest.

She arrived unseen at the Baron's door and with great apprehension she tried to inserted the newly coined key into the lock. Unfortunately the key appeared stuck and refused to turn, while pearls of sweat formed in her brow and a sense of panic began to take over during the challenging moment.

She looked around fearing the Baron's early arrival and the possibility of the key remaining stuck inside the lock. With some effort and after jiggling the key for sometime, it finally rotated in the lock relieving her trepidation. She slowly turned the knob and entered the room, then stepped inside and carefully relocked the door before placing the key in her pocket.

Curious, she looked about the room. The chamber appeared similar to others in the splendid palace, with a high vaulted ceiling beautifully decorated with splendid frescos of mythical figures. Torches were strategically placed on the walls, illuminating the magnificent tapestries and the shining suits of armor placed everywhere. Splendid velvet drapes framed stately windows, giving a grand aura to the private studio. She noticed the desk she had formerly spied through the keyhole.

On closer inspection, the piled manuscripts were nothing more than accounts from the Duke's vassal states and proprieties. Many revealed great expenses incurred by the Duke to pay for his guards and mercenaries, but nothing seemed unusual or suspicious to her. The Baron's daily visits appeared to be for the work of overseeing of the Duke's power and proprieties, shedding no light on Arsenio's whereabouts.

Polyxena was demoralized by this setback, but continued undeterred in her stubborn pursuit of any possible clue in the large chamber. She spotted an imposing bookcase against the wall, filled with a great collection of rare books. She investigated it without knowing what she looked for or hoped to find.

She removed a few books from the shelves and carefully turned the delicate pages. They were mostly religious books, while some contained love sonnets and poetry. All had been hand engraved by talented monks throughout the centuries.

As time passed, Polyxena become aware that her pursuit seemed to be futile. "Nothing," she said in despair. "My dear Lord, there is nothing here to help me. I have no other place to look and no one to ask. Please heavenly father, if Arsenio truly lives, help me. Show me the way to find him or he will be forever lost."

Stubbornly, she continued to search the room in a desperate hope that silent walls would reveal their secrets. She hoped that she had some time left before the punctual Baron's habitual visit, so she remained wrapped in her mission.

But unexpected footsteps sounded in the corridor. The Baron was more than half an hour early for his usual visit. Polyxena was trapped in the room with no way out. She looked around for shelter but the magnificent chamber was well lit and sparsely furnished, making it impossible to find a hiding place.

The velvet drapes at the windows provided the only place to hide. She took a place there and held her breath. With her heart beating wildly, she heard a key turn into the lock and saw the sinister Baron Van Halt enter the chamber.

As usual, he locked the door on the inside, leaving the key in the hole. Then he went to the sculpted desk. Polyxena watched his movements from behind the drapes, which provided an advantageous viewing position.

He placed a small parcel that he had carried into the room with him onto the desk, then sat and feverishly wrote something onto a sheet of parchment with a duck feather pen. He rolled up the document, placed his seal on it, and put it in a desk drawer.

Polyxena watched the Baron's movements, holding her breath for fear she would be discovered if she made the slightest sound. Adding to her frustration, the Baron spent plenty of time

Adriana Girolami

reading the manuscripts on the desk and keeping her trapped behind the drapes.

Finally, he stood and walked to the bookcase, selecting a large, timeworn volume. Polyxena was distressed at the sight, fearing the Baron would spend additional time reading the book and extending her entrapment there.

But to her happy surprise, he showed no interest in the book and merely set it aside on a nearby chair. Instead, he returned to the bookcase and searched for something in the empty space left by the manuscript. As if by magic, the heavy, sculpted bookcase moved to the side, revealing a cavernous opening visible in the room's shadows.

With the haste of someone wasting precious time, the Baron picked up the parcel he had left on the desk and entered the mysterious opening.

Polyxena watched shivering with anticipation and filled with hope. She remained behind the drapes for a few additional moments, listening while the Baron's footsteps gradually became more distant until at last there was complete silence.

She ventured out from behind the velvet drapes and went to the bookcase to peer into the empty space on the shelf that had been occupied by the Baron's book. There she saw a metal lever, obviously the hidden trigger that opened the secret passage.

Polyxena approached the mysterious opening and gazed inside. A small, dimly lit room opened into a long stairwell. She wondered if it connected to some ancient dungeon hidden deep beneath the palace.

The Baron had lit several torches on his way down, but their soft reddish glow wasn't bright enough to illuminate the passage well. It was dangerous to descend the treacherous staircase and though she feared being trapped there, her desire to unveil the mystery remained paramount in her mind. She decided to take the risk.

No handrails were present. The stairs were humid and the walls were damp with mold. She noticed a liquid sludge leaking through the live stone. A disgusting stench of decay prevailed. In contrast to the stifling heat outside, a bitter chill hung in the air. She wrapped her cape tight to her body.

With resolve she carefully descended the staircase, she finally reached the bottom and stood on a large platform surrounded by brick walls. A rusty metal door obstructed the way, partially off its hinges. The door was open and allowed her to move through it and into a dark corridor on the other side. She could see a soft light at the end, so she went ahead, startling a bat into flight. It loomed from the darkness and skimmed her face, screeching as it passed. She stifled a scream and fought desperately to regain her composure before she could accidentally reveal her presence.

When she finally approached the lighted area, the sound of voices encouraged her to go forward. Finally, she reached the end of the corridor and cautiously investigated the lighted area from the safety of the shadows. She saw an enormous room with a high vaulted ceiling. Ominous metal objects hung from the walls, revealing an ancient torture chamber. The room was lit well enough for her to see a man chained to the wall.

The baron stood between her and the prisoner, partially obstructing the victim's dismal form. Metal cuffs connected to long heavy chains that had been anchored in the rock wall restrained the man's wrists and ankles. It was impossible to guess his age. His face was covered with dirt and he had a matted beard entwined with his tangled hair. His clothing had been reduced to dirty rags.

She clearly heard the Baron address the prisoner.

"Well my lord. I see that my presence displeases you. Strange. Considering the solitude of this dismal place, you should be eager for my company."

The chained man responded in a voice filled with contempt. "Rest assured that the bats who reign supreme in the squalor of this place are more welcome to me than your presence."

The Baron grabbed his sword to show his impatience and in a sharp sounding voice responded, "You forget, my lord, that without my daily visits, you would die of hunger and thirst." The Baron threw the small parcel he was carrying at the feet of the prisoner, but the man ignored the package.

"It would be better for me without your visits. My death would come sooner. It would be a way for me to leave the torment of this place."

"If your life is such a burden to you, why don't you kill yourself? With the powerful chains that bind you, you could easily accomplish it."

The prisoner looked at the Baron and Polyxena saw, even from a distance, that he had temerity and courage left behind those tormented eyes. "No," he exclaimed. "Is not by my hand that I will end my life. You have placed me in a tomb before my death, so I leave it to you to perform the one cruelty I would welcome."

The Baron sneered. "Nothing would please me more, your grace, if I had the power to choose it. But as you well know, your cousin prohibited it. He is enslaved by superstitions unworthy of any man in power. Perhaps this makes him undeserving of such an exalted role, one that should belong to someone with greater intelligence and fewer scruples."

Polyxena realized her hunt had proved successful and the prisoner was indeed Arsenio, long believed dead by his people. With her purpose achieved, she quietly climbed the long stairwell and returned to the private study. There she hid once again behind the velvet drapes and waited for the Baron.

When he finally left the dungeon and reappeared in the room he was clearly restless and angry. He approached the bookcase and reached for the hidden lever. The heavy cabinet moved and closed off the hidden passage, returning the room to its innocuous appearance. He put the book back in its original position, then quickly left.

At last, Polyxena heard the metallic sound of the key turning the door's lock from the outside. She listened to the distant sound of his footsteps until there was silence.

She emerged once more and again went to the bookcase to pull the hidden lever. When the secret passage opened she took a lighted torch from the wall and hastily entered the long staircase, shivering in the putrid cold air. Finally, she arrived at the entrance to the dungeon and after placing the torch on a metal hold, entered, and descended the last few steps.

She saw Arsenio leaning motionless against the wall. His head dangled and rested on his chest, and he appeared to be oblivious to her soft footsteps. Once she was close to him, she spoke in a voice tightened with emotion, "Arsenio, Duke of Lorengard-Lorraine, I bring you greetings."

At the melodious sound of her greeting, Arsenio woke from his torpor and opened his eyes, which widened with surprise at the sight of a stunningly beautiful girl regarding him with a benevolent smile.

He gasped and rubbed his eyes in disbelief. "Am I finally dead? Has a merciful God ended my torment and sent an angel to gather my soul?"

Polyxena answered, filled with compassion, "No my lord. God be praised, you are alive. Look around at your horrible surroundings and you will know this is not Heaven, but a cruel dungeon on earth."

The Duke continued to stare at Polyxena, incredulous. He finally asked, "But then…who are you, my lady?"

She smiled. "I am Polyxena of Nemours, Duchess of Lorengard-Lorraine."

"Oh my God! My bride," Arsenio cried out. "I didn't understand the cruel depths of my loss."

Polyxena gently touched the metal cuffs restraining the young Duke. "My lord, I shall return tomorrow with the tools necessary to free you from these chains and remove you from this oppressive place. With the help of God I will do my best to restore you to your people, who so desperately need your help and divine justice."

"Oh! I'm not mistaken," the Duke said in a voice shaking with emotion. "You are truly an angel sent from Heaven to free me from my torment. I have harbored no hope of ever returning to my people."

Then Arsenio's voice sharpened, "My vengeance will be merciless to those who have willfully betrayed me. There was one person I loved and trusted above all others and she also betrayed me. The vile ingrate should tremble with fear for I will take revenge."

"Calm yourself, my lord. You must be patient. I fear it will not be easy to remove your cousin from his control of the Dukedom. He is very powerful. Perhaps more then you suspect. As for the other person you despise so deeply, you should know that Lady Flavia De Brezzé paid the price for her betrayal. A few days ago, she died in horrible agony and torment, a victim of the plague. But she repented at the end and confessed to me that you were still alive. This is why I took the risk of searching for you. With her last breath she begged your forgiveness."

Arsenio sorrowfully lowered his eyes and fell silent. Gently, Polyxena touched his shoulder to interrupt his bitter reflection.

"It is time for me to leave, my lord. But do not fear, I will be back tomorrow. After the Baron's daily visit, we will have time to remove your chains and free you."

"My lady," Arsenio gratefully responded. "Permit me to kiss your hand with the respect and devotion you richly deserve."

Polyxena smiled and offered her hand to the Duke, who kissed it with such gratitude it made her uneasy. The open wound in her heart constantly bled and she perceived any loving overture toward her as a betrayal to Duccio's memory. She removed her hand abruptly from his loving touch, causing Arsenio to misunderstand her gesture and recoil in embarrassment.

"Forgive me my lady. In my pitiful state, I can only inspire disgust."

"No my lord. You must forgive my haste," she answered. "But time constraints make it imprudent to stay longer. I will go make the necessary preparation for tomorrow's event and return to you as I have promised."

As Polyxena was about to turn from him, she noticed a look of anguish in Arsenio's eyes. She approached the unfortunate Prince and addressed him in soothing words, "Have faith my Lord, your cruel imprisonment will soon be over. I believe in destiny and the power of goodness that somehow led me to you…it will continue to protect us until you are restored to your legitimate place and your people."

"My lady, you have already placed yourself in terrible danger on my behalf. It is not death I fear, but the unbearable loneliness of this horrid place. I am deeply grateful for all you have done on my behalf. You have brought the blessing of hope to this chamber of death and I will not ask for more."

His courage moved Polyxena and she lightly touched his shoulder. "I bid you goodnight, my lord. And I thank God in his mercy for sparing your life."

Polyxena bowed and quickly left the chamber while A grateful Arsenio followed her with his eyes.

†††

CHAPTER THIRTEEN

FREEDOM

The next day, armed with necessary tools to free Arsenio from bondage of his chains, Polyxena prepared herself for a novel encounter with the unhappy Prince. She chose men's clothes that would not restrict her movements. She also placed her sword at her side for added protection.

She sneaked to the Baron's chamber and hid in the usual place to wait in the dark for his nightly visit. She felt especially anxious, for even if the Baron arrived on time and his visit with

Arsenio was brief, she knew the stressful wait would feel like an eternity.

Finally, the Baron showed up and quickly opened the secret passage and made his way down to the dungeon while Polyxena could only wait in her hiding place, feeling as if she stood on live coals.

At long last he returned, sealed the secret passage and left the room, re-locking the door behind him.

She cautiously emerged and followed the usual ritual to open the passage and reveal the stairway to the dungeon where she knew Arsenio anxiously awaited. When she arrived and he saw her appear before him, he inhaled deeply and gave an enormous sigh of relief.

"Finally, my lady, you are here," he exclaimed. "I must confess I have been overcome with the fear that you were a hallucination, a figment of my distressed imagination. I thought your angelic apparition was just a beautiful dream."

"As you can see my lord, I am real. Try to relax if you can, for you have suffered much." She smiled. "I brought several tools, a metal cutter, hammer, and a pry bar. If we work together, you will soon be free."

Without further ado, Polyxena and Arsenio began the grueling task, focusing their youthful vigor on breaking the heavy chains. But although they worked with enormous effort to toil against the thick chain links, it soon became apparent that the chains refused to yield. They kept up their labors for nearly an hour while sweat surfaced on their flushed faces. But their frantic efforts were interrupted when a male voice cut through the air and delivered a nasty jolt of surprise.

"What a touching sight. The bride and groom finally reunited."

They turned with ashen faces to see Baron Van Halt staring at them, radiating cruelty. "My lady, why are you toiling hard to cut those heavy chains, ruining those beautiful aristocratic hands? You should have asked me for help, since I have the keys to free the Duke right here."

After speaking those venomous words of mockery, the Baron laughed and showing the distressed couple several large keys hanging conspicuously on his belt.

"How did you know I'd be here?" Polyxena asked, filled with dread.

"Oh, so simple, my lady," the Baron triumphantly answered. "Every day I place a special tiny object at the entrance of the secret passage, a detail you obviously failed to notice. Since it was moved, I knew someone other than myself had entered. It was not difficult to guess it was you. Judging by your unusual friendship toward me, I should have been suspicious. It would appear our beloved Flavia confessed her dark secrets to you before giving her soul to the devil."

The Baron accosted Polyxena. "You have given me no choice. With great regret, I am forced to kill you, since you have proven to be dangerous and invasive. It's too bad, because you are so beautiful." He approached and caressed her raven hair with utter disrespect. She recoiled in disgust.

"My lord," Arsenio exclaimed. "If you ever loved anyone, in their name, I beseech you to spare the Duchess. She is helpless against you and there is only dishonor if you kill her. Kill me instead. With me gone, her knowledge of my existence will no longer matter. I beg you, my lord, have mercy."

"Oh, calm yourself, Duke," the Baron sadistically replied. "There is no logic to your argument. First of all, I never loved anyone except myself and I want the Duchess to die. Besides, mighty Duke of Lorengard-Lorraine, you are not in any position to bargain. Offering your life in exchange for hers is futile because you shall die together. I am tired of coming to this infested place and tired of serving you, even if you are a Prince of the blood. The Duke of Saxe-Hanover will concur with my actions after he learns the facts and understands that keeping you alive causes danger for everyone, especially him."

The Baron took a deep breath. "I am tired of this useless chatter. It's time to die. And you, my lovely Duchess, if you have a final prayer, say it without delay."

Polyxena defiantly addressed him. "My lord, I want the keys you hold on your belt to free Duke Arsenio."

The Baron's laughter erupted at her audacious words. "I must admit, my lady, you have plenty of gumption. Your courageous behavior makes you even more appealing to me, and I am tempted to possess you right here, but I am restrained by the squalor of this place. Too bad you have such unusual taste in your choice of men."

The Baron venomously addressed Arsenio, pointing to Polyxena, "Your pure, lovely bride, my lord, is a woman of high birth with plebeian tastes. She scorned intimacies with the rich and powerful, only to fall into the arms of a mere servant. You should know that she was the lover of Duccio Degli Uberti, a knight with high ambitions. You knew him as your mercenary, and I had the singular honor of killing him with a well-placed thrust of my sword."

Polyxena screamed with rage at the Barons words. "It was you! Miserable assassin. You plunged your sword into the back of my Duccio. You are a despicable traitor and coward!"

The Baron flushed with anger, but restrained his rage. "Such abusive, insulting words my lady. They are not worthy of your high station. You do not understand that I am a modest, intelligent man. I am no coward…I'm simply not a fool. Your lover had amazing fighting skills and unparalleled courage. He had already killed five of my guards and was about to escape. I stuck him prudently from behind and as a memorable souvenir of my triumph, took a special remembrance from him that couldn't be of use to a corpse."

The Baron removed a heavy gold chain holding her splendid ring from around his neck with its engraved coat-of-arms of Nemours and its magnificent, large emerald. Polyxena gazed at it with anguish.

Tired of his sadistic game, the Baron removed the sword from his side and approached Polyxena menacingly. "I think it's time to end this useless chatter."

Arsenio tried to rise and shield the Duchess, but she daringly distanced herself from him to prevent him from being killed on the spot, then once more addressed the Baron, "I demand you give me those keys, my lord. And I am asking you for the last time."

"Yes my lady," he sneered. "This will be the last time you ever speak." The Baron raised his sword and lunged forward to deliver a powerful strike against her. Arsenio, helpless and chained, was filled with horror upon seeing the woman who valiantly tried to save him, about to die.

But instead of falling to the Baron's cruel blow, she sidestepped the fatal strike and swiftly drew her sword. The Baron laughed at the sight.

"What can you accomplish with those lovely hands, which you might have used instead to caress a worthy lover? That ridiculous sword will not save your life." With renewed ardor he struck at Polyxena, but she easily deflected the blow. With agility and speed, she inflicted a painful wound on the Baron's left arm, causing him to drop the chain holding her ring.

The shocked Baron recoiled in pain, she grabbed the chain, and quickly she put it around her neck after kissing the emerald ring.

"Accursed woman," the Baron hissed. He commenced a renewed, ferocious attack. Polyxena compensated for her lack of brute strength by quickly moving about the room, drawing him away from Arsenio.

The Baron was amazed and filled with horror. Never had he seen a woman who could fight with such masterful skill. He completely lost his bravado and became eager to end the contest. He attacked again, more aggressive and violent this time, but less efficient because of his fear. He initiated powerful strikes, and the clashing swords echoed throughout the torture chamber.

Polyxena continued her defense with consummate ability and boundless energy, forcing the vile Baron to keep moving at top speed, using his years and his girth against him. He was burdened by his heavy weapon and depleted by the enormous effort he had wasted in wild and aimless strikes against Polyxena's sword. His stamina became so impaired by his protruding belly that he gasped for air, quickly losing energy.

Meanwhile Polyxena continued to evade the Baron's wild swinging blade with tactically placed parries and thrusts that inflicted painful wounds. The Baron was soon losing significant amounts of blood.

"Accursed woman," he shouted. His breathing grew more labored while the blood loss depleted his strength.

She remained silently determined and coldly continued her relentless assault like an avenging angel. By this point, the Baron realized he was in mortal peril. Isolated without the help of his guard, he renewed his attacks in desperation.

Polyxena continued to defend herself against his strikes, but lost her footing on the slippery stone floor and fell backward.

The Baron triumphantly lunged to finish her, but she swiftly rolled away and evaded his blade. An instant later, she leaped back to her feet taking her sword in both hands and swinging it with all her might at his extended right arm. The sword connected with her target and severed his hand away—it and the sword dropped onto the floor at his feet.

He screamed in pain and in terror at being suddenly unable to defend himself. The Duchess advanced on him, her eyes flaming with hatred. He desperately retreated but lost his balance and this time he was the one to fall helplessly on the floor, shaking with terror. Polyxena mercilessly placed her sword tip on his neck.

"Look death in the eyes, you miserable coward who strikes from behind. You who have killed my beloved Duccio…May God have mercy on your soul."

With a swift trust, she buried the blade in his throat. He tried to scream, but choked on his own blood and quickly died.

Polyxena remained silent, staring at the Baron's bloody body and shaking with exertion. In spite of her victory, she felt stunned by her actions, dropped her sword on the floor and fell to her knees. Her trembling hands went toward the emerald ring while tears streamed down her face.

"Rest in peace, Duccio, my love. My husband. You will be in my heart as long as I live…Heavenly Father, I place my soul in your hands and ask for your mercy and forgiveness. Help me cleanse my soul of my hatred and thirst for revenge."

She leaned toward the body and took the Baron's keys from his belt, and then walked to Arsenio, who stared at her with wonder and relief. She knelt next to him and used the key to release him from the cruel shackles.

As soon as he was free, Arsenio fell on his knees before Polyxena, gratefully kissing her hands. "My lady, praise the Lord for your safety. I bow with humility to the most valiant person I have ever encountered. You are as courageous as you are beautiful."

"Thank you, my lord," Polyxena humbly answered. "But the merit is not mine. My father and his friend, the Count of Rozenberk were both Knights Templar of the first order, instrumental in teaching me how to fight. My athletic disposition responded well to their relentless training."

"How will I ever be able to properly thank you for saving my life?" he asked. "I owe you my eternal gratitude and devotion."

"It is my honor and privilege to help restore you to your rightful place, my lord. I have seen for myself that the people love and respect you as their honorable leader."

Polyxena picked up the Baron's discarded cloak from the floor and handed it to Arsenio. "Place this garment around your shoulders, my lord. It will keep you warm and help disguise you while we make our way to my private rooms."

The Duke eagerly obeyed, relishing the warmth of the mantle. He wrapped the garment closely around his body, amazed and grateful for the simple comfort of its warmth after so much unbearable suffering.

Polyxena stepped over to her fallen enemy, unable to rejoice at the victory. "It's easy to learn cruelty when you live with evil," she said. Then she turned to the Duke. "I will make arrangements to give Baron Van Halt a Christian burial. He has paid for his crimes in this life and we will leave it to the Lord to judge him in the next."

Arsenio continued to be amazed and impressed by Polyxena's rare and special traits of humanity and justice. He allowed her to help him leave the torture chamber. His legs were weak from disuse, but thanks to his youth and his great joy at being liberated, the revived Arsenio slowly climbed the long stairwell. With each step, he regained a bit more of his vigor and strength.

When they reached the Baron's study, they closed the secret passage and left the room, quietly entering the long corridor. Polyxena had become expert at eluding the palace guards, and with her guidance, they quickly reached her private rooms without hostile encounters.

Once inside her apartment, Davina exclaimed with delight and joyfully welcomed them, greatly relieved to see Polyxena return from her dangerous quest. She believed it was a miracle that they were alive and she cried with relief and joy while she immediately began to attend to Duke Arsenio's desperate needs. His months of captivity had left him in a pitiful physical state.

Once Arsenio was finally bathed to remove the grime of his long imprisonment, he ate a welcome meal and dressed in clothes worthy of his high station. Then at last, he was able to lie down and rest in a comfortable bed for the first time since his capture.

Polyxena waited for many hours while he slept like the dead and his body restored itself. When she finally saw him once again, clean and rested, she was surprised to see that the pathetic captive she met in the dungeon was a very handsome young man, with long blond hair and finely chiseled aristocratic features. His dark eyes were refined and expressive, and despite his patrician demeanor, his kind, and benevolent aura was evident even in his weakened condition.

With their adversity behind them, Polyxena now addressed him in the same slightly cold manner that had become her habitual behavior with all men since Duccio's death, "My lord, it is imperative you leave the palace and find shelter in safer surroundings," she said. "The palace has become the unholy nest of the Duke of Saxe-Hanover. I am certain his mercenaries will shortly notice the absence of Baron Van Halt and make a thorough search for him.

"You should be pleased to know, my lord, that you have many loyal friends who are fearlessly fighting for freedom against the tyrant, and against terrible odds. I know you were loved by your people, because I was privileged to witness their despair and sorrow when they thought you were dead. Their devotion honors you and the justice of your compassionate reign."

Arsenio lowered his head with a pained expression. "The poor people of Lorengard-Lorraine," he exclaimed. "How much they have suffered. May God forgive me for my failings and help me bring justice once more to them."

The Duke's nobility and compassion touched Polyxena's heart. "I will be by your side in this effort. But we must leave the palace at once. I will guide you to a mutual friend who will be overjoyed at your return."

Late that night, shielded by darkness, Polyxena and Arsenio cautiously left the palace using the secret passageway to the stables. Once on horseback, they hurried to the old section of the Dukedom and stopped before a decayed edifice where they secured the horses on metal rings imbedded in its stone. Then they approached a large wooden door.

Polyxena knocked several times using a code and the rubicund face of Berthold Ballon appeared in the torch light. His face revealed concern over receiving visitors at such a late hour, but when he saw it was the Duchess, he uttered a joyful greeting, "Your grace," he exclaimed. "It's such an honor to be in your presence. Please enter and be welcome. I will inform the Countess of your unexpected visit."

The genial host stared curiously at the Duchess's mysterious companion, who was shielded by the hood of his mantle. Since no one moved to introduce him, he deferentially bowed and led Polyxena and Arsenio in a humble room decorated with elegant furniture that seemed out of place in the modest surroundings.

Their wait was relatively long, since their unexpected arrival was late at night, but eventually they heard hurried steps in the foyer. A woman appeared in the archway of the room, conservatively dressed in black, with her hair pulled back at the nape of the neck and covered with a white linen cap. She bowed respectfully to the Duchess.

"Welcome to my humble home, my lady. My heart rejoices at the honor you have accorded me."

"Countess De Vargas'," Polyxena answered. "The honor is mine to be welcomed by a noble and distinguished lady. Forgive our visit at this late hour. It is prompted by the need to provide a safe place for this man, whom I believe to be a dear friend of yours.

While Polyxena spoke, Arsenio removed his hood to reveal himself. The Countess grew deathly pale and trembled lightly. For a long moment she was stunned speechless. "My lord, Duke Arsenio of Lorengard-Lorraine," she exclaimed. "How can this be? Is it a miracle that brings you back from death?"

"Oh yes, my dear friend," the Duke answered with a smile. "It is indeed a miracle that I am back, but is not from death that I return, but rather a cruel grave where I was buried while still alive."

The Countess trembled, beset by emotion, and placed her hand before her face to shield the joyful tears streaming down her cheeks. "May God be praised. My humble prayers were answered. You have returned, my lord, and thanks be to God!"

The Countess so overwhelmed that she appeared to be near fainting. Arsenio stepped forward and held her warmly in his arms to prevent her from falling.

"I also thank the Lord," he told her. "Not only for my life, but for loyal friends like you, Countess. You are as dear to me as my mother. I honor you great lady, now and always."

"Arsenio," the Countess exclaimed, finally regaining her composure. "My house is yours, to be used as you deem necessary. I am sorry I can't afford you better comfort. All my wealth was confiscated by the Duke of Saxe Hanover. Except for a few pieces of furniture, I have no other possessions."

"I am aware of it," Arsenio answered with his anger showing. "If the generous Lord spared my life, he must have done it for a good reason. Now I am here to regain my legitimate place, and I must erase the atrocities inflicted upon my people by that evil Duke, a man I am ashamed to call my cousin."

"God willing," the Countess affirmed. She bowed and left the room to prepare a shelter for him. Polyxena and Arsenio were alone once more and for a few minutes, they remained silent, feeling suddenly uncomfortable together. Polyxena was the first to speak.

"My lord, it is necessary to speak with you about issues vitally important to both of us. Baron Van Halt was an evil man, but despite his faults, I cannot call him a liar regarding my love for the noble knight, Duccio Degli Uberti. The story is true. We were in love and celebrated our own wedding, beseeching God's blessings to our union. He was the only husband I've ever known. Therefore you are free, my lord. Our marriage is null and void because our union was nothing more than an alliance I have honored on behalf of the people, using my position for the small amount of good I could offer them. I will continue to honor it until you are restored to your rightful place and the tyrant is defeated. I pledge my life to this end, knowing my father and Duccio would have wanted it this way."

Arsenio appeared saddened by her words. "You have your freedom, my lady," he exclaimed. "I am in no position to make demands of you. I owe you my life. I cannot begrudge your love for the valiant Duccio Degli Uberti. You were certain I was dead. You were free to love whomever you pleased. You chose the noblest and most gallant Knight I've ever known. He honored me with his loyalty and service, and he was a dear friend who placed his life in danger on my behalf countless times. He would have died defending me if destiny had willed it. You chose someone to love who was a better man than I...I know you gave your affection to a worthy person."

Arsenio took a deep breath and his voice became more somber while he continued, "However, I wish with all my heart that you would remain by my side as my wife. I would accept it on any terms, taking into consideration your broken heart and overwhelming pain. I would comfort you in any way I could, with endless devotion and affection. I may not be worthy of this great honor, but I confess my feelings for you are more intense than anything I've ever experienced..."

Polyxena interrupted, "I beg you to refrain from speaking to me about a possible union between us. I am in mourning for my beloved husband and it causes me pain. If you truly care for me, respect my sorrow and my broken heart."

"Your words are painful, but they are true. I have no right to ask for anything because I owe you too much. I only want you by my side because I need your comforting presence, but I make the request of you without asking for anything else in return until you are healed and ready to love again."

"It is not possible," Polyxena firmly responded. "I beg of you not to speak of it anymore."

The uncomfortable conversation was interrupted by the Countess De Vargas reappearance, now wearing a bright smile.

She was followed by the man known as the Mysterious Templar, strikingly dressed in black with the Templar's cross on his chest and the familiar red mask on his face.

The unexpected guest approached the Duke and addressed him with elation. "Arsenio of Lorengard-Lorraine. It is a glorious day that returns you to your home and people. God be praised for his mercy."

Then, with a single dramatic sweep of his arm, the Mysterious Templar removed his red mask, showing for the first time to the stunned audience the noble and proud face of Polyxena's father, Alexander, Duke of Nemours.

"Father!" she cried. "Is that truly you?"

"Yes, my daughter," he exclaimed. "It's time for you to know the truth."

Without a word, she ran to him and fell into his arms with joyful tears streaming down her face. "Oh father, thank God you're alive."

He lovingly held his daughter tight and caressed her flowing hair. "Forgive me my child, for all the pain I caused you, but it was imperative that you believed in my death, not only to protect my mission, but because you would have been in mortal danger if the evil Duke suspected the truth.

"When I learned of Arsenio's death, my first impulse was to wage war against the Duke of Saxe-Hanover, but the move was too risky because he had great military power. Such an action could have become a blood bath. I thought it would be prudent to bide my time, because tyrants are always hated and sooner or later they become victims of their own injustice.

"In the shadows, I decided to instigate the people against him. Depending upon the wealth I have at my disposal, I used my gold to pay mercenaries and corrupt the Duke's own guards. They are men without scruples and serve whoever pays better. With their help, I have inflicted humiliating defeats on Ludwig.

"Even if our work has not yet been sufficient to remove him from power, I have accentuated his vulnerability and given hope to the people. Only the Count of Rozenberk, my trusted friend, has been aware of my actions. Thanks to his help, everyone believed I was dead and no one suspected that I was this man who has come to be called the Mysterious Templar."

The Duke of Nemours turned toward Arsenio. "Now, as if by magic, the legitimate lord of Lorengard-Lorraine returns. After so many desperate and challenging months, real success is within our grasp."

"What an incredible day this is," Polyxena said, staring at Arsenio and her father.

"It's a day of destiny, my daughter," the Duke of Nemours answered. "A day when the dead rise to destroy infamy and blind ambition. It is time, Arsenio, to brandish your sword and regain control of your Dukedom. We will stand by you. With the help of God, victory will be ours."

The Duke of Nemours held Arsenio in a fatherly embrace and the young Prince warmly responded.

THE MIRACLE

Heated air pressed down on the land like a thick wool blanket. Menacing clouds and an overcast atmosphere had no wind to accompany them and cool the stifling atmosphere. Late in the day, Cathedral bells broke the stillness with their tolling. The sounds spread throughout Lorengard-Lorraine and drew consternation and wonder from the citizens. They responded in large numbers to the bells and assembled in the cathedral square. In a short time, it brimmed with people while the bells continued their incessant ringing.

Abruptly, the tolling stopped and silence returned to the square. The heated stillness created an aura of mystery, disturbing and hypnotic. The citizens stared at each other with apprehension.

As if by magic, the large cathedral doors opened and allowed the imposing dark figure of a knight dressed in a black mantle to step forward and solemnly descend the many steps before the edifice. A sudden murmur rose from the crowd.

"The Mysterious Templar!" voices repeated across the square at the sight of his familiar red mask.

The Duke of Saxe-Hanover's mercenaries were present at the scene, but instead of moving against the Templar, they remained immobile and silent. The Knight faced the multitude and raised his gloved hand in greeting. "Citizens of Lorengard-Lorraine," he called out to them. "The supreme hour for retribution has arrived. The tyrant's enormous cruelty and oppression toward innocents has challenged justice decreed by

271

men and God. By his divine will and mercy, I was sent amongst you as an instrument of justice."

As if Heaven was in union with the Knight, a lightning bolt illuminated the livid sky where a summer storm boiled in the air. Booming thunder reverberated in the piazza, igniting an ominous fear in the people.

At last, a strong wind burst through the piazza, sweeping away the stale air as if invisible hands had opened windows in the sky. The mighty wind flapped the Templar's black mantle and gave him a spectral look.

"People of Lorengard-Lorraine. I entreat you to arm yourselves and follow me." Though the multitude appeared confused by his words, the Templar continued his invocation, "In the name of God who loves us all, follow me," he cried at the top of his voice.

With that, the Templar ripped off his mask and allowed the crowd to finally see his face. When they realized who he was, the voices in the crowd screamed out, "Arsenio, our Duke! He is alive. He has been resurrected. It's a miracle. A miracle."

Arsenio stared proudly at the multitude, deeply moved by his subjects' joy at the inexplicable return of their leader from the dead—another miracle.

The Duke of Saxe-Hanover's guards were terrified at the sight. Ignorant and superstitious, they feared retribution from a vengeful ghost.

Arsenio took advantage of their confusion to rapidly descend the stairs and mount a magnificent Arabian horse awaiting him at the bottom. He raised his sword to the sky, taking up the invocation. "If you love me, follow me to the palace. Death to the tyrant!"

"Death to the tyrant!" the cries rose from the crowd as if in a single voice. The guards were terrified at the sight of the massive, indomitable crowd spurred to violent action. The people attacked them and easily overwhelmed their numbers.

They continued to shout, "Hail to Arsenio of Lorengard-Lorraine. It's a miracle... a miracle."

Attracted by the tremendous upheaval, the town's citizens curiously opened their windows and doors to look out onto the square. They were astounded when they saw their beloved Duke, sword in hand, but eagerly joined the rest, following that beloved ghost who exalted them and made them feel invincible.

The day was spent in a grueling fight. Most of the weapons used by the citizens were pitchforks and bats. But they fought with the ferocity of lions, inflicting shameful defeats upon the well-armed guards.

Untouched by the mercenaries, Arsenio stirred irrational terror in them. They thought he was an avenging spirit who, by the will of God, had returned from the grave to punish them. Few even dared to test him. Those who did quickly fell.

After much bloodshed, the people captured the greater part of the Dukedom. They were euphoric at their success even though Arsenio reminded them that only by taking the palace could they claim victory. But the palace was a fortress filled with massive artillery and many guards. The task remained, deadly and grim.

The thick cloud cover caused darkness to fall early, so it became necessary to light torches. Their reddish light only rendered the scene more horrifying, with mutilated corpses everywhere. Still, the determined crowd continued to move by torch light toward the Ducal palace.

When the giant assemblage arrived there, palace guards informed the Duke of Saxe-Hanover that a terrible revolt was in progress and danger was imminent. The tyrant looked out a window with horror at the huge approaching mass. He furiously ground his teeth and ordered his guards to prepare an immediate defense and to destroy the revolution in any way possible.

The battle was violent and deadly. Hundreds of arrows were shot from the palace walls against the helpless crowd, killing many dissenters. The strong defense made the palace impregnable and the coveted victory eluded the people. But with indomitable will they continued an assault even though it appeared to be fruitless and tragic.

Arsenio, sword in hand, fearlessly incited his people to press onward. His conduct inspired many to bravery when they saw him fighting with ferocious energy, oblivious to the danger from the deadly arrows flying everywhere. Orange-yellowish lights from the torches illuminated his face and he appeared as an ominous ghost.

Suddenly a mercenary who had been busily defending the palace looked and recognized Arsenio, whose menacing stance looked like an avenging Angel. He screamed, beset with fear, "The ghost of Arsenio of Lorengard-Lorraine has returned. God's vengeance is upon our heads!"

General panic erupted among the superstitious palace guards, greatly weakening the defense. The attackers came on with renewed ardor, aggressively pounding the palace doors with heavy logs.

The Duke of Saxe-Hanover arrived at the battle scene and was furious to see that the determined people had gained ground and the heavy palace doors were giving way to the massive pounding of the logs. His anger quickly turned to fear. "What are you doing, you fools?" he shouted. "Get back to your places at once, or you will pay with your lives."

But the guards were oblivious, aware of nothing but their superstitious fear. "The ghost of the dead Duke has returned from the grave," they exclaimed. "The curse of God is upon us."

Only then did the Duke of Saxe-Hanover become aware of Arsenio's presence, fighting boldly, sword in hand. He was stunned to see his 'dead' cousin and went deathly pale.

"Damn him!" he shouted. "How is it possible that he escaped?"

Now the despot was nearly out of his mind with dread and horror. He ran back into his private rooms and quickly dressed himself in splendid bronzed armor, then with that small protection in place he returned to incite his men to fight on.

"Miserable fools!" he shouted to them. "Go back to your places or you will pay, I swear it. Don't you see, you imbeciles? He is alive. He never died, I tell you. He is not a ghost, he is alive."

The tumult and the imposing palace doors that finally gave way to the pounding logs drowned out his voice. Arsenio led many of the patriots into the palace courtyard, where they accosted the tyrant's armed guard and overwhelmed them.

The Duke of Saxe-Hanover watched from a safe distance on the summit of the central staircase, looking like a man possessed while he continued to attempt to incite his men to action. His fury overtook him at being unable to control his guards, so he plucked a spear from the wall and threw the lethal weapon at Arsenio with all his strength, shouting, "Look, you fools, how your ghost dies."

But Arsenio, who was agile, jumped swiftly from his horse, causing the spear to miss and instead strike the body of a nearby guard. As the guard fell, a determined and vengeful Arsenio brandished his sword and advanced toward the hated tyrant.

"Defend yourself, you miserable traitor," he called out, closing in. "Fight as a man of honor for the first time in your contemptible life."

Ludwig of Saxe-Hanover looked as if he would have preferred to run, but there was no escape. Though he launched into an aggressive duel with Arsenio, his terror made his sword strikes wildly unpredictable. Arsenio was the superior sword fighter, and had used his sword in battle on many occasions, unlike his cousin, who had always hidden behind hired assassins.

Arsenio deflected Ludwig's wild blows with ease while he attacked the tyrant with expertise and consistency, making good use of his strikes, nicking and cutting the exposed parts of the Duke's body. Still, because of his protective armor, the Duke remained basically unharmed.

The Duke knew his guards would not interfere in a fight against a man they considered a vengeful ghost. Forced to rely on his dubious expertise, he struck wildly in a desperate effort to kill Arsenio. The fighting stopped and everyone focused on the mortal combat between the two cousins, knowing the result would be a clear demonstration of God's will.

The fighters struck at each other relentlessly, sending up sparks when their blades collided. Arsenio, a few steps below Ludwig, attacked relentlessly, gaining ground until he reached the top of the staircase.

A cold sweat bathed the tyrant's face and he realized he could not continue to repel Arsenio's masterful strikes. He turned and fled for his life up the long marble staircase connecting to the palace summit.

Arsenio pursued, contemptuous of his cousin's cowardice. But the tyrant had suddenly disappeared. Fear seemed to give wings to his steps, allowing him to reach the palace summit in a short time. He hid behind the battlements and remained out of sight, hoping for some miracle to intervene.

The sky darkened and torrential finally rain fell on the scorched earth. Arsenio had reached the summit, but looked in vain for the evil Duke, blinded by the downpour and darkness. A bolt of lightning illuminated the scene and Arsenio, in his disadvantaged position, failed to see his cousin hiding behind him.

When Ludwig saw his mortal enemy in such a vulnerable position, a triumphant smile flashed across his face. Without hesitation, he raised his sword with both hands and prepared to plunge it into Arsenio's back. The metal blade reflected a flash of light from the distance while he prepared to thrust the sword.

But in that instant another lightning burst lit up the gloomy sky and this time the electric charge struck the Duke's copper armored body. He cried out, allowing Arsenio to turn around just in time to see his cousin shrouded in red and green flames falling off the battlement. It gave the appearance of an infernal spirit diving back down into the bowels of Hell.

EPILOGUE

A NOVEL GOOD BYE

The rain fell in torrents, wetting the arid soil at long last, washing away the terrible scourge of the Black Death, and purifying the land and its people.

When the sun finally shone once more in a clear sky, the people staged a festive gathering of celebration. They crowded the massive square before the Ducal palace, joyful and full of gratitude.

In the central balcony, Arsenio appeared. He was moved by the overwhelming expression of love from his people, who were not interested in learning specific facts or logical reasons for his reappearance. It was easy for them to believe in a divine, miraculous return from the impenetrable shadows of death. They assumed he was awakened from his eternal sleep by a merciful God for the purpose of saving them.

After a final, affectionate wave to his people, Arsenio left the balcony and briefly returned with Polyxena and the Duke of Nemours on either side of him. He raised their arms, solemnly proclaiming, "People of Lorengard-Lorraine, who so warmly welcome me and give thanks to God for my safe return, I express my gratitude for those who were his divine instruments of justice." Arsenio looked at Polyxena and her father, and spoke in a voice filled with emotion.

"Our Duchess, Polyxena of Lorengard-Lorraine and her noble father the Duke of Nemours," he exclaimed. "Honor to them, now and forever!"

Joyful shouts inundated the piazza, and the people offered homage to their heroes. "Hail to the Duchess and the Duke!" they shouted, a thousand voices in unison. "Long life and prosperity to them!"

After a final bow, the trio retreated into the palace followed by members of the court, including the Countess Amelia De Vargas and the jovial host Monsieur Ballon, all dressed in splendor. Berthold's new garments were the finest brocades and silks, and he was at last adorned in a manner fit for a Prince.

Even after the people reluctantly dispersed, they still hailed their beloved Prince and ended their historical day with joy. Meanwhile Arsenio arrived in the throne room, followed by

Polyxena and the Duke of Nemours. Arsenio invited Polyxena to join him.

"My lady," he said. "Our people greeted you with such affection and love that I beg you not to abandon them. Please remain by my side as the Duchess of Lorengard-Lorraine and share with me the heavy burden of power."

Polyxena looked at him sorrowfully, but remained undeterred in her response. "I simply cannot, my lord. It's useless to persist. My mission has ended and God willing it was a success. Allow me to return with my father to Nemours where finally, after so much upheaval, I can mourn in solitude and remember my beloved Duccio."

The Duke sadly lowered his head. "How fortunate and privileged was the valiant knight, to know your love. My destiny appears cruel. Perhaps I have not paid enough for my past indiscretions and thus have the misfortune of knowing you too late."

Arsenio's feeling moved Polyxena. "Please understand, my lord, that my decision remains unchanged. I have experienced too great a loss. I am unable to feel anything else at this time. But it is not in any way your fault. I've known you to be noble and kind, worthy of being loved."

"I understand how much you suffer, my lady," Arsenio answered. "My heart breaks for you, and I wish to be of help with my support and caring. You saved my life. You are most generous and courageous. Forever, you will be my special angel. I make no demands on you, no matter how painful it is to withhold them and I will abide by your wishes."

"Thank you for your understanding," Polyxena gratefully responded. "I must soon depart and leave for Nemours with my father."

The Duke of Nemours had remained discretely apart, but now came forward and spoke with concern. "Yes daughter. Return with me to Nemours, because it is predestined that you should be like your father in every way. Let's go back to the place that will be our spiritual tomb, while we await our death. Following my tragic example, you may waste your life there, while still in the flower of youth."

Polyxena looked at him in surprise at his words, so far removed from his usual taciturn nature.

"I thought I had paid in full for my many failings," he sadly continued. "But it is inevitable that I experience immense pain when I see my daughter close the doors to life at such a young age. You should know my child, that the life you disdain is a divine and sacred gift. By destroying it, you are guilty of ingratitude toward the One who so generously gave it to you. And as for the gallant Duccio, who loved you so deeply, do you wish to make him responsible for your sorry end? Do you think that is what he would desire for you? This stance of yours is certainly unworthy of the nobility of your nature…because it is in living that you prove your real courage."

The Duke paused and approached her. His hands trembled with emotion and he gently took her by the shoulders to emphasize his words. "Hear me, child, the deep feelings you experienced for that noble knight will always be in your heart. He was your first love, enhanced by the burning passion of youth. He will be forever young in your memory, and the gift of love you shared will never be tarnished by time. Perhaps you will not love again with the same passion, but you will not be denied other experiences, no less intense or important. Please stay here, my daughter, and in the name of God be more courageous than your father. Remain by Arsenio's side and do not be oppressed by your pain on this glorious day of his triumph. I know he will be patient and wait for you to regain your peace of mind and the joy of living.

"The people need the united strength of both of you after so many injustices have been done to them. It will be your place to lighten their burdens and be worthy of the high station in life that is your destiny. Take your husband's arm and gain strength from his noble spirit."

The Duke gently pushed Polyxena toward Arsenio. She looked at the handsome Prince, so deeply tormented by the thought of their separation. Suddenly, in that pivotal moment another image materialized before her, seen through her eyes alone, and it was a splendid vision of a knight whose features reflected his valiant nature. Magnificent, dark eyes gazed into her.

"Duccio, my love," she whispered, her heart breaking.

The beloved vision did not disappear. Duccio continued to regard her with joy and love, as if encouraging her to go on living. The vision made no sound, but he looked at her and nodded. She knew his meaning without asking.

Deeply shaken, Polyxena ran into her father's arm and held onto him. The elder man understood from that loving gesture that his daughter had somehow changed in that moment and was now saying good bye to him. Then Polyxena walked with a confident stride toward the young Duke, having made up her mind to stay.

Arsenio joyfully extended his arms toward her, holding her hand in his. When he gazed into her eyes, she saw his boundless appreciation of her.

A smile crossed Polyxena's face. Behind the sad veil she had kept over herself for so long, there now glistened the light of hope.

TIMBER CREEK PRESS

PREVIEW

PART II

of

THE TEMPLAR TRILOGY

THE CRIMSON AMULET

by

ADRIANA GIROLAMI

CHAPTER ONE

LORENGARD-LORRAINE

Arsenio saw Polyxena at a distance. Her graceful figure strolled among the tree-lined pathways brimming with flowers in bloom. She was resplendent in a loose fitting purple gown with oversized sleeves lined in ermine. Her long, raven hair hung loose upon her shoulders and caught the sunlight. Arsenio was thoroughly enticed, and approached her with a bright smile.

When their eyes met, she extended her hands in greeting. He clasped them raised them to his lips.

In the closeness of the moment, he noticed an unusual glow radiating from her. It was so unlike her customary somber and dignified demeanor. He felt pleased and encouraged by the change in her.

"My lady, your smiling face brightens the beauty of the day. I am delighted to see you so cheerful."

Polyxena took a deep breath to control her excitement, and looked at Arsenio with joy. "I have received some wonderful news, my lord, and I am eager to share it with you." Her voice became softer. "I hope you will be pleased..."

"I am intrigued," He answered." What is the news?"

"Yes. I have been informed by the court physician that I am with child. Of course the news is unexpected, but so very welcomed."

A shadow of pain crossed Arsenio's face before he caught himself and concealed his feelings. He offered her a comforting smile.

"My lady, this... is a blessed day that... brings forth such news. After much sorrow, you have reason to rejoice."

He took a deep breath, then looked into her eyes and added, "The noble Duccio will be much more than a loving memory, because his sacred blood will continue to flow unhindered through the child."

Polyxena gasped in delight. "Arsenio. Oh, thank you. Thank you for your kindness..."

"I rejoice with you, to see again that smile upon your face. After so much sadness for us both, there will be a great celebration of the coming birth of a new Prince or Princess of Lorengard-Lorraine."

But instead of showing him that smile, her face darkened."Duccio's child is not of royal lineage my lord. I will not falsify a birthright and deny the father's name."

Arsenio felt as if he had just stumbled down a flight of stairs. "Forgive me Polyxena," he quickly replied. "I have no desire to usurp Duccio's rights as a father. He was my friend and I honor his memory. I only wish to bestow upon his child the protection and love he will not have otherwise."

"Please do not apologize, Polyxena. No explanation is owed for your behavior, considering all the suffering you endured. You placed your life in great peril to save mine. I am forever grateful to you."

"Thank you, my lord." She studied his face. There was a sensual, aristocratic demeanor in Arsenio, coupled with a warmth and approachability that was disarming. She moved closer to him and smiled, looking directly into his eyes.

Arsenio beamed and slid his arms around her waist in a warm embrace. "I am not your lord, Polyxena. I am your husband who loves you above all others. I also know that Duccio would want you to be happy. Please, allow me to share your life."

Passion and love were etched on Arsenio's face. Polyxena was startled, but the sight moved her. She felt as if she again saw him for the first time, and was overcome by the same intense and sensual feelings that had struck her then. She responded to his embrace and pressed into him. He held her in his arms, caressing her with all his ardor and desire.

When her arms remained tightly wrapped around him, he dared to press his lips against hers, and when he felt her respond to his kiss, it stirred all his longing. He gasped and began taking fast, deep breaths while she returned the kiss with warmth. He reveled in the softness of her lips, ripe and full of promise.

Arsenio's desire remained bound by her delicate condition, regardless of Polyxena's tantalizing beauty. He could feel that the memory of the man whose child she was carrying still cast a long shadow over them. Nonetheless, he was elated that the woman he loved was in his arms once more after so long, responding to his passion.

"Polyxena, my wife, I love you so much." He immediately regretted saying it, fearing he had gone too far. But Polyxena's smile widened.

For her part, she had grieved alone for so long that she reveled in the comfort of Arsenio's arms. Coldness and sorrow were replaced by a deep glow of sensual warmth. "Arsenio," she whispered. "my husband…I love you, too."

Somehow, hearing herself speak such passionate words amplified her own emotions. She was finally able to release her pain and felt herself freed from the torment of guilt that she had not earned over betrayals which she had never committed. Such feelings had plagued her ever since Duccio was killed. Now she allowed herself to nestle in Arsenio's arms and drink of the comfort in his embrace. After so much time lost, she felt as if she and Arsenio had finally found one another again.

News quickly spread about the impending birth of an heir to the Dukedom of Lorengard-Lorraine. The people were overjoyed and eagerly awaited the blessed event. The birth of a new Prince or Princess was considered a good omen, a blessing from God that would assure peace and prosperity for the Dukedom.

For Polyxena, the months could not go by fast enough. She waited with great anticipation. Arsenio's reassuring presence and comforting words were always available during the stressful moments. The respect and affection she felt for her husband grew with each passing day.

She had been emotionally impaired, almost paralyzed, not just by the pain of loss, but by the fear of disrespecting the noble Knight's memory so soon after his passing. The secret she nurtured was the news that she was carrying Duccio's child had greatly relieved her torment with the knowledge that the man she had loved would live on through his child. The splendid interlude of passion that they shared for a fleeting moment had not been in vain.

Finally, the bell towers of the churches in Lorengard-Lorraine rang a festive sound that resonated throughout the Dukedom, tolling the news that the Dukedom now had a new prince. Pandemonium ensued, and elated citizens shouted with delight, "Long live our new Prince. Honor to the noble house of Lorengard-Lorraine."

A massive crowd gathered in front of the ducal palace, waving banners with the crimson coat-of-arms of Lorengard-Lorraine. Their joy was palpable and the sound of their voices resonated throughout the walls of the palace, reaching the stately room where Polyxena cradled her newborn son in her arms.

Arsenio was by her side, beaming with joy despite the challenges of his wife's pregnancy with Duccio's child. The baby boy looked healthy and was sleeping peacefully, unaware of the excitement he was bringing to so many people.

"My lady," Arsenio said. "Our people rejoice at the arrival of their new Prince. After all the suffering they endured under Ludwig's evil reign, his little life is bringing needed joy. This is truly an eventful day."

Arsenio remained silent for a moment, then placed his hand gently on the infant head, intoning a heartfelt prayer. "Heavenly father, we thank you for all our blessings and the gift of this precious child. Endow him with wisdom and kindness; make him worthy of the high station in life that is his destiny."

He smiled at Polyxena and continued, "Duccio, this is your son that is given in my care. I promise to love him as if he were my own child. I pledge to protect him against harm and guide him in the righteous path, hoping he will be as noble and chivalrous as his father."

Polyxena took Arsenio's hand with gratitude and love. In that pivotal moment, peace and contentment filled her. The three of them were a family now and she rejoiced.

THE CRIMSON AMULET

DUCCIO RETURNS

Nearly a month passed since the birth of the new Prince, and already Duccio's likeness was apparent on the child's face. Polyxena was keenly aware of it and secretly rejoiced that the handsome features of her first great love would live on through their son.

The young prince was named Alexander in honor of Polyxena's father, the Duke of Nemours, and Edward, in memory of Arsenio's father. Preparations were made for the stately baptism according to the tradition of Lorengard-Lorraine, with the festivities scheduled to occur in the infant's second month of life.

Young Alexander's nursery was lavishly decorated with delicate mahogany furniture, richly inlaid with semiprecious stones. The splendid ceiling frescos depicted mythological scenes of fawns and unicorns giving the room a whimsical allure. The golden crib was a priceless heirloom of the ducal family, crowned by precious Venetian lace. The privileged infant's comfort was of paramount importance, with a wet nurse always at hand and several handmaidens catering to the child's every need.

As a new, doting mother, Polyxena was at first reluctant to give Alexander's care to strangers, even if required by the court's etiquette. Despite her aversion, she finally relented, knowing it was a traditional and necessary requisite.

Because of her many duties as Duchess, the compulsory separation from her child was necessary, even though she spent every available moment with him and cherished the precious time they were able to share. Her nightly visits to the nursery were joyful, and she was always reluctant to retire to her adjoining bedchamber.

One evening, Polyxena found the separation from her child unusually challenging. Disturbing thoughts plagued her and she was unable to find solace in the luxury of her lonely room. She tossed aimlessly in her bed searching for elusive relaxation.

Finally, no longer able to endure her distress, she jumped out of bed, placed a dressing coat over her nightgown, and walked impatiently toward the tapestry that separated her room from Alexander's bedchamber. She felt herself filled with uncontrolled anxieties and yearned to hold him in her arms, searching for comfort in the warmth of his little body.

But when she was about to enter the nursery she was startled by the sight of Arsenio leaning over her son's crib and lovingly caressing the child. The tender scene filled her with warmth. She was gratified to witness this genuine affection for little Alexander by stepfather Arsenio. She had feared that his acceptance of another man's child was only due to his sense of gratitude toward her. Now she was finally certain that he truly loved and accepted the child as his own.

She eagerly entered the nursery and joined her husband, whose face brightened at the sight of his beautiful bride. He encircled her waist in a loving embrace and they stood together silently, gazing at the sleeping child.

When the time came, Arsenio reluctantly escorted her back to her sleeping quarters. They were chosen for her because of the close proximity to the nursery, but Polyxena had dwelled alone in the lavish bedchamber since the birth of her child. Now the young Duke felt reluctant to leave her and return to his own lonely rooms.

Throughout their marriage, no intimacy had existed between them, and the situation had become difficult for Arsenio to sustain. However, dominated by his inflexible sense of chivalry and pride, he wanted her love to be freely given and passionate, not dictated by some sense of duty.

The closeness of her body accentuated his longing and erotic desires, but Polyxena remained silent without extending an invitation to join her in the bedchamber. Arsenio bowed and with reluctance prepared to leave her. But Polyxena surprised him by firmly holding his hand to stop him from departing. She gazed in his eyes. "Thank you Arsenio," she finally said. "I am so grateful for all your generosity and kindness toward me and my child; you are truly my very best friend."

Arsenio could not hide his disappointment at the sound of those words. The offer of friendship hardly fulfilled his passionate nature and only added to his feeling of rejection. Polyxena noticed his reaction and moved closer to him, snuggling against his body and pressing her breasts invitingly against his chest.

"You are not only my best friend Arsenio," she whispered. You are also my love." She blushed violently as she uttered those last words, while she brought her lips so close to his that he could feel the warmth of her breath.

Arsenio was stunned by the revelation and beset with desire. He placed his strong arms about her and caressed her curvaceous form. He kissed her lips with hunger. The ecstasy of the moment was volatile, overwhelming them while he lifted her off the floor and carried her in the bedchamber and closed the tapestry behind them.

Once inside, he placed her on the bed while their bodies trembled with desire and he kissed her once again with unbridled passion. Polyxena's response to his loving overture took his breath away. He had never been so much in love with any other woman before, and having her so receptive to his passion was almost unreal. Polyxena's body seemed untouched by the recent pregnancy and Arsenio reveled in the silkiness of her skin and the loveliness of her form. The intensity and heat their bodies generated in their passionate embrace was exhilarating.

For her part, Polyxena was stunned by the depths of her feelings. All the emotions and desire that her grief had stifled were resurging.

She wondered if she be in love with two men at the same time. Was she being disrespectful to the Duccio's memory? Or was she following his desire that she should go on living and fulfill the path of her destiny?

She had been fearful of being vulnerable to the pain of a loss if she ever allowed herself to love again, and yet in her husband's arms she felt the love and contentment that she never expected to feel again.

Strangely, the catalyst that brought them together was Duccio's son, since the child's eventful birth had been instrumental in giving Polyxena the necessary strength to go on with life. The child was the ultimate gift from the noble knight, and his message to her was to go forward with life, to once open herself to love with a noble and proper person.

Great plans were in the making in celebration of the baptism of the heir apparent of Lorengard-Lorraine. Duke Arsenio spared no expense for the grand occasion. It was an opportunity to share the eventful day with the citizens of the Dukedom and they were eager to rejoice and celebrate after so much turmoil and suffering.

Arsenio was truly happy for the first time in his life. With the woman he loved by his side and the birth of a healthy new son, he felt grateful for all his blessings.

He doted on Polyxena and considered himself fortunate that this courageous woman was his wife. And so he showered her with lavish gifts and loving devotion, eager to please her and bring her joy in every possible way.

Polyxena was overwhelmed by the attention and reveled in the warmth of the relationship. Her passionate nature, long repressed, was finally reawakening, and her romantic feelings toward Arsenio grew with each passing day, coupled with renewed respect and trust she had for him.

One afternoon, while busily performing her many duties as Duchess, Polyxena received an unexpected but welcomed visit from Arsenio. He approached her with a bright smile, then placed his arms around her and lovingly kissed her cheeks.

"This visit is a pleasant surprise, my husband," she told him. "I thought affairs of state were occupying your time today."

"That's true, however, I have some wonderful and surprising news for you that I am eager to share without delay. This gift is truly special and I am certain it will bring you great joy."

"Thank you Arsenio, but you are far too generous," she said in a mock reprimand while caressing his face and rearranging an unruly lock of his hair. "You have already showered me with so many presents that I am overwhelmed and humbled by them."

Her voice became softer, alluring, "The greatest gift of all is your love Arsenio and I will not ask for more."

"I believe this is one gift you will not wish to return," he added with an enigmatic smile.

Intrigued, she replied, "Then please don't keep me in suspense."

"Your noble father, the Duke of Nemours, will honor us with a visit," Arsenio exclaimed joyfully. "He is already on his way and will soon be here. He is very anxious to meet his new grandson."

Polyxena threw her arms around Arsenio's neck and kissed him on the lips with joyful ardor, disregarding the court etiquette and the presence of nearby ladies-in-waiting. "This is such wonderful news Arsenio and the best present of all. When will he arrive?"

"In just a few days, according to his message, and he will remain with us until Alexander's baptism."

Polyxena laughed in delight. Nothing could have pleased her more than a reunion with her father. She savored the thought of introducing him to her son.

"But wait," Arsenio added. "I have one more surprise for you Polyxena, and although is of a different nature, I am certain you will be greatly pleased." He squired her without delay toward the adjacent reception room of the palace.

The stately chamber was crowned by splendid ceiling frescos and chandeliers brimming with a thousand lights, and as they entered, Polyxena noticed a striking man in his late twenties, dressed in a distinct Italian style. His appearance was refined and elegant, with an unusual flair. A flowing mantle draped his shoulders, and a black velvet cap topped his reddish brown hair. A long beard framed his sculpted features, and the face was highlighted by his piercing blue eyes.

The man exuded an aura that seemed benevolent, but also quite intimidating. The instant he saw her, the man removed his velvet cap with a sweeping gesture and bowed to the royal pair in courtly fashion. Arsenio introduced him.

"My lady, it is my pleasure to introduce to you, Master Leonardo Da Vinci, who has graciously consented to oversee the festival honoring our son's baptism. His artistic contribution represents a special gift from our friend and ally, Ludovico Sforza, Duke of Milan."

Polyxena walked eagerly toward the distinguished guest and extended her hand in greeting. "Welcome to Lorengard-Lorraine Master Leonardo. We are honored by the presence of such a great and distinguished artist. We joyfully extend our hospitality to you, and we are most grateful for your artistic contribution to our son's festival."

"Thank you for your warm welcome, your grace," Leonardo kissed her hand with courtly flair while his piercing eyes focused on her lovely face. He was silent for a long moment, then added, "Rumors of your beauty have been greatly understated my lady, I am overwhelmed by the grace and loveliness of your presence."

With those parting words, Leonardo bowed deferentially to the royal pair and exited the room.

After many days of eager anticipation, the arrival of the Duke of Nemours was welcomed with ceremonial splendor in Lorengard-Lorraine. He was accompanied by the festive sounds of trumpets as he strode by the ceremonial guards honoring his arrival.

No expense was spared to welcome the Duke. Arsenio was eager to honor his heroic father-in-law, who had been instrumental in saving Lorengard-Lorraine from an evil tyrant.

Polyxena was pleasantly surprised by her father's healthy appearance and relaxed demeanor, so unlike the usually stern and reserved man. She embraced her father and Arsenio warmly greeted him. They offered to escort the Duke to the comfort of his rooms, assuming after such an arduous journey he needed a proper rest. But to their surprise, the vigorous Duke dismissed the offer and professed his desire to meet his new grandson without delay.

Unable to dissuade the stubborn man, Polyxena and Arsenio acquiesced and squired him to their son's nursery, where he was finally introduced to the little Prince. The elder gentleman was overwhelmed; tears of joy blurred his vision at the sight of the beautiful child. He struggled to maintain his dignity and his face shone with delight. Polyxena felt as if she could glow in the dark while she placed the baby Alexander in his grandfather's arms.

The Duke gazed lovingly at the child, focusing on the striking beauty of the dark eyes and the perfection of his features. The excitement of the tender moment between father and daughter was palpable and Arsenio graciously left the nursery to allow his wife and father-in-law to share the wonderful occasion alone.

"This is one of the happiest days in my life." the Duke of Nemours finally said. "This precious child brings so much joy to us."

"Yes father, that is true," responded Polyxena. "Nothing could have been more helpful to heal the wounds in my heart than the blessing of his presence."

The Duke of Nemours remained silent for a brief moment, then exclaimed with pride. "My grandson has a brilliant future before him. As the heir to Lorengard-Lorraine, he will be groomed for his great destiny as the future leader of the people."

Sadness flashed across her face. The moment sagged. She turned away from her father, unable to face him while she spoke. The beauty of the moment was suddenly ruined by escalating emotions and deep seeded feelings of guilt. "My son is Duccio's child, father. He is not of royal lineage. It pains me to think of hiding that fact and denying him his true heritage."

Her father, surprised her when he smiled and lovingly placed the child in the crib. He embraced her and spoke in a soft voice, "I am aware of it, Polyxena. Even at this early stage of his life, the child's resemblance to the noble knight is apparent. Those luminous dark eyes and the perfection of his features tell the tale.

"However, my daughter, there is no need for distress in sharing this knowledge with me. I place no blame and have no desire to judge your actions. You have shown amazing courage and chivalry despite impossible odds and I am proud you are my daughter. In truth, I am happy because it will comfort you to know that the chivalrous Knight you loved will live on through his son.

"However," the Duke continued. "the child's welfare must be paramount. He is in need of a father. I believe Arsenio is the person to can fulfill such an important task. He is a kind and noble man who truly loves you.

"Polyxena, you must remember that your marriage to Duccio was celebrated in secret and was never duly recorded by the church. Consequently, Alexander will be unfairly marked with the stain of illegitimacy. It will certainly complicate his young life. He will also be denied, through no fault of his own, the high station in life that I believe was willed to him by Destiny."

"But what about Duccio?" Polyxena interrupted. "Aren't we denying his son his true heritage?"

The Duke's response was stern. "He was a noble knight, and thus would have been in full agreement that the present course of action is the proper one. Unquestionably, his son's welfare would have been paramount to him."

Polyxena remained silent. Tears streamed down her face. She understood the wisdom in her father's words, and his understanding gave her comfort.

The Duke wiped away her tears. "The child is an immense source of joy to everyone and a precious gift of love. Cherish him without regrets. And if the occasion should ever arise, it will be your choice to determine whether Alexander's true heritage should be revealed."

"Thank you my father. With your wisdom and understanding you give me peace."

They remained silent for a moment, savoring the joy of their reunion, until Polyxena looked into her father's face and noticed concern in his eyes. The Duke moved away from her, cleared his throat, and addressed his daughter with concern in a tighter voice.

"Polyxena, did you share the knowledge of the Templar's treasure with Arsenio?"

"I did not. I swore an oath of silence and allegiance to the Knights Templar. It is a manner of honor."

"It isn't mistrust on my part, for I believe in your honorable nature. However, Arsenio is chivalrous in his own right and I thought, perhaps, you made an exception with him."

"I considered it, I must confess. However, I would never break a promise of such importance without your knowledge or consent."

The Duke was visibly relieved. "I am very glad you used discretion, Polyxena. Knowledge of the treasure would only place Arsenio in peril."

"How can there be danger, since no one knows of the treasure but us?"

"Over the past century, going back to the times of Wilfred the Valiant, many have had knowledge of the existence of a great treasure. We are the only ones who know its location...

"Enemies of our ancestor were aware that Wilfred took possession of the fabulous plunder from the holy land, but they never learned where it was hidden. For generations, a long list of ruthless people has been on the quest to find it. They have used barbaric means at times to achieve their aim. Through the decades, several heroic members of the house of Nemours were captured by our ruthless enemies, tortured, and even put to the sword. All of this was done in the search for the treasure."

Polyxena was overwhelmed by a feeling of dread. Her son was also a member of the house of Nemours.

The Duke put his arms around her. "This is the reason, Polyxena, why we must be vigilant in dispensing the wealth. We must not attract attention, since we are the direct descendents of Wilfred the Valiant. There are too many people who would do anything to possess such a treasure."

Polyxena finally said, "Why don't we try to find trustworthy individuals who are not connected with the house of Nemours to join our quest? They could help us dispense a greater portion of the treasure to needy people."

"Unwise…given the risk." Her father shook his head. "Wealth brings about great responsibilities. Even trustworthy people can be corrupted by the awesome power of gold."

"But with so much suffering out there, that treasure could do great good in many places."

"No, daughter. Involving more people who would have knowledge of the great treasure will bring too much danger. You must remember that the treasure rests within Nemours Castle and the Dukedom would be in grave peril if the secret became known to our enemies. We would be vulnerable to attack from every direction.

"Polyxena, I know the kindness of your heart and your generous nature. But if the secret becomes known and the Templar's great treasure falls into the hands of our enemies, it will be lost forever. We must be vigilant, in order to protect it.

"Much good has been done through the ages, dispensing the wealth successfully to thousands of needy people, while many evil tyrants have been toppled. To succeed in our quest, it is essential that we stay the course. The safety of the house of Nemours depends upon it. It would be preferable for the treasure to be forever lost rather than fall in evil hands."

"I see your reasoning and I bow to your wisdom, father. The present course of action is the right one. I pledge my life to the protection of the Templar's treasure."

†††

TIMBER CREEK PRESS

www.ingramcontent.com/pod-product-compliance
Lightning Source LLC
Chambersburg PA
CBHW021310250626
47155CB00002B/463